SKERRID MAWR

Nick Davieson

First published 2024
by Rowanvale Books Ltd
The Gate
Keppoch Street
Roath
Cardiff
CF24 3JW
www.rowanvalebooks.com

A CIP catalogue record for this book is available from the British Library.
ISBN: 978-1-914422-75-1
Hardback ISBN: 978-1-914422-76-8
eBook ISBN: 978-1-914422-74-4

To everyone connected with Team Davies.

CONTENTS

Chapter One – The Gift 7

Chapter Two – Argent...15

Chapter Three – Westward 24

Chapter Four – Arrival in Skerrid Mawr 35

Chapter Five – New Dawn 47

Chapter Six – Brotherly Love....................................53

Chapter Seven – Stepping Out 63

Chapter Eight – Intricate Pathways.........................74

Chapter Nine – Weaver Birds....................................86

Chapter Ten – Open Your Heart................................93

Chapter Eleven – Actions Speak Louder.................101

Chapter Twelve – A Persian Princess.....................107

Chapter Thirteen – Inevitably Omni.......................114

Chapter Fourteen – Girls' Talk................................123

Chapter Fifteen – Love and Understanding............127

Chapter Sixteen – Mutual Appreciation 139

Chapter Seventeen – Frankfurt Am Main...............144

Chapter Eighteen – Refuge......................................157

Chapter Nineteen – Face the Music........................164

Chapter Twenty – Tonic 167

Chapter Twenty-One – Seek and You Will Find 174

Chapter Twenty-Two – Sandpiper...........................179

Chapter Twenty-Three – The Spider and The Fly 184

Chapter Twenty-Four – Plans 190

Chapter Twenty-Five – Sugar and Spice 198

Chapter Twenty-Six – Evening Out 203

Chapter Twenty-Seven – The Power of Truth 210

Chapter Twenty-Eight – So Gullible 223

Chapter Twenty-Nine – Stronger Together 231

Chapter Thirty – Skirting with Trouble 236

Chapter Thirty-One – Need You 243

Chapter Thirty-Two – Reality Strikes...............................251

Chapter Thirty-Three – Gone 256

Chapter Thirty-Four – Isolated 260

Chapter Thirty-Five – The First Responder 267

Chapter Thirty-Six – The Fold 273

Chapter Thirty-Seven – Say Nothing, Do Much.............282

Chapter Thirty-Eight – Taking the Mantle 290

Chapter Thirty-Nine – The Steps 295

CHAPTER ONE – THE GIFT

For the second time in a week, Tam Kendall took delivery of an unwanted gift.

She had opened the front door in order to check the mailbox, only to find a bunch of lilies lying there at her feet. No card, no explanation, nothing.

Lilies, she noted; associated with funerals and grief. She hadn't been expecting any flowers, but especially not these.

Outwardly, this could have seemed like a case of mistaken address, were it not for the fact that a similarly mysterious delivery had met her upon her return from work the previous week. In that particular case, it was a large, white plastic bag, purporting to contain horse feed but actually containing a consignment of fresh horse manure.

She looked up across the leafy cul-de-sac in the forlorn hope that the perpetrator of the lily delivery may still be visible. They weren't.

Her heart sank. These mysterious deliveries were becoming a serious problem, adding to her many matrimonial woes, and one that was obviously escalating.

"How I wish someone would buy me flowers," came the call from a female neighbour as she emerged from her own front door with two teenage children in tow.

"Not lilies you wouldn't," Tam replied, picking them up and waving them in her direction.

"Yes, perhaps you're right," the neighbour replied, thankfully understanding the symbolism of the flower.

"Did you happen to see anyone around this morning, at all?" Tam tentatively asked.

"No, sorry. I suggest you report it to the police if it bothers you. There are so many freaks around these days, you just never know. Costs nothing to report it, even if they do nothing about it, at least you have logged it on their system, yeah?" She gave a nod of affirmation and closed the car door.

Tam felt it was her neighbour's way of being polite but not really wanting to get involved, but it was a fair point. Yes, she would report it, to make sure there was a paper trail should any other incidents arise.

Sadly, Tam knew it was an incident that the police, in this modern day and age, would be unwilling to investigate, despite the anguish it was causing her. There was little evidence she could offer them. Even if she could locate CCTV footage showing the deliveries taking place, the chances were that the culprit's identity would be concealed. The police would just fob her off with a crime number—if they deemed it a crime at all, that is.

Tam was intelligent enough to know the difference between a childish prank and something more sinister. This was definitely the latter.

Her hand shook as she tried to insert the small key into the wall-mounted letterbox. She had got up that morning already dreading opening the mailbox, knowing it was likely to contain yet another dismissive communication from her estranged husband's solicitors.

True enough, in with the mix of junk mail, there was their trademark large, cream envelope embossed with their name. With a deep breath, Tam prepared herself for the worst and, whilst opening it, unwittingly proceeded to lightly slice her finger on the edge of the sharp envelope, drawing blood.

Each little thing sent her spirits down further.

Yes, as expected, it was a notification from Felton's solicitors rejecting the previous valuation of the house and insisting upon "a truer market value". This was their third attempt to get her to climb down from what she felt was a perfectly reasonable market valuation. However, their collective haranguing was starting to affect her delicate state of mind, and she was seriously considering caving in to their demands.

The truth was that Felton wanted a lower value because it would reduce his payout to her, whether he bought her out of the property or it was to be sold. Tam had found Felton's logic baffling at the best of times throughout their topsy-turvy marriage of twenty-seven years, but this was getting ridiculous. It was just as well she was due to visit her own solicitor that very afternoon, to determine his view on the matter and hand over important information that may be required should things turn any darker for her.

All that she really wanted, at fifty-two years old, was a fair settlement so both she and the children could move on with their lives. Not that the children had time for their father anyway; their respect for him had long since disappeared.

The pressure being put on her was now becoming intolerable and the loneliness harder to bear, despite speaking to the children frequently by phone or text. There was no way she could tell them about the two deliveries; it would alarm them, and Tam didn't want to spoil their respective vacations with their friends. However, her ability to absorb much more upset was waning.

She stepped back inside and pushed the front door shut with her back, before sliding down to the bristle doormat to cry once more.

Some minutes passed before Tam's tears abated, her brain trying to reason through the possibility that Felton could be the one behind these deliveries, perhaps in some bizarre attempt to force the issue and get his own way. But this wasn't his style; he would usually be more direct and physical given the chance.

Tam had wisely changed the locks some weeks before, preventing any possibility of him returning unannounced to their former matrimonial abode. A modicum of security, at least.

It could only be one other person causing her this much distress, a person who had caused so many problems for their marriage since her arrival in the country—namely, Felton's latest concubine: Brig Huddlestone.

Had the drama been confined to just the three of them then their divorce may have been heading for resolution sooner and with less acrimony, but Tam had stupidly brought a fourth person into the equation a few weeks earlier, a person Brig Huddlestone had more than a passing interest in. It had weakened Tam's position, and Felton clearly wanted to capitalise on it.

Of all the damned people in the world Tam could have fraternised with, it had to have been someone that Brig knew, and intimately at that.

Tam accepted that she was partially the architect of her own undoing and would have to face the consequences of her one-night stand with Grant, even though it had meant nothing to her. How could life be so unfair? Was she never meant to find true happiness?

Conversely, Brig, someone whom Tam had seen only once, briefly at an American Consulate function, had everything going for her. She was young, attractive and able to play the field without a care in the world, supported by her diplomatic status and immunity to prosecution whilst working in Britain.

It was a power Brig must now be wielding in revenge for Tam's liaison with Grant. Whether that involved Felton or not was still the big question.

Tam's heart thumped uncontrollably in her chest as she remained sitting by the front door. She was vulnerable, isolated and unsure where to turn.

She decided she would need to cancel the appointment with the solicitors. For all she knew, Brig could be waiting outside for her.

Before she could make the call, an incoming call appeared on the phone. It was Elinor, her daughter.

"Hi, Mum, how are you?"

"OK, thanks, El. How are you?" replied Tam, her voice a little gruff.

"I'm good, but you don't sound so good. What's going on?"

"I'm just a bit tired and I have to see the solicitor today, so it's on my mind."

"Is Dad being a pain again?"

"Yes, but when isn't he? He wants another valuation."

"Oh, for God's sake, I am going to phone him. Me and Anthony discussed this earlier."

"No, please, don't do that. Let me speak to Mr Argent at the solicitors', first."

"I am not happy, Mum. He's bullying you again, isn't he? You surely can't be eating and sleeping properly if he's being like this again. He makes me mad. I hate him."

"I know you are angry, love, but I'm sure it will get resolved soon."

"I think I should get back home, don't you?"

"No, please, El, don't do that. It wouldn't serve any purpose other than to spoil your holiday. Your father won't listen to anyone anyway."

Elinor's threat to return home was the last thing Tam wanted to hear. There was no possible way she could allow Elinor to be open to a threat from Brig, or whoever was responsible. If things were to escalate, then physical harm seemed to be the next step up. Tam couldn't tell El the true story behind her decision; she had to protect her, and Anthony too for that matter.

"In fact, Mum, go and book a cruise somewhere for singles," Elinor playfully suggested, trying to lighten the mood. "You've got enough money and you've still got your looks. Perhaps you could meet a millionaire toy-boy and buy Dad out of the house."

"Nice thought, but no thanks, El. Anyway, how is your holiday?" said Tam, quickly deflecting the conversation away from her woes.

"Aw, we are all having a great time, but you're always in my mind, Mum. Now, listen, all joking aside, I will stay away from home on one condition: that you go and stay with Uncle Norm and Auntie Amey in Skerrid Mawr. You have kept on about wanting to visit them again, especially after the last time got cut short, so do it, please. You said there is so much you would like to do down there, so here's an opportunity. Either way, you definitely need looking after, plus you can still speak to your solicitor down there via numerous apps that Uncle Norm can probably set up for you. There are no excuses, Mum, it's early June and the sun is shining, so stop rattling around in that sodding house alone and get away from it all to the coast—you know it makes sense. Don't say there are things to be done, because we all know the house will get sold, so don't waste your time on it, do you hear me?"

Elinor's case was more compelling than she knew. Nevertheless, Tam didn't want to bother her busy brother and Amey with her problems. They both knew of her indiscretion with Grant—after all, Grant worked for Norm and news had got out via an unknown third party. The whole affair had caused him great embarrassment professionally, and she didn't want to burden herself on them under such a tainted scenario.

"Mum, are you still there?"

"Yes, dear."

"You paused for too long. I think you know I am right."

"Maybe."

"There's no 'maybe' about it. You deserve to be happy and you are clearly not. You have loads of holidays to take, so take them, for crying out loud. Phone in and extend them. Just get Uncle Norm to pull rank on them if they say no," Elinor said with a laugh.

"OK, OK. Let me get through today and think about it on the train," Tam said in an attempt to abate Elinor's ranting. "In fact, I think I had better get myself ready to go right away, or I will be late for the appointment."

"OK, Mum. Let me know how you get on. Take care and speak soon. Love you... Bye."

Tam gave a sigh of palpable relief. It wasn't nice to be fending off her own daughter, but at least Elinor wouldn't be coming home to potential danger. Now she knew she had a little more time to consider her immediate options.

Yes, Elinor's holiday suggestion was probably what she needed, but by the same token, Tam couldn't possibly leave the house unattended now—anything could happen. Another conundrum to add to her list of worries.

Time was passing; she really did have to leave to meet with Mr Argent or be very late. As tempted as she was to cancel the meeting, she knew it was delaying the inevitable.

However, using her car was out; it was under repair for an electrical fault. Taking the Tube would not ordinarily be a problem, but things were not ordinary any longer; she felt vulnerable and open to attack.

As much as she hated using taxis, she knew it was either that or protract the whole divorce case even longer by cancelling the appointment. Continual indecision was making matters worse.

On the wall was a card for a taxi firm that Elinor used. Tam picked it up and put it down again several times before finally making the call. She really couldn't delay any more; she wanted Felton and all his baggage out of her life as soon as possible. It usurped anything else.

CHAPTER TWO – ARGENT

Mr Argent, a long-time solicitor, wasn't the most dynamic of people, more of a tortoise than a hare in today's fast-moving society, but very thorough nonetheless. He was a good friend of Norm's and had acted for their family for many years.

The financial options he had unveiled against Felton were promising, dismissing the "juvenile tactics" his solicitors were employing as "poppycock". Furthermore, he had delivered the welcome news that his "special team" had uncovered various secret bank accounts that Felton held solely in his name, ones he had obviously kept secret from Tam. Argent then reeled off values appertaining to stocks, shares, Premium Bonds, Individual Savings Accounts and even a small flat in London, none of which Felton declared on his tax returns. It gave Argent more to bargain with. More interestingly, he suspected that someone was blackmailing Felton, judging by the regular weekly amounts that had been leaving one of his accounts.

He even offered Tam the recipient's name. It wasn't a surprise. In fact, it helped Tam make more sense of the ongoing situation and understand why these attacks had only started recently: Brig Huddlestone must be seeking some form of revenge by targeting Tam for the absence of payments due, but where would it stop?

Now, Mr Argent had friends in very high places and had devised his own methods of finding out such intricate details, methods Tam would not question nor divulge, of course. Ultimately, he advised her that she would be due, in his own words, "a considerable windfall after he had finished with Felton". At last, a crumb of comfort, but that would be for tomorrow, not today.

Tam finished the meeting by handing over a large, padded envelope that she had brought with her.

"Only to be opened by Mr Argent should anything fatal happen to me" was written on it in Tam's own handwriting, which Argent thought a little dramatic. Tam didn't agree. It was important to her to leave its contents in safe hands, contents she was unwilling to openly discuss with anyone right now, not even her own children.

As she left his office, Mr Argent's secretary informed Tam that she had called a cab to take her home. This was a welcome relief. At least she would get home safely.

The taxi took her southeast over the Thames, passing those everyday types of places she took for granted. The parks where she had spent many happy hours with the children, their primary school and the horse stables where, until relatively recently, she had spent much of her spare time.

Her fond reminiscences were interrupted by a phone call. It was a telephone number she didn't readily recognise. With trepidation, she accepted the call.

"Hello, this is BVL Security. My name is Kyle; I work in the contact centre. We have an alarm activation for your property and we cannot reach the main keyholder, Mr Felton Kendall. We have a Mrs Tamsin Kendall as the second keyholder on this number, is that you?"

"Yes, I am Mrs Kendall. What is the problem?"

"Can you confirm your password, please, Mrs Kendall?"

"Password? I didn't even know it had a bloody password for Pete's sake. Listen, Kyle, you have phoned me, and I am Mrs Kendall, now tell me what's wrong."

"Sorry, I don't set the rules, Mrs Kendall. Could you give me your date of birth, then?" he requested in his awful monotone.

Tam duly provided the information.

"OK, Mrs Kendall, can you call us back on the number stuck to the alarm box, or this number if you prefer, should you not be able to reset the device with the PIN code?"

"What bloody PIN code?" Tam demanded, her blood pressure now rising in anger.

"I will send an engineer out, then, as you sound distressed. He will probably be an hour, OK?"

As if Tam needed this as well. It had only been serviced recently, for crying out loud.

"Have the police been informed?" Tam enquired.

"According to us, it is an ARVS, 'Alarm Report to Vendor Service', not to the police, I'm sorry to tell you, so you will need to contact them yourself."

Tam was now incensed. Why hadn't Felton set up an automatic link to the police when it was installed? It wasn't as if he was short of money!

Luckily, Tam was almost home and curtailed the call immediately.

As she did so, the black cab swerved to avoid hitting a hoody-wearing cyclist recklessly emerging from the cul-de-sac, likely the culprit of the alarm.

She could now see that several of her neighbours were starting to congregate outside her house as the cab pulled up. Tam was scared to go inside—anyone could be in there.

"Go on, love, off you go. The cab has been paid for by Mr Argent. Hope everything's alright," the driver called over his shoulder.

Before she could catch her breath, her neighbour, Terry, approached.

"Hi, Tam," he said. "I saw a kid in a hoody throw something through your window. When the alarm went off, he scarpered on his e-bike. Would you like me to check the building and call the Old Bill?"

Terry was a burly former firefighter and a renowned club doorman in his day. If anyone could deal with a commotion, it was him.

"Yes, thank you, Terry, but don't call the police just yet. It's a long story—one I haven't got time to tell you right now," Tam shouted over the deafening tones of the alarm as she unlocked the front door. "The alarm engineer is due. He will have to turn the alarm off if I can't," she added.

"You will need your window boarded up," he shouted back.

"Yes, I know, thank you. Leave the window for now, in case Forensics want to do anything. My brother will sort it all out, I'm sure."

"Well, only if you're really sure?" he asked. The warble of the alarm continued unabated.

Tam nodded as she approached the alarm keypad. Somehow, she steadied herself sufficiently to punch in Anthony's birthdate, and the alarm instantly ceased its deafening din. It was an inspired guess.

Terry slowly opened the door to her lounge and Tam followed quickly behind.

Her heart sank.

There was a single rock lying on her glass-strewn carpet.

"That's taken some bloody force, to break your double-glazing," said Terry. "Little shit. I'd love to get my hands on him."

Tam stood motionless, looking around the damaged room, silent but distraught.

This was no random attack. It was a cowardly one, but most likely a serious warning of intent. The kid on the bike had been paid-off, no doubt. This was pure intimidation.

Here stood the last vestiges of her already fragmented home life, now in greater tatters.

The weight of everything that had happened over the last few months bore down on her, strengthened by this latest callous act, and she retched. Her hand rose to her mouth as her stomach churned. She swallowed hard and took a few deep breaths to prevent the personal embarrassment of adding to the mess that already lay before her.

"We'll get the glass tidied up for you, just give me a few mins to get some kit and some of the boys together and we'll have it done."

"No, please, Terry, leave it for now. You've been a great help and I really appreciate it."

It was far more than just the window that needed fixing—the whole situation was getting out of control.

"It's no trouble. I just feel angry for you, Tam. No one deserves this."

Terry was right—no one did deserve this—but what was coming next?

"Terry, would you be kind enough to wait outside and stop anyone else coming in, please, whilst I make the call?" she requested so there was no risk of Terry overhearing her conversation with her brother.

Terry duly obliged, leaving the front door slightly ajar as he took his post outside, like a nightclub doorman might.

Now, as Tam stood alone in the hallway, her hands started to involuntarily shake so violently that she had to sit on the bottom step of the stairs to even contemplate making the phone call to Norm. She needed him and the power he could bring to bear upon this escalating situation, not just as a brother, but as someone of national standing and extensive influence.

Within two rings, Amey had answered the phone, at first overjoyed at hearing Tam's voice, but then she stopped, as Tam's sobbing made her words inaudible, and quickly passed the phone to Norm.

Norm asked her to speak slowly and concisely, as best she could, so he could fully understand the gravity of the situation. She gave him the chain of events leading up to the rock incident and told him that Terry was there to protect her from any further intrusions.

"OK, you have done tremendously, Tam. I will get my people there as soon as possible to safeguard the house, make the repair and even get someone to stay there for a few days, in case they try anything more. You must pack a bag and be ready for collection within the next hour or so, do you understand?"

"Where am I going, Norm?"

"Down here to Skerrid Mawr, with Amey and me, so you can be safe. Don't argue, just do it and do it now."

"I will, I will, Norm."

"The first person there will be from the police. Make sure you see their identity first and ask for a security word, which will be 'Burgess', OK?"

"OK, Burgess, yes, OK," she repeated back to him in a muddled state.

"Right, Tam, get packing, right now," Norm impatiently told her before ringing off.

Adrenalin shot through her, and she rushed upstairs. She grabbed anything that seemed even somewhat useful, throwing the stuff at random into her case, rucksack and handbag.

After half an hour of frenzied packing, she was interrupted by a shout from Terry from downstairs, confirming that the alarm engineer had arrived to reset the alarm and that he would keep him out of the living room as requested. Thank God for Terry.

Tam looked around her bedroom in case she had overlooked anything vital.

Her eye caught her jewellery case, and something stirred inside her mind, something buried deep and dark.

She walked around the bed to the small rosewood case that her mother had given her as a present when she had turned eighteen years old. Carefully opening one of the small drawers, she found two brown, packet-style envelopes inside, neither bigger than a credit card. One contained a couple of rings that had belonged to her late mother, and the other a silver, heart-shaped pendant embossed with the letter "T" upon a silver chain.

It was what had drawn her to the case, something she hadn't looked at for years, not since the day she'd had the chain repaired.

Tam unclipped the slim gold chain she had been wearing and laid it gently upon her dressing table before sitting down to face the mirror. She picked up the ends of the silver chain and clasped it around her neck. Delicately, she eased the heart-shaped locket along the chain to rest above her cleavage and looked back up into the mirror.

She stared at the locket lying against her skin and then into the reflection of her own eyes.

"Well, I never thought I would see the day," she said aloud to herself. "Never."

Standing, she opened the curtains and looked into the back garden. Gardening was one of very few activities that had kept her going recently. The rewards of her hard work were there to see, the roses and the trimmed lawn. On the decking, a single chair sat next to the small circular table, where an empty wine bottle kept a wine glass company, another one of her solo activities after work.

She gave a sullen yank of the curtains, and the darkness surrounded her.

Tam wondered where fate was about to take her. Was she just running away from the problem or was she actually taking a vacation, like Elinor had suggested?

Either way, she had to go—if she could move this overloaded case, that was.

Despite its wheels, Tam struggled to drag the case over the carpet and out of the bedroom, finally getting it onto the tiled flooring of the interior balcony and pushing it along to the top of the stairway.

As she stopped, she saw a female police officer arrive in the hallway below, with Terry in close attendance.

"Tam, this is Becca. Becca, this is Tam," he announced. "Becca will look after the house for the next few hours, apparently. The alarm engineer has left, I signed his worksheet so you didn't have to. Now, shall I give you a hand down with that case? It looks heavy."

"Hi, Becca, and yes please, Terry," said Tam gratefully, leaving the case and making her way downstairs with her two lighter bags.

"Hello, Mrs Kendall. I need to say 'Burgess' to you, if that makes sense?" Becca said, to which Tam nodded in agreement. "I am sorry to hear about the damage. The scene-of-crime people will be along shortly," Becca informed her as Terry struggled down the stairs with the heavily laden case.

"Thank you, both of you, for looking after me like this," Tam said, slightly overwhelmed by their kindness.

Despite her troubles, she knew she was extremely privileged to have a brother in such an exalted position within the nation's defence hierarchy, able to help her at a moment's notice in a time of crisis.

Tam was handing the spare house keys to Becca when a stocky man, announcing himself as Morgan, suddenly appeared through the front door. He presented his identity card to the three of them in turn.

"Norm sent me. Are you ready, Mrs Kendall?" he asked Tam.

"Yes," she replied.

"OK, let's go. Is this your case?" he asked, clearly tasked with a fast turnaround.

Tam nodded once more, as the significance of leaving started to hit home.

Morgan assumed control of the case from Terry and wheeled it out toward the front door.

"Where are you going, Tam?" Terry asked, and Morgan paused at the door.

"I can't tell you right now, Terry. I told you it was complicated, didn't I? When I get back home, I will explain, I promise." Tam kissed his stubbly cheek before stepping back and taking a last look around.

When she would be back here, if ever, was something she would need to find out herself.

CHAPTER THREE – WESTWARD

Being ushered into an unmarked police car and whisked westwards to Wales wasn't exactly how Tam had envisioned spending this warm summer's evening, but there it was.

As Tam made her way along the paved drive, with Terry escorting her, Morgan dodged past them with her suitcase and lifted it into the open boot as if it were a bag of feathers.

He returned a moment later, reaching for Tam's remaining bags, but Tam was not going to relinquish them.

"No, I want these bags with me. Thank you all the same," she stated, and Morgan quickly retracted his offer.

He dashed back to close the boot of the shiny black car and open the rear door for her. Tam thanked Terry once more for his invaluable help before pitching the holdall and handbag through the open door and onto the back seat, quickly following them in herself. Her trailing ankle had barely made its way over the threshold before the door was firmly pushed shut. Tam sought the sanctuary of her safety belt as Morgan clambered in behind the wheel.

"OK, Mrs Kendall?" enquired Morgan as his door shut, engaging a loud clunk of the auto-locking mechanism.

"Fine... fine..." Tam replied, a tad flustered. "And I am Tam, not Mrs Kendall. Just so you know."

"Understood, Tam. Can I just ask you to turn off your phone, please?"

"Why? I need to let my children know that I am not at home. I was going to do it on the way."

"I fully understand that, but whoever is doing this, and we think we do know who, could well have the power to trace your movements. Whilst it may seem unlikely right now, we cannot leave it to chance. I have instructions from your brother, my boss, to make sure it is done, to protect you," Morgan explained, as tactfully as he could.

Tam knew he was only doing his job.

"Can I send one last message before I switch it off, just to let my children know, please?"

"Of course you can. I have a couple of things to do too." Morgan inserted an earpiece into his right ear before adjusting the small monitor in the middle of the console.

Tam watched, somewhat worried by seeing the front and rear views of the car appear on the small screen.

"Sorry, Morgan, but am I safe in here?" she asked. "It seems that we could be followed."

"It's very unlikely. If you were deemed high risk, then there would be a couple of motorcycles here too. I know you are frightened by what has happened, Tam, but your brother views any kind of interception tonight as a low risk. The cameras just help me keep track of anything untoward, in which case I could call for backup, hence my earpiece."

This assuaged Tam, for the moment anyway.

"Could you send the text, please, so we can get going?" added Morgan, firing up the car and peering into his rear-view mirror, somewhat impatiently in Tam's opinion.

A blast of cool air jetted out from the air-conditioning, very welcome after the heated hour she had just gone through. She keyed in the message that she wished could say more:

Ant & El,
I am taking El's advice and spending a couple of days
away from it all.
If you need anything then contact your auntie, as my
phone will be off.
Love you both.
Mum XX

With a final press of the button, it was successfully sent.

As she turned off the phone, she hoped that this message wasn't too cryptic or alarming, nor a giveaway to the likes of Brig or Felton, should either be tracking her movements.

Morgan turned in his seat to face Tam. His sleek, ginger hair sported an expertly gelled side parting, and his beard and moustache were also well groomed, as befitting someone in Norm's employ.

"Are we done?" he asked politely.

"Yes, all done. My phone is off now." Tam waved it at him as proof.

Morgan smiled as he proceeded to double-check his own safety belt before commencing the journey by slowly driving away from the house.

Tam's head was buzzing with so many different thoughts as she looked back at the house she used to call home, the shattered window a sad metaphor for her current life. At least the window could be boarded up, but how she would get through this turbulent episode and find some type of resolution, she didn't know. She knew she had much to think about now. At least staying at Norm's house would give her the opportunity to escape some of her worries and properly assess the threats against her, with the invaluable support of her brother and sister-in-law, of course.

She reached across to her holdall and unzipped it on her lap, wanting to double-check that she hadn't forgotten something vital and, in doing so, proceeded to dig everything out and chuck it all back in again. It was all nervous energy expending itself, and she knew it. It wasn't as if she was leaving the country—well, not immediately anyway.

The zip was drawn back across and the bag pushed away. Her phone lay dormant beside her. Ordinarily, she'd be using it to check out the limited social media sites she used, listen to one of her favourite radio stations or watch a programme whilst she travelled, but not today.

She was trying to relax, and knew that particular action in itself, "trying to relax", was a contradiction in terms.

Tam reached down to the floor to collect her handbag with the intent of putting her phone away for safekeeping. As she did so, her locket swung out before her. When she sat back, her phone safely tucked away, the locket rested upon her tee-shirt.

She noticed Morgan's eyes looking in the mirror, not so much checking the traffic behind but more like checking on her, as if he wanted to say something. If there was something, he wasn't saying it.

A few minutes passed as they made their way through the borough, neither saying anything. Tam toyed with the locket, running it up and down the slim silver chain in an attempt to alleviate her agitation, as she looked out of the window at the manor so familiar to her.

There was the local park where she regularly volunteered at Parkrun on a Saturday, one of the few places she could ever socially relax and enjoy herself, namely because she was helping others. Then there was the narrow lane that led to the stables that she used to frequent every day. It had been at least three months since she had last set foot there, since her last horse had lost its battle with an inflammatory bowel disease. It marked the end of a predominately pleasurable chapter in her life. So many years of riding alongside the children on their ponies, and the competitions they took part in, now all gone. So sad.

Tam caught Morgan's eye in the mirror once more.

"Is there something you need or want to say, Morgan?" she asked, quite sternly.

"Er, yes actually, there is. I wanted you to settle in first. It's nothing ominous, it's just that I took the liberty of getting you some water and a sandwich, that's all," he confessed in his strong Welsh accent.

Tam broke into a smile. "Sorry I was so curt. That was very thoughtful and sweet of you, Morgan."

As the car came to stop at a red traffic light, Morgan reached across to the front footwell and extracted a plain white plastic bag, which he held aloft for Tam to collect.

Tam was impressed. She hadn't eaten anything since early morning; she had felt too stressed.

"I hope it's one you like?" he asked.

Tam checked the packaging.

"'All Day Breakfast'. Well, that's appropriate, isn't it?" she announced, seeing as it was nearing teatime.

"I can stop if you want a takeaway coffee or something else, just let me know," he offered.

"Thank you, that's most thoughtful of you. My daughter would love you," Tam replied before settling back in her plush leather seat, noticing the smile in his eyes via the mirror.

She unzipped her handbag once more and pushed out a paracetamol from its blister packaging, then washed it down with a large gulp of water. The headache she had tolerated all day was still there, probably caused by the involuntary hunching of her shoulders, causing her neck to feel tight. Remembering some of the exercises she would do at work when staring at a monitor for too long, Tam started to move her head to the left, pointing her ear down toward her shoulder, where she held it still for ten seconds. The crunching sound made it feel as if she had a skull full of gravel, which sounded even worse when she repeated the move to her right.

She put the water in the cup holder then placed her cool fingers under the base of her skull on both sides and gently started to massage the pressure points, a technique a friend had mentioned to her, finishing a minute later with a hard press on the nerves she had been massaging.

The tightness in her neck and tension in her shoulders seemed to have abated a little as, for the first time today, she actually felt a pang of hunger.

Like the water, the sandwich was cool and actually tasted good. Perhaps it was knowing that she was in safe hands and escaping to her brother's house that let her enjoy food for the first time in a while.

The combined effect of the day's trauma, the self-applied physiotherapy and the filling food made Tam feel drowsy. Sure of Morgan's loyalties, she finally allowed her guard to drop and let herself relax, drifting into the repose she so desperately needed.

***

A loud blast caused Tam to wake suddenly.

It took a few moments before she comprehended where she was.

"It's OK, Tam, just motorway traffic getting a bit fractious. Nothing to worry about," Morgan informed her.

Tam felt a little shaken by being so rudely awoken and reached down for the bottle of water.

"Feeling better after your snooze?" asked Morgan.

Tam finished the remaining water, then replied, "Much, thank you. I don't think I have slept so deeply for ages. When will we get to Skerrid Mawr do you think?"

"Hopefully in the next half hour. I was hoping to get down before it got dark, but there were a few hold-ups. I've let Norm know."

"Thank you. It's probably past his bedtime by now," she said, looking at the time on the car clock. "Norm has always been an early bird. Tell me, Morgan, are you a local Skerrid Mawr man?"

"No, not far away, though. My home is in Llynocre, about four miles away. Llynocre means 'amber lake' in Welsh, by the way. There used to be a small quarry there that mined for ore, way before my time, of course."

Tam enjoyed his pronunciations and explanations in equal measure.

"So how did you get into this job? Did Norm have anything to do with it, by chance?" she asked, knowing the likely answer to be yes.

"Yes, actually. Norm wanted someone with my credentials on secondment in London. He made enquiries with the local police force to see if anyone met the criteria and, when I was put forward by the force, he invited me to meet for an informal discussion. Only six months back, it was."

Tam nodded. This sounded very much like Norm's style of recruiting personnel.

"Probably the best interview I ever had. It was in The Dragon's Tail in Skerrid Mawr—well, I say the best, apart from the intrusive landlady, Omni."

"Omni? That's a strange name."

"No, her name is really Gayle, but everyone calls her Omni. Wherever you go in the village you seem to bump into Omni, in the pub, on the beach. She's hilarious and a local legend for sure, but not exactly who you want around in an interview. She could talk and drink for Wales. You're bound to meet her, but you need to make up your own mind. Anyway, I thought you had been here before, Tam?"

"Once, about ten months ago, but it was a very brief visit thanks to my argumentative pig of a husband, Felton. He and Norm drifted apart, and now we finally have too. Surely, you must know who Felton Kendall is?"

"Only his name, never met him in person. I gathered Norman didn't get on with him but I didn't ask why. He is a very high rank, so it's unlikely we would meet," Morgan explained.

"Pompous and arrogant, with an eye for the ladies, if that is what you're thinking? If so, it would be true," Tam responded in a vehement mood.

"You wouldn't expect me to comment on that, would you?"

"Yes, I would. You can say whatever you like about him, I don't care."

Judging by the elongated pause that followed, Tam sensed that he wouldn't be drawn any further with regard to Felton so she changed the subject back to the village.

"So, you clearly know the village well, then?"

"Yes, I certainly do, we used to go there as kids and I have never stopped visiting, work permitting, of course."

"So, what, in your qualified view, makes it so special, then?"

"I always say to people that Skerrid Mawr doesn't have a harbour, posh boats or a promenade and it's all the better for it. In fact, it doesn't have a fish and chip shop either, but the dunes and the beach are something else, wild and unspoilt. You can lose yourself there, on foot or on horseback, it's magnificent. It's a fair walk to get to Skerrid Beach, but well worth it when you do."

Tam could feel his passion for the village.

"And don't forget Sker Lake, plenty to see there too, all year round. Wonderful hides where you can view the birds close up. You should borrow Norm's binoculars if you can," he suggested.

Tam had never fully understood why Norm and Amey chose to move to Skerrid Mawr, but she was beginning to now. It sounded truly idyllic, with a big beach on their doorstep upon which they could ride horses together, with a lake they could walk around, if the choice so took them.

Tam started toying with her locket again, anticipating the amazing opportunities that Skerrid Mawr afforded her. Riding horses, in what would be the first time in months, across the dunes to a deserted beach, was a childhood dream. Alternatively, long walks to the beach on her own, where, as Morgan had said, "you can lose yourself". It made her think back to a comment made at the housewarming, where a couple had reported seeing people naked, availing themselves of the sunshine and lack of public intrusion. This was another reason Amey would like it there—after all, naturism was second nature to her and her kind, back in the days of the old East Germany. Skerrid Mawr was starting to sound ideal, a perfect escape from Tam's tribulations.

Morgan snapped her out of her daydream.

"Not too far to go now, Tam. Pity it's almost dark, but there's always tomorrow."

"Indeed, there is," Tam buoyantly responded. "And thank you for sharing your invaluable insights with me, Morgan. You saw how uptight I was earlier, and you have been most kind and attentive. I will let Norm know what a good man he has in his team."

Tam could see his instant response to her statement as he shuffled in his seat, seemingly pleased that he had done a good deed.

Pouring out her feelings to anyone, let alone a stranger, was something she rarely had the chance to do. Her closest confidante, Michelle, now lived in South Africa, and chats had become few and far between. When it did happen, the conversation mainly kept to reminiscing and generalities. Michelle was too far away to really help now, which was a crying shame. Meanwhile, everyone else around Tam in London was an acquaintance, nothing more. This exchange with Morgan had been a very welcome fillip.

As she strained to take in the outside view through the descending darkness, Morgan spoke about Norm.

"Now, I shouldn't really say this, but if we are handing out compliments, you should know that, in your brother, you have a tactical grandmaster on your side. He's been there, done it, and done it his own way too. The morale in our section is second to none and that is because he treats people like people, not imbeciles. Mind you, if you get it wrong, he will be quick to tell you!"

Tam laughed. Morgan was right—Norm was clever. Always the big brother to her, protecting her when she needed it, never more so than now. Of course, they had argued over the years, like any brother and sister would, but he was never malicious. The only person she had ever truly heard him be vindictive toward was Felton, primarily because he thoroughly deserved it.

It was good to hear the respect that Morgan had for Norm, very gratifying.

Tam freshened up her skin with a travel wipe from her bag before pressing the interior light above her so she could see her face clearly in her compact mirror. She gently dabbed her soft skin with foundation, before applying a little balm onto her lips. A quick pout in the mirror confirmed she was ready for her arrival.

She snapped the compact shut and dropped it away into her bag, remembering to switch off the light above her. The roads twisted and turned as they made their way toward Norm and Amey's house, passing the brightly lit Meadow Pipit public house, as the road sign proclaiming "Welcome to Skerrid Mawr" came into view. At last, she was here.

With one final turn, Tam could see Norm's house ahead, the halogen headlights bouncing off the stainless-steel balustrade that surrounded the first-floor balcony.

As the car slowed, she could make out the tall figure of Amey emerging from the illuminated side door, waving furiously, complete with Hertz, their sleek black Labrador, crazily twirling around and around with excitement. It was so nice to feel welcome here again.

CHAPTER FOUR – ARRIVAL IN SKERRID MAWR

The car had barely stopped before Amey wrenched the back door open and dragged Tam into her clutches.

"It's so good to see you, Tamsin," she said, squeezing Tam so tightly she hardly could breathe, whilst the dog jumped up at them both.

Morgan hauled Tam's heavy case from the back of the car, up and into the side entrance of the house, then quickly returned to the vehicle.

"*Danke*, Morgan. Good man," Amey said, in her soft German lilt, as he extracted Tam's remaining bags.

"Just need to use the facilities, Amey, OK?" he informed her, as he hotfooted it back to the house.

"Is he staying here too?" asked Tam.

"Not here no, but at his mother's house in Llynocre. It's why he volunteered for the job. Norm will have promised him a couple of days off in lieu, I am sure of it."

Tam and Amey made their way to the house, arm in arm.

As Morgan re-emerged, Tam opened her arms and gave him an appreciative hug.

"Thank you so much for looking after me and listening, you are a star!"

"No problem at all, Tam. Right, I will say, *Nos Da* to you, Tam, and *Nos Da* to you, Amey. My mam has cooked me a dinner and I'm starving. Anyway, no doubt I will see you both soon," he chirped as he trotted back to the car with a wave, understandably keen to get home.

Amey led Tam into her brightly lit kitchen. It was a blend of light grey cupboards, charcoal-grey walls, white quartz worktops with black glass splashbacks and a vintage porcelain sink, one that Tam remembered from their previous house in Sussex.

"Wow, this is new. How lovely, Amey! Are you pleased?"

"Oh, very much so. I have claimed this as my territory. Norm isn't the best in this department, is he?" Amey smiled, knowing Tam was well aware that his catering skills weren't his strong suit. "I even get to put up my own pictures and mementoes," she added, pointing around the walls.

Tam walked over for a closer look.

"Aww, your late brother's football shirt—and is this you?" she asked, pointing to a small, framed photograph.

"Yes, in Oberhof, on a skiing trip back in 1982 with school."

"Were you teaching the others how to ski, given your family connections there?"

"Maybe, maybe." Amey was too coy to admit her strong skiing credentials.

Lovely Amey. Her humility was to be admired.

Tam knew, from their chats over the years, that East Germany hadn't been blessed with the wealth of options that its divided neighbour enjoyed, but sport and community were very much part of her upbringing, something she was devoutly proud to discuss. Since moving to the UK, she had been proactive in putting herself forward to talk about the old and new eras of both East and West Germany at any opportunity, including the obligatory Women's Institute circuit in and around Sussex, and was now doing likewise in South Wales.

"What are you looking for, Tam?" Amey asked her, as she moved around the large kitchen.

"Your equine pictures... where are they? I can see you swimming here, and there is the one of you running, of course, but no horses."

"I can't ever bring myself to look back at them in the same way. They are in a box in the spare room. One day perhaps, one day. Now, enough about me, Tamsin. Let's talk about you. We have been so worried. Tell me exactly what has been happening."

Tam noticed Amey had changed the subject away from herself as quickly as she could.

"I am sure you know what has been happening," she said. "I made a mistake and it looks like I am incurring the wrath of God. Well, Brig Huddlestone, anyway."

"You will have tea, yes?" Amey asked as she switched the kettle on.

Tam nodded, but she, like Morgan had done, needed to excuse herself first to use the toilet following the long journey. Despite her welcome snooze during the trip, she was still a little tired and hoped that Amey might not press her too much tonight on the in-depth details of her indiscretions.

A couple of minutes later, however, when Tam returned to the kitchen, Amey was swiftly back onto the delicate subject.

"Let's sit here at the table and you can tell me more. I know it is late and Norm is in bed already, but I really need to hear it from your own lips. Tell me about Felton, this girl Brig and how it has all gone so wrong for you," Amey insisted, pulling out a chair from under the large farmhouse-style table for Tam to sit on.

There were no shortcuts to be found. Tam now felt resigned to pouring out the whole sordid story as Amey poured out the tea.

"Help yourself to a biscuit, or two," said Amey, gesticulating toward a plate of chocolate chip cookies.

Tam picked one up. "Homemade, I assume?"

"Yes, your favourites. Made them this afternoon when Norm told me you were coming down. When you're ready, Tam," said Amey, obliging Tam to tell her the full, unexpurgated story.

There was no way out of this, Tam realised. Might as well get it over with.

"It all went toxic after that Majorca trip, at the end of October. We had agreed to disagree after we left here last August, you may recall, which resulted in me claiming the master bedroom for myself. There was no way on this planet I could ever share a bed with him again. He begrudgingly moved into the spare room. It seemed to be an easy way for us to cohabit yet hide our problems from the children."

"Like they didn't know already," tutted Amey.

"Of course they knew; it was just that I couldn't think of an exit plan at that point, one that would best serve us all."

"So, you took the brunt of it, then, like you always do, Tam. That man annoys me so much. So, yes, Majorca, go on, please."

Tam cleared her throat with a shallow cough.

"One of the girls from work offered me an eleventh-hour invitation to go abroad with a hen party. Apparently, someone had dropped out, and I took it, on the spur of the moment. It seemed like a real chance to escape the confines of the house. I never told Felton; I just went. Sadly, after just one day, I realised I was out of my comfort zone. There was no escaping the hen party's blatant escapades."

"Not my sort of holiday either, Tam, by the sound of it. Couldn't you go off and do your own thing?" asked Amey.

"Well, on the second day, I tried to do just that. I went swimming and sought a quiet corner to sunbathe, but they found me and insisted I join in with their silly antics. Now, Amey, bear in mind that I am at least ten years older than my colleague and probably twenty years older than most of the other girls. When my colleague is in work, she is fairly reserved, but she was an absolute lunatic among their gang of alcohol-swigging women, who were all trying to get me to do things that just aren't me. I wanted to go to bed just as they were about to go out!"

"Oh, I see," said Amey, crunching her way through her second biscuit.

"To cut a long story short, I got through it, somehow. When I got home, you can imagine the abuse I had from Felton. Had I enjoyed it, perhaps he would have had a point, but I'd hated it, hated it all."

"Such a shame, Tam, you deserved a nice break. What exactly did Felton say to you?"

"Apparently, I was 'a common slut'."

Amey's eyebrows rose.

"You know what, Amey, the irony of that bloody trip is that I was the only one who stayed true—even the bride herself decided to have one last fling. So I get tarred with that brush yet was totally innocent. Keeping my fidelity was the right decision, and that is all that counted to me, despite being called frigid by one of the other girls. Frigid I am not! Anyhow, things deteriorated further at home."

"What happened next?" interjected Amey, leaning forward onto the table.

"Felton was acting all annoyed and jealous, yet I knew he wasn't being true himself. He was, and still is, a philanderer and not a very good one at that. You know full well that I had my suspicions that some of his lads' trips were euphemisms for dirty weekends away, based on what I found in his case when he returned. Disgusting."

Amey sat back and sighed.

"I know what I am about to say is wrong, Amey, and if I could turn the clock back I would, but all of his transgressions played on my mind. Finally, I decided that, at some point, I would actually get my own back on him, having passed up the dubious opportunities on the Majorca trip. Cheap, I know, but I felt so unhappy and worthless."

Amey was looking down, arms folded, as Tam continued her explanation.

"I honestly thought that Christmas might bring me some cheer in that sense. Of course, it didn't. The work party was fun, food and frolics, but not even a Christmas kiss for me, the oldest, ugliest woman there. To make matters worse, you and Norm were back in Thuringia for the holiday season, so I didn't get to see you at all. At least the kids were home, well, some of the time, at least.

"As it transpired, something happened in February. A guy I knew through work kept flattering me, often over the phone and on a previous visit to the office. I suppose his flirty suggestions subliminally crossed my mind, yet I still did nothing about it."

"Grant, you mean?" said Amey, topping up the teapot with more hot water.

"Yes, Grant. When he said he had to stay over one night for work, I arranged the hotel for him as part of my job. Luckily for me, it was a night hubby would be out with his cronies. As part of Grant's stopover, I had offered to drive him to the hotel, quite openly you understand, as it was common practice for someone to do this, given he had travelled over by train that morning."

"OK... carry on," said Amey, more interested now.

"He was a player for sure, and I knew it, but I just wanted the thrill by that time. Was that wrong?"

"Never mind what I think, it's your life. Go on..."

"Naturally, I had showered and 'dolled up' in the morning, creating saucy comments from the girls in my office. They were envious, I think. Grant played his part, telling them that there had been a change of plan and I would be dropping him back to the station, after all."

"Clever ploy by a clever boy," Amey said, dabbing Tam's hand.

Tam was surprised. She knew Amey was liberal, but not this liberal!

She had gone this far with her confession, she might as well tell the full, sordid story.

"After work, we met in the multi-storey car park and I drove him across the borough, well away from work. Sure enough, I got the chat I expected. When we got to his hotel, he confirmed he wanted me to stay for a drink, so I gladly agreed. Deep down I felt ashamed by my actions. Nevertheless, I remained committed to seeing it through, primarily because I knew he was leaving the department to go back to Norm's department, following his recall."

"Yes, I knew he had recovered from his injury and that the secondment was due to end; Norm did say," agreed Amey.

"The chances of us meeting up again in the future were slim, so it was a risk, in this instance, I was prepared to take. I dropped him off at the front of the hotel and he checked-in whilst I parked the car and made my way to the bar. It was already fairly full of single businessmen, so my presence was met with dirty eyes. Standing at the bar alone, I ordered the drinks. I could almost hear their disappointment as I took the two drinks to the nearest vacant table, where I sat and waited for him to return."

Amey's attention remained fixed on Tam's story, pausing only to offer her more tea, which she declined, opting for a glass of water instead. As Amey filled her glass from the tap, Tam felt the pangs of embarrassment welling up inside. Best to get it over and done with.

"He turned up fifteen minutes later, showered and changed, and we ordered food whilst he started his patter. Some of his revelations were amazing and he soon realised we had a connection that neither of us could ever reveal, as it would be too damaging to those around us."

"To Norm, you mean?" asked Amey pointedly.

"Yes. To Norm, you, everyone really. I should have stopped there and then. Stupidly, I didn't. To cut a long and obvious story short, we went to his room, and it all took place. In all honesty, I panicked. I wasn't relaxed, so I told him what he needed to hear, in the hope that the ordeal would finish sooner rather than later. I shouldn't have been there and I knew it. The guilt took over."

Tam hesitated for a moment, picking at some loose nail varnish on her ring finger, primarily to avoid making eye contact with Amey, such was her shame.

"Dragging myself from under his body, I made my way to the toilet whilst he lay prone on the bed, clearly dead to the world. Nevertheless, I expected him to stir. When he didn't, I knew it was my cue to leave. Quietly and quickly, my escape took place."

Amey just sat there, tapping her fingers on the table, prompting Tam to continue.

"Grant wouldn't have cared. At best, he would probably phone or mail me in the morning at work, as if nothing had happened. He was that type of player, that's why I played with him. It was wrong. Anyhow, with adrenalin overriding alcohol, I drove home. My second big mistake of the evening."

"This is when the violence happened, yes?" Amey enquired.

"Unfortunately so, Amey, yes," Tam replied, now recalling the awful outcome. "I had noticed several missed calls and texts from Felton, but seeing as he never answers mine when he goes out, I stupidly ignored them. Consequently, I didn't realise he was back in the house at all, so didn't even bother to lock my bedroom door. Why would I? He was away, or so I believed."

Amey's hands went to her head, and she grimaced.

"I must have drifted off quite quickly. Then, sometime later, I became aware of someone getting into bed with me. From the reek of drink and cigars, I instantly knew it was Felton.

"His hand went over my mouth, so my screams could not be heard, as he attempted to force himself on me. However, he got the shock of his life. Exactly how, I will leave to your own imagination."

"That vile man tried to rape you, Tam, didn't he?"

"Theoretically yes, he did, but he got more than he bargained for. Even in the semi-darkness, the look on his face will live with me forever. The moment of realisation, he withdrew, spitting in my face before hurling a string of obscenities at me. It was then I felt him slap me across the face in his drunken rage. Somehow, I managed to push him off and escape to the bathroom, grabbing my phone as I did so. Through a locked door, I had to threaten to call the police before he stopped his shouting and threats. Luckily, the kids were away."

"Tam, this is so terrible," said Amey, taking hold of Tam's wrists across the kitchen table.

Tam looked squarely into Amey's steel-grey eyes. "Believe me, it was. The arrogant pig even asked me why I had done this to him. You know what, Amey, I couldn't believe his gall, so I took the opportunity to reveal to him that I knew of his serial cheating and named the latest girl involved—Brig Huddlestone. Based on that information alone, he relented. He asked if it was revenge and I said, in part, yes, but moreover, that I was undervalued, treated with disrespect and had been for years."

"Good for you, Tam. Norm always knew he was a wimp and totally unworthy of your love. He told me he tried to make Felton's life as difficult as he could at work. He even said he didn't want him here at the housewarming, as you know full well," said Amey bitterly.

"I know. He even had the temerity to say it was stress, caused by his job, that made him act that way."

"Nonsense, he was having a whale of a time. He makes me sick," said Amey, thumping the table with the side of her hand.

"Me too, Amey, me too. It was his pathetic attempt to play the victim card. That is why it led to an immediate separation between us, pending divorce. Basically, I told him to move out there and then or I would cry rape that very night. And he did."

"Do you know where he went? Was it to Brig's place?"

"Well, he probably stayed at his own flat, the one I never knew he had until Mr Argent told me, amongst many other facts, earlier today."

"What a conniving, horrible man. Do Anthony and Elinor know any of this?"

"Not exactly, no. I explained to them that we had fought, which upset them. They're not stupid, they knew we had grown apart and that divorce was inevitable. To be honest, neither of them care for him at all and both independently said that we should have started divorce proceedings sooner!"

Tam was relieved that Amey had taken her confession so well. It was a burden she had been carrying alone for far too long.

"It must be awful for them, going through all this. But it is good they were not involved and are old enough to see him for what he is—a waster—and that you weren't happy."

"Thank you for not judging me, Amey. You must know that I've never been self-centred, but it seems to me that the minute I try to do anything for myself, it just goes wrong. I've given up ever trying to be happy."

Tam's chin dropped and the inevitable tears began to flow. Amey swiftly made her way around the kitchen table and put her arm around her shoulders.

"You weren't to know, Tam, you weren't to know it would turn out like this. I admire your strength. You are a strong woman and absolutely have the right to be happy too. I know we aren't in the best place right now, but keep fighting and you will get there, I'm sure. Now, is there anything else you want to tell me?" Amey handed Tam a tissue to dry her eyes.

Tam shook her head.

"OK, let's leave it for tonight, it's very late now. Thank you for being so frank with me, Tam. I must confess, I am a little shocked at it all. Anyway, let's get you up to your room. We can talk more tomorrow, yes?"

"Yes, we will, thank you, Amey. I never wanted anyone else to be involved in this mess, least of all you. Thank you for listening. You know, I really don't deserve you or Norm," said Tam, standing up with open arms to give Amey a massive hug.

"Come now, Tam, quietly upstairs so as not to wake Norm. I will be out early at an appointment, so help yourself to anything you need. If I get time, I'll leave you something in the fridge. Norm will be up early, working in the front room as usual. He has converted it into his new office, so he can watch the golfers, I think," she said with a wink.

"By the way, Amey," said Tam, "if you a receive message from Ant or El, it will be because Norm got me to switch my phone off."

"No problem. Don't you worry about anything now, please. You will be safe here," Amey assured her.

CHAPTER FIVE – NEW DAWN

Tam awoke to the sound of male chatter drifting in through the half-open window of her bedroom. Casting her thin quilt aside, she edged herself out of the double bed and moved over to sit on the wide windowsill, looking down on the lush green grass of the common. Nearby was a neatly mown tee area where three golfers stood talking, waiting to play their shots. Over their heads, in the middle distance, lay the vast swathe of dunes that buffered the village of Skerrid Mawr from the sea beyond.

Tam took in a deep breath of fresh air. There was no taste to it, unlike the congested smog of diesel fumes she would normally inhale in suburban London.

For Tam, the early weeks in June used to be the loveliest time of year, even in London. Long days, warm weather and a new sense of hope. Not so much now, of course.

She reflected back on her previous visit to this very bedroom-—the ill-fated, extremely brief visit to Skerrid Mawr with Felton on a very arid August day, just ten months before. Then, she recalled, she'd looked out from this self-same window, on the grass so scorched it resembled parchment. Even then, it had mirrored the dried-up state of her marriage.

What had promised to be a wonderful August weekend was soon spoilt by the niggling arguments between Felton and Norm. The disagreements weren't just about politics; they also included a heated debate about the new girl at the American Embassy. The girl, Brig Huddlestone, was "running loose and fancy free", according to Norm, since being appointed. She, Brig Huddlestone, certainly wouldn't have been Norm's choice of a sound candidate. He would have preferred someone much more experienced, or even someone he already knew, being promoted from within, but as Felton pointed out, it wasn't up to him who the Americans employed.

Norm conceded that to be true. However, since her arrival in the consulate, she had been continually upsetting his backroom staff, the ones who actually had to deal with the fallout of her actions. Norm had been far too busy organising his move to Wales with Amey to deal with it properly, and it had spiralled out of control since he had temporarily handed the reins to Felton.

Felton was vehemently defending Brig and asking Norm to give her a second chance and not complain to the Americans, on the basis that "she was new" and things would be sorted out by him in conjunction with them. That never happened.

Norm must have known at that point that Felton's relationship with Brig was more than professional, but he never divulged it to Tam, his little sister. Always the protector.

Later that very evening, Felton had instructed Tam to pack immediately, as they would be leaving first thing the next morning, citing personal differences as the reason. By eight o'clock the next morning they had left, heading back to London. Hardly a word was spoken en route.

During the journey, Tam had received multiple text messages from Norm as to the nature of their disagreement.

Norm, without outwardly saying anything, implied enough for Tam to make up her own mind. Ultimately, she trusted her brother more than her philandering husband and informed Felton that she wanted him to sleep in the spare room from then on and not with her. She was done with his shenanigans.

It had been clear to Tam at that point that the marriage was over and, truthfully, had been for some considerable time. Consequently, it made her feel even more isolated and lonely. The children were hardly ever at home to cook for or, more importantly, to talk to.

She looked up, drying a single tear with the sleeve of her nightshirt. It was approaching ten o'clock—perhaps it was time she went downstairs to discuss the current situation with Norm, before he came up looking for her.

Norm would, no doubt, already have a plan, given that—according to him, anyway—the entire future of the Western world very much depended on him being at the helm, even though he was technically semi-retired! "In the world of public service, you never retire. They engrain you in the system and then own your very soul forever under the Official Secrets Act" was Norm's view of Whitehall retirement.

Tam knew she had been lucky to have the children that he and Amey were never fortunate enough to be blessed with. Amey was Norm's rock and he doted on her. Tam had always found Amey upbeat, witty and the perfect foil to Norm, and she had clearly relished the move to Skerrid Mawr, given the abundance of lifestyle choices the village had afforded to her.

Tam felt a little easier knowing that Amey was fully up to speed with the whys and wherefores behind the ongoing drama with Felton and Brig.

She now had to decide what to do with her day, as Amey would be out and Norm was busy working downstairs.

Remaining on the windowsill, Tam wallowed in the spectacular view of the vast dunes. From here, she could see vehicles arriving in the car park, their occupants heading to the beach no doubt. Tam decided she wanted to join them, if she could. A good long walk would help clear her mind, if nothing else.

Then an outlandish thought drifted into her mind. Why not take a leaf out of Amey's book and find somewhere secluded, where she could enjoy her solace "au naturel", without clothes, naked.

The idea instantly excited her. She hopped off the windowsill and grabbed her open holdall, rifling through the meagre range of clothing options within. Success! She found both her swimming costume and bikini. Yes, her bikini, a good start, and clean knickers for her bag, of course.

Throwing off the baggy tee-shirt that had improvised as a nightdress, she took hold of her flimsy bikini top. She engaged the clip around her stomach and swivelled it around before adjusting her breasts into place. Looking in the mirror, it appeared not to cover her as well as it used to. Too much indulgence in the form of gin, wine and comfort eating in the last year had added to her midriff, not to mention the increased effects of the menopause, but it would have to be good enough for today. Not "cover model" potential any more, but at least no one would bother talking to her on the beach.

But what if they did?

She panicked.

Wiping her fingers under her arms, she noticed she smelt less than fresh. She scrambled for her travel-sized deodorant and applied it accordingly.

She was sending herself into another indecisive spin. Insecurity caused by a trauma when just twenty-two years old, and then slowly exacerbated by living with Felton for far too long, was getting the worst of her.

She ripped off the bikini top and stared at the mirror.

What the hell are you thinking? her alter ego yelled inside her head.

"Fat, useless, unloved, not needed by anyone anymore, causing problems to everyone around you... What on earth are you doing, woman?" she said out loud, as the self-deprecation continued.

At that point she detected a creaking noise. Someone was making their way up the staircase.

Tam now found herself in an unfortunate state of undress, a complete state of terror and absolute self-loathing, all at the most inappropriate time.

"I've made some tea, if you're up, that is?" It was the familiar voice of Norm, asking quietly, as he knocked gently on her door.

"Just going to take a shower if that's OK, then I'll be straight down," Tam managed to reply, whilst covering herself quickly with a towel to hide her modesty, should he open the door.

"Knowing you, that will be two hours, then," responded the acerbic wit of her lovely brother.

"Ha, ha. Give me ten minutes and you can microwave it," Tam replied, hoping she was covering the upset in her voice.

"OK. By the way, your case is outside your door. Bloody heavy, that was," he added, before his footsteps could be heard returning to the stairs.

Now, at least, she might be able to find something more flattering to wear to the beach.

Feeling re-inspired, she decided that all negativity must be set to one side. The chance to realise a dream was here for the taking. Grabbing her shower gel, and that damned bikini top, of course, she tiptoed naked to the bathroom to take a shower.

Today is the first day of the rest of your life, flashed into her head. *Do it... come what may.*

CHAPTER SIX – BROTHERLY LOVE

In the front room downstairs, Norman Weaver sat facing one of three computer screens.

He had adapted the room into his new, state-of-the-art office. It was a contradiction of styles comprising sleek, modern technology mixed with a typical Whitehall office of yesteryear—mainly old government surplus furniture, stuff that he had bought at a clearance auction. The furniture was dark and bulky but was offset by the incoming morning sunlight. It made him comfortable and reminded him of his heyday in service.

Shelves containing files and papers threatened to fall from their moorings at any given moment. Others might view it as organised chaos, but Norm knew where everything was, apparently.

Above his desk, the whitewashed wall held reminders of his sporting past, including an epee mounted on a beech plinth. One small display cabinet, lit by an old fluorescent strip-light within, held his most treasured prizes, including several medals of various denominations that covered county, national and international successes. Pride of place was given to a large gold medal that lay upon the bib number he had worn throughout the competition. It read:

Modern Pentathlon
World Event
Frankfurt, Deutschland 1992
GOLD

and was embossed with both the logos of the World Pentathlon Organisation and the recently reunited Germany, the hosting country.

Norman Weaver was one of life's achievers.

Driven by his own father's sporting prowess and influence, he had been afforded opportunities to compete in one of the toughest multi-discipline events one could do, Modern Pentathlon. As a youngster, his parents had taught him to swim, fence, shoot and ride, and his strong physique meant he ran well too.

Such abilities and provenance were attractive to the military, and it was obvious he would suit service life which, in turn, would allow him to compete on the Modern Pentathlon world stage.

Norm was a true sportsman in every sense of the word, excelling in team events, captaining many and being a flagbearer for Great Britain and Ireland on several occasions.

The gentle tapping sound coming from outside his open window was the clinking of metal eyelets on a flagpole bearing a Union Jack, one he had been gifted by the British team manager after winning a European Championship. It was his show of national pride.

Tam emerged from the bathroom as a ringtone emanated from downstairs. She stood still to avoid the creak of the floorboards as she strained to hear Norm speaking.

"Hi.

"Coping yes... somehow.

"I don't know how to play it. At least we've got Tam here now with a modicum of protection and have a little time to think.

"Well, you are closer to her than most, so what do you suggest?

"I hear what you are saying, but the Yanks won't like that. Thank God that Tam didn't take matters into her own hands or it would have been a major diplomatic incident.

"I know we have to draw her out somehow. They need a good reason to deal with her the way we want them to. Hard proof, or we will look like fools.

"Listen, I no longer dictate the game, remember?

"You know yourself that this is way outside police jurisdiction, and we just can't involve them anyway, can we?

"It's not just Tam's argument anymore. It has far wider implications that we have only just uncovered. It involves me and Amey now.

"No, no, it *directly* involves me and Amey, because of something that happened years ago.

"Yes, seriously. I won't go into it now, but it muddies the water even further, let me tell you.

"OK, look, she's in the bathroom but due down any moment, so have a word with the others and let me know what you think. I will keep tabs on Tam.

"Right, best go. Bye."

Tam stood still, now starting to shake with shock. This confirmed her worst fears.

As if her present predicament wasn't bad enough, the harrowing trauma of 1992 was back to haunt her, but how these events were interlinked, she didn't know.

She definitely needed to get out and think. It didn't make any sense.

A brave face was needed if she was to evade Norm's emotional radar. He couldn't know that she had heard something she clearly shouldn't have.

Tam reached back to the bathroom door, purposefully slamming it shut to create the pretence that she was just emerging.

"Be with you in a moment," she called down the stairs.

"OK," Norm called back.

She stepped into her bedroom, her heart still pounding through her chest.

Frankfurt. It must be Frankfurt. Norm was playing with something behind her back. Why, she didn't know, and it absolutely irked her.

Tam opened the window wider and then sat on the bed, taking a few minutes to compose herself by using one of her breathing exercises. When she felt calmer, she unfurled her towel, allowing it to fall to the floor, repositioning herself in front of the mirror once more. Tam literally started putting on a brave face by dusting some light foundation on her flushed skin, applying some dark eyeliner to cover any redness and a balm stick to her lips.

She tied back her damp, straggly hair before applying a rapid coat of factor-thirty sun lotion for later. The ill-fitting bikini would be covered by loose shorts and a matching top, items she had quickly extracted from her suitcase in the hallway.

As she padded barefoot down the wooden staircase, Tam took one last deep breath, then she turned and walked into Norm's office.

"Fifteen minutes. Not bad, seeing as you've dressed for the conditions too," Norm proclaimed. He clearly wasn't going to mention the telephone call. "Do you want one of my berets to go with your outfit?" he cajoled.

"Shut up and pour the tea," she said with a grin, before rushing forward for the hug she had been longing for.

"It's good to 'cwtch', as they say down here," he said, almost crushing her in the process.

"Cwtch? What's a cwtch?"

"It's the Welsh for 'hug'. Even we use it—now that we are natives of the parish, of course," he exclaimed, making Tam relax slightly.

It definitely helped knowing he was in a good mood as he poured out the tea from its pot, like Amey had done the night before. Norm, dependable Norm, his salt-and-pepper hair freshly combed, his face cleanly shaved as if an inspection were due to call in at any moment. He never changed. His discipline and dedication to his vocation were blatantly apparent.

"It's so good to see you here, although I wish it were in better circumstances," he said. "Sorry I couldn't stay up last night, but I heard it was a smooth transition."

"Transition... your words reflect you so very well, don't they? Most people would say journey, Norm." Tam giggled as she picked up her mug and took a sip of the lukewarm brew. "I have to say that Morgan was wonderful, very courteous and kind. You have a good one there, so you need to keep hold of him."

"Yes, he's a good man. Promising career ahead for him, I forecast."

Now was as good a time as any to ask, Tam realised, if she wanted to catch Norm in a good mood.

"Norm, I would like to get out and about this morning... to the beach, if you're agreeable to that, of course, given the circumstances?" she tentatively enquired.

"Well, that should be fine. It's a pity that Amey has her appointment this morning—although she will be back lunchtime, probably—and I have a few issues on my plate, or we could have spent the day with you. Obviously, it's all been a bit last minute, but we had to make you safe first and foremost," said Norm, as if giving a debriefing.

"It sounds like I've added to your issues, is what you are trying to say?" said Tam playfully.

"In a fashion yes, you have. Hopefully, Brig will give up this vendetta. Let's see."

Tam hoped he would volunteer more information to her, perhaps something from his cryptic telephone call. She gently pressed him. "So, how long do you think, Norm, before she relents?"

"Give it a week or two to blow over. Just make yourself at home down here, then she can't get at you, can she?"

Norm didn't seem unduly fazed by her plight, now that she was in Skerrid Mawr, housed in his fortress. Admittedly, compared to the nationally important issues he probably dealt with day in day out, this was, to use his own vernacular, "piffling". But whilst that might be the case for him, it was monumental to her. After all, she was the one who had been forced from her home by Brig's attacks.

Tam decided to maintain her line of enquiry. "So, what makes you think she will give up?"

Norm was taken aback. "She doesn't know you're here, does she," he said in a harsh tone.

"True, but she has travelled across the Atlantic to be here. Even you must agree that it's not a coincidence she's got herself close to all of us, surely?"

"The only coincidence is Grant, is it not?" he responded with a raised eyebrow.

Tam smiled, letting Norm think his pointed remark had won a mini battle with her. He was clearly deflecting, as befitted one of the Government's top negotiators.

Tam surmised that the content of the call she had overheard went much deeper than she thought. Norm sounded rattled, too, most unlike him. Tam felt powerless to contribute anything further. After all, what could she actually do, other than wait and see?

"Maybe you can go out with the dog this morning?" Norm suggested in what Tam believed was an attempt to move her away from the subject.

"Would you mind if I go out for a walk to the beach alone? I could do with a long walk, without the dog, to be honest, in the clear light of day. Time to think. I didn't sleep very well last night—it's all been going around in my mind, as you can imagine. Hopefully, fresh air will help."

Norm nodded, before becoming distracted by incoming messages on both his phone and laptop.

Tam felt it might be the prudent time to go out and leave him to his work. She put the mug onto the corner of the messy table and turned to go to the kitchen.

"Wait, Tam," he said and reached down into a deep drawer in his desk, a drawer that was full of cables and gadgets. He extracted a phone. "You will need this phone if you are going out alone. It will be tracked the moment you switch it on. I primed it up for you last night, for just such a situation."

"Morgan told me to switch my phone off, before we left London, so what good will this do me?"

"I told Morgan to ensure your own personal phone was switched off. Standard phones, like yours, can be traced and hacked. We don't want to hand Brig any advantage. This one is secure.

"Listen Tam, there is danger from the prime source, as you know, but we don't know if she has any cohorts... This is what the team have been working on, since your call to me yesterday. In order to counteract any threat from Brig, we have put a trace on her movements. She isn't stupid, and the devices we are using aren't infallible, but at least we have some insight as to her whereabouts—currently Ealing, West London, according to the latest update from Parv."

"Parv was the beautiful, young Persian girl I met here last year, at the housewarming party, wasn't she?"

"Yes. She also has a connection to Brig, shall we say?" Norm raised his eyebrows suggestively.

"You mean Brig and Parv are involved, in some way, romantically?"

"Yes, they have been."

"Can you trust Parv?"

"That is what I am about to find out."

"Interesting and potentially dangerous," replied Tam.

"Talking of dangerous, have you spoken to Felton at all? I don't suppose he has bothered to call you recently?" Norm enquired.

"Good God, no, he's too busy living his glorious life, isn't he?" she said sarcastically.

"Well, Tam, I can tell you that he is on the brink of departing the Service. We suspect he will be bombed out soon, with a golden handshake. That's what I've said to the Home Secretary, so let him decide, eh?"

"Indeed, Norm. Let's hope he delivers good news sooner rather than later. If he does, let me be the first to know, won't you?"

"You definitely will be, and don't forget to tell Argent next time you see him so he can get you your cut of it, because it will be a handsome amount, and his pension too."

"Nice. It will be good to see him squirm for a change," Tam gloated.

Norm brushed some food crumbs off the phone from his desk drawer and handed it to Tam.

"OK, Tam, we digress. The phone you have in your hand is a VPN phone: Virtual Private Network. The members of my team have one too, including Parv. If yours is used at all, then we will know almost instantly. Now, I suggest you only switch it on and use it should an emergency arise. Is that clear?"

"Clear," Tam responded, as if one of his underlings.

"Secondly, if there is an issue, we may shut down certain digital channels. If this new phone doesn't work for any reason, it's because we have made it so, do you understand?"

"Yep, got it."

"Additionally, should this latter situation actually occur, and I have told Amey this too, you are to check the status of the house flag."

"The flag? What the hell has that got to do with anything?" she asked, somewhat bemused.

"Anything other than a fully masted flag means do not come back here, under any circumstances. Whilst I might be old fashioned in my ways, it provides us with a form of contingency, yes?"

"Yes, OK, so what would I do then?" she asked.

"Go to the caravan over at Sker Lake. Here, I have even drawn a map for you," he said, passing her a page, one he'd ripped out from an old diary by the look of it.

"It isn't up to your standards for graphics, sis, but I suggest you check out the location of number fifty-four, 'Burgess', on your way out to the beach. It's only a minor detour, but it could save your life later. It is that serious."

That name, Burgess, again. She'd wondered where it had come from yesterday when the female police officer arrived. Now, she knew.

"It's only a contingency and unlikely to happen, but we need a way to direct the play. Essentially, you need to stay vigilant, which I know you will, sis. Right... enough. Here are the caravan keys, in the unlikely event that you will need them. Amey told me she has made you a sandwich, which is in the fridge along with a bottle of water, I think she said. Just take anything you want."

Whilst these instructions raised a modicum of alarm in her mind, he'd still given her the freedom she required.

"Daft question to finish, Norm. Which way is it to the beach?"

Norm beckoned her to the window.

"See that car park ahead? That is where you will cross the West Bay Road. Head left at that point, along the golf fairway. After a short while you will start to see the top of The Steps, you can't miss them. They are a set of black steps, similar to the ones they use at horse races, like the Grand National."

"Ok, I'm following you. Go on," Tam said, thinking it was starting to get a little complicated.

"Then follow the path to the left, which takes you to the beach. Don't take the undulating bridlepaths to your right, they are too tough. However, as I said, you need to find the caravan first, please, which you will see to the far right of the car park when you cross the West Bay Road. If you head to the right-hand side of the nature reserve building, you will see the path itself, lined with bracken, or ferns, I never know which is which."

Neither did Tam, but she got the picture.

"What would Mum and Dad have thought of all this mess?" she said.

"Dad would hunt them down and deal with it in his own way," said Norm, casting his gaze to the messy table covered with papers barely concealing the end of their father's old pistol.

Tam followed his eyeline to the tip of the gun.

"Yes... I think you're right. Perhaps we should invite another guest to dinner tonight," said Tam jokingly.

"If only. Then all our problems would really be solved."

CHAPTER SEVEN – STEPPING OUT

Tam added the VPN phone to her bag and turned for the kitchen, only to be met by Norm's ageing and somewhat overweight cat, Olive, struggling to get onto her favourite corner chair.

Tam scooped her up, giving her a cuddle and a kiss in the process, before placing her down onto the equally plump cushion.

"You're too soft—let her do it for herself. She needs the exercise, fat old moggy," Norm commented, before returning his gaze to his screen.

"Aww, don't listen to the grumpy old man, Olive. Like the rest of us, you're not getting any younger, are you?" Tam said, stroking Olive's soft tortoiseshell head.

Tam partly regretted her decision to offer Olive such assistance when she saw her blouse was now covered in cat hair. Norm looked up and threw a roll of Sellotape at her.

"I told you, didn't I? Why do you think I keep the tape so close to hand?"

Tam expertly caught the roll in mid-air.

"Can never find the end, though," she said, picking away at the roll with a jagged fingernail.

"Let's hope we can soon, eh?" came his wry reply, referring to her predicament with Brig.

Tam gave him the stare she usually kept for rude people in London, as she began dabbing the front of her top with the tacky side of the tape.

"Don't forget your sandwich now, will you, sis?" Norm said with his craggy smile.

Tam immediately threw the roll towards his head. He ducked, and it hit the open window behind his head then disappeared outside. Tam playfully shrugged and turned, once more, for the kitchen with a smug smile.

The sandwich, water and an apple were easily found at the forefront of the fridge, with a handwritten note attached:

Elinor replied to my message. She is fine and enjoying herself.

I haven't said anything to her about the situation, she thinks you are just visiting on a pleasure trip.

So GO AND ENJOY YOURSELF.

See you later.

Amey x

Yes, she damned well would enjoy herself.

Her eyes fixed upon a stunning monochrome photo, tucked away by the side of the fridge. There, with her bare back to the camera, sat the then Amey Vogler astride a large grey horse. Her beautiful young face, looking over her shoulder, was mesmerising. It served to entice Tam into that clothes-free world that many might disapprove of. However, Tam no longer cared for the opinions of others on the subject; she found the picture incredibly powerful and evocative.

"You have always been an inspiration to me, Amey, never more so than now," she said, then headed out of the house with renewed vigour.

Stepping out into the mid-morning haze, Tam was finally free to roam the dunes of Skerrid Mawr alone. Whilst her heart desperately wanted to get to the beach as soon as possible, her head told her that she should check out the caravan park first, just in case. She owed Norm that much, at least. Surely, it couldn't be that difficult to find the only caravan facility in the area.

Tam headed down the very short lane to the junction with the West Bay Road. It effectively marked the dividing line between inland and coastal, grass versus sand and, hopefully, old problems against new horizons.

Tam stopped for a moment, turning around to take a panoramic look back at the village of Skerrid Mawr itself. It was like nothing she had seen before.

Apart from the lane that led up to Norm's house, there were no side streets as such, just a long line of differing properties hugging the arterial West Bay Road. There was no significant depth to the village's housing, no overcrowding like one might usually see in many a small British seaside town. Refreshingly, its unique layout, style and character was further supported by a verdant backdrop dotted with sheep, bestowing a special feeling of space and quaintness in equal measure. It had a certain serenity.

She looked forward to finding out more about the village in the next couple of days when, hopefully, Norm and Amey could give her a proper tour of the area.

Crossing the road, Tam reached the nature reserve building, a wide, low structure that dominated what she had seen of the village thus far. The upper tier bore a modest atrium, clad in dark wood slats, making it sit well in the encroaching dunes behind.

Opting to go round the right-hand side of the facility, on her way to find the pathway to the caravan site, she passed by a very tall, carved wooden statue of a woman. She only had the merest glimpse of it, but a few steps later, she realised the vision had instantly lodged deeply into her brain, making her literally stop in her tracks. Tam swivelled on the spot and returned to look at it again, this time in much greater detail.

Almost ankle-deep in the warm sand, Tam stood in front of the intricate carving. She was entranced by its weather-beaten magnificence. Here, before her, was an awesome sculpture, already touching something deep within her own psyche.

The carving stood tall, rising several feet above her. It was unlike any art she had seen before, the nearest being the stone carvings on Easter Island, which she had never had the chance to visit. Her fingers touched its legs and continued their contact around its torso, engaging with the small hands that lay peacefully behind its back. She marvelled at the extended hair, seemingly blowing in the strong sea breeze.

Returning to view the beautiful features of the statue's face, she felt compelled to speak.

"I want to feel how you feel," Tam let slip, louder than planned.

"Do you?" came a voice from behind her.

Tam jumped.

It was a lady, clearly from the nature reserve in her beige trousers and green polo shirt embroidered with "SMNR Warden". Her lanyard confirmed her identity, with the name "Hannah" printed in large letters.

"It is a fantastic symbol, isn't it?" she said.

"Very much so. I love art, and this is amazing." Tam shook her head in wonderment. "I have never seen anything like it. Wow."

"It's known as 'Our Lady of the Dunes'," Hannah informed her.

"What a great name. Very ethereal, isn't it?"

"It's exactly that—ethereal. I was at the side door and noticed the way you halted and came back to look at it. Here, you might like a brochure that tells you about her and all about the nature reserve," said Hannah, presenting Tam with said item.

Tam had a quick look through the leaflet. "Oh, I see you host school trips."

"Indeed, the primary schools love coming out here because it offers so much to them, not only in terms of nature studies but also in terms of getting out from the classroom too," Hannah informed Tam in what Tam now realised was a Yorkshire accent. "We give them a brief talk in the Sker Suite, telling them how Skerrid Mawr was founded on an ancient village that once sat close to the sea yet was forced back by the waves to reside behind the safety of these magnificent dunes. After that introduction, we then provide them with some activity books, pencils, crayons and so forth, and let them enjoy themselves, as their teacher decides, of course.

"If it's warm, then they can sit outside. If not, they can draw from the pictures posted around our function room or even walk over to the hides on the lake, where they can watch the wildfowl, even in the winter—it's all year round here, you know."

"What a wonderful place, so quiet," said Tam. "There's very little like this in London's concrete jungle, of course, with the odd exception here and there. But the cost of doing anything up there is always so high."

Hannah nodded in agreement. "Recent cut-backs here mean that there are very few of us staffing the facility now. We survive on a mixture of council funding, lottery grants and donations. Any profit we glean from our small gift shop or letting the function room gets ploughed back in. So, if you know anyone, send them here!"

"Well, my sister-in-law, Amey Weaver, may be one of your helpers actually. Sorry, my name is Tam, by the way," said Tam, offering her hand somewhat formally, to which Hannah dutifully responded.

"Oh yes, Amey has been one of our saviours since she arrived in the village. A very interesting lady. Actually, were it not for volunteers like her, we may not survive. She has worked so hard, giving her time to fill the facility when we don't have any school visits, with talks from invited guests, plus other social gatherings like photography clubs and also a small book club on a Friday, which she hosts too."

"That sounds like Amey, generous to a fault," Tam added with a smile. She felt proud that Amey had made her presence felt to such a deserving cause.

As she finished speaking, a large white coach appeared, ambling slowly toward its allotted parking bay in the car park.

"Oh, here are today's pupils," said Hannah. "I had best away. Nice talking to you, Tam. Send my regards to Amey, won't you? Bye for now."

Tam waited a couple of minutes more, to watch the excited children filing from the bus into the building, remembering similar school trips she used to help with when Anthony and Elinor were little.

Spending a little more time here couldn't hurt. She tucked the pamphlet into her bag and took out a pencil. The carving was such an amazing addition to the landscape— she couldn't help but want to draw it.

Tam rummaged for some paper; she usually kept plenty close at hand for writing copious lists. Digging deeper into her bag, she found a tiny, plain-sheeted notepad, no larger than a postcard.

She took a few steps across the sand to the edge of the bracken and sat down cross-legged, like the children might now be doing, to face her subject, placing her baseball cap on her now dry hair to keep the sun out of her eyes.

Her sketching technique was simple and swift, and within ten minutes, she had completed a very reasonable representation of "Our Lady of the Dunes". She decided to show it to Amey later, who would surely be able to tell her more about its provenance, should the leaflet not do so.

Checking her watch, Tam carefully put the pad and pencil back into her bag, then securely fastened it before standing up and harnessing it to her warm back. Although she wasn't exactly in a rush, she still wanted to reach the beach sooner rather than later. After all, she had something else she wanted to do whilst the opportunity presented itself: find a quiet spot and bare herself to the sun.

From her position, the roofs of the caravans were now apparent, as was the bracken-lined path that would take her away from the coast, toward the large lake and into the caravan park itself, should it be needed.

Having satisfied her brother's demand, Tam now opted to explore the labyrinth of paths that lay before her. If she branched left at some point she would, based on Norm's instructions, hopefully meet the main path to The Steps, where she could take her bearings again.

Tam knew she must have been heading in the right direction, as the wide sandy path started to undulate, signalling entrance into the main dunes system, as did the tall, dense scrub which reached above head height. Together, the sand and the scrub helped to create a noticeable funnel of heat, as the sun, now way up high to her left, burned down.

Her pigeon instincts had served her well and Tam soon arrived at the infamous Steps, a large, jet black, metal construction several metres high that sat on the back corner of a golf teeing area.

However, the path that lay in front of her was snaking further left, away from the direction she thought she would ultimately be taking. The only other choice was to take the path denoted by a small blue circle on a post to her right, but that was a bridlepath, the one Norm had advised her not to use. She was a little confused.

To her left, the rattle of metal could be heard, and she was met with three cap-wearing men making their way up to the tee area where The Steps lay. It was a trio of middle-aged golfers with their motorised golf trollies, heading her way. Their attention seemed to quickly focus on her as they climbed up the woodchip path.

"Alright, love, fancy shimmying up these steps to watch our drives?" chirped up the one with the awful dress sense.

"Not really. I was just wondering if you know how I can get to the right-hand side of the beach?"

"No idea, we're not from 'round yer', but perhaps that guy there behind you can help. See you again maybe, love?" he optimistically added.

"Thanks, but probably not," came her less-than-tactful reply, returning back to the path to be met by said man behind her, who was donning a cap and rucksack.

"Excuse me..." she began to ask, but he held his hand up to stop her question mid-track. With a winning smile, he made her world rock in an instant.

"I know where you are heading, and I can take you there if you would allow me to do so," he said, whilst his brown eyes scored a direct hit into hers.

She smiled a bashful smile. "The beach," she weakly replied.

"Yes, of course you are... but, excuse the expression, you want the far end, don't you?"

His eyes remained fixed on hers, obviously awaiting a response. He was sharp, witty and dangerously attractive. She had no choice but to launch a smile that Helen of Troy herself would have been proud of.

"So that's a yes, then?"

Tam felt like a seventeen-year-old, bowled over by the school smooth-guy. There was no other choice but to accept his offer. She hadn't factored this into her plan, but, after all, she did ask.

"My name is Kee, by the way. Are you on a break down here?" he asked politely.

Tam wasn't sure if she had heard him correctly. Was he asking her if she was on a breakdown here? How would he know?

"Sort of," came her unconvincing answer.

"What does 'sort of' mean exactly?"

"It means... well... sort of."

There was a pause as she realised that they were talking at cross purposes, followed by a spontaneous and simultaneous outburst of uncontrollable laughter from them both. In that moment she knew, despite the gibberish, they had connected on a very instinctive, human level and, moreover, he seemed to know it too. The electricity was there; they both felt it, and there was no going back. Tam felt giddy; this guy was already in her head, and she loved it.

"My name is Tam. Sorry for being so ditsy. I'm not usually like this," she said, not sure whether to shake his hand or how to move on from here.

"Hello, Tam," he said with a broad grin of his own. "Let's walk this way." He gestured for her to continue along the left-winding path, thus easing any awkwardness. It was immediately apparent he knew the dunes well.

As he led the way, she noted his beige cargo shorts and his jaunty blue training shoes. He must have walked this path many a time, she thought; his calf muscles looked strong, too. A small black rucksack sat on his white polo shirt, lightly swaying in rhythm with his purposeful stride. Tam realised she needed to walk a little quicker to keep up with him, her own footwear now filling up with the excess sand from the softening pathway between the steepening, grassy dunes on either side.

She wasn't sure if she should start asking him questions, he could be anybody. But she didn't want to get too intrusive, so she stuck to a few generalities.

"I think I should clarify something, Kee—I am staying with my brother and his wife, here in Skerrid Mawr, for a couple of days probably before I head back to London, all being well."

"Yeah? I was a Lewisham lad originally. You?" he asked.

"We moved around a bit, due to my father's work, but mainly Kingston upon Thames."

"Nice place. Close enough to London and far away enough from London too, isn't it?"

"Yes... and it sounds as if you know the area," Tam replied, pleased that he knew where she had spent most of her life.

"I do. My ex-wife was from that neck of the woods."

Tam didn't want to respond by asking why he had an ex-wife; it could be any number of reasons. If he wanted to tell her, then that was up to him. She changed tack.

"So, Kee, do you regularly visit Skerrid Mawr or do you actually live here?" she asked.

"I'm a regular visitor here. Basically, it all depends on the weather and when I can actually get down, with work commitments and the like," he said, allowing Tam the opportunity to delve deeper.

"What is your work, then, if you don't mind me asking?"

"Mobile hospitality. That's a posh way of saying I attend events and turn up with my trailers to provide food and drink to the punters. It's sporadic, which suits me. When I work, I work very hard for a few days and then I have time off, just like today."

"It sounds interesting."

"It can be. It depends on the event and who I am working with."

Tam had started to notice the little tag on Kee's comments—it was as if he wanted her to ask him more. Maybe she would.

CHAPTER EIGHT – INTRICATE PATHWAYS

Tam could soon hear the sea, as they approached a small descent in the narrowing path.

"Excuse us, please," came a call from behind.

It was three teenage girls on horseback. Both Kee and Tam stood back to allow them to pass.

Leading the pack was a strong bay, around sixteen hands, whose dappled hind quarters shone in the bright sun, closely followed by two ponies, both nearer fourteen hands. The first pony was iron grey, sporting a bushy black mane and tail, similar to one Elinor used to ride. The second one was a chestnut, complete with a flaxen mane and tail, with a clean white blaze down its face.

The sight reminded Tam of the hours spent riding her own horses with Anthony and Elinor, her leading and them following, as they hacked through Richmond Park on a Sunday. She was envious of these girls being able to ride on the sands. Never, in all her equine days, had she ever been lucky enough to ride along a beach. Hopefully, Amey would allow her to ride Hektor, their Bavarian Warmblood, if time allowed during her stay.

"Welsh Cobs are my favourite," Kee commented loudly to Tam as they trooped by.

"Oh, know your horse breeds, then, do you, Kee? Very impressive. Do you ride at all?"

"It has been known," came the enigmatic reply.

He was getting more and more interesting by the minute.

"So, if you had the chance to ride on this beach, would you?" Tam put to him.

"I already have," he said, somewhat smugly, as they moved forward to watch the teenage trio head down toward the sands below.

"You really are a dark horse, aren't you?" she cheekily suggested.

"When women are involved, yes," he quickly replied.

Tam now knew she had met her match when it came to banter. Kee had a very sharp wit and wasn't afraid to use it. As she contemplated her next line of enquiry, he spoke again.

"Here, Tam, take a real good look at the panorama," he said, standing on the front edge of a small tump, inviting her to join him.

"You are looking across to Mumbles Lighthouse, at the end of Swansea Bay," he informed her, "and the hills of the Gower beyond. It's something special to behold, isn't it?"

It was, and so was he.

Saying nothing more, Tam allowed him to savour the view. This was clearly an element that had repeatedly drawn him here, to this particular spot above Skerrid Beach. How lucky was she to be sharing his special moment, she thought, looking at his kind, tanned face. Yes, the views here were, indeed, something special.

Tam waited for Kee to break the silence, not wishing to interrupt his moment of tranquillity. She didn't mind waiting; in fact, the longer the better.

"By contrast, I think I need to show you this, too: the infamous 'Omni's Shack'," he said, pointing to Tam's left.

Sure enough, tucked neatly above the end of the beach and the reddish rock of the jutting headland, stood a structure comprising two conjoined former shipping containers set at right angles to one another and surrounded by well-worn, rough, brown ground. Its corrugated dark green metal shell sat surprisingly well in the landscape, with the end of the dunes almost camouflaging its presence.

A small flag, a yellow cross upon a black background, sat fluttering above a row of solar panels that covered its roof. Kee explained its significance as the standard of St David, the patron saint of Wales.

Tam wanted to know more about Omni. Having received some information about her from Morgan on the drive down, she was curious to see what Kee's impression of her was, given that he was a regular visitor.

"I have heard a little about Omni," she said, testing the water.

Kee's hand went to his chin and started rubbing it, delaying his response. He looked a little unsettled by her statement.

"OK then, Tam, what have you heard about Omni, exactly?"

Tam quickly contemplated her response, as he sounded a little defensive about the subject. Could this be her chance to open him up, or would he continue with his minimalist answers?

"She is everywhere, apparently, hence the name, and she also owns one of the pubs in the village. The Dragon, I think it is," she stated.

"The Dragon's Tail, to be exact. Omni is a very 'interesting lady', shall we say, with a heart of gold."

Tam waited for Kee to elaborate, so she could compare his thoughts to Morgan's. When he stayed quiet, she prompted him,

"I take it you've been to her pub, then?"

"Many people have been to her pub, Tam. What of it? It's just a pub."

"I heard she is single and not shy when it comes to men," she teased.

"Well, I don't know what you've heard and from whom, but don't include me in that list. Tell you what, Tam, you take in the wonderful view whilst I go and use the facilities in The Shack," he said, exchanging places with her. "And... just for your information, I can see that Omni isn't here, her trademark quad bike is missing. See you in a moment or two, then."

As he made his way down the dirt path to The Shack, Tam wondered if she had overstepped the mark with her intrusive questioning. Kee clearly wouldn't be drawn about Omni, not that she had any right to know about his personal life. Even if he were closer to her than he made out, it was none of her business. Tam regretted asking and hoped it wouldn't cause him to find an excuse to part company, which would leave her to walk the far end of the beach alone.

Why did she have to overthink things so much? At least he hadn't taken off to The Shack in a huff; he had remained nice and polite.

She decided to let the subject go, moving up a few feet to a new vantage point.

Below her, a vast expanse of beach arced like a giant boomerang into the distance, exacerbated by an outgoing tide. There seemed to only be a smattering of people dotted along its length, all of whom looked like tiny ants. Likewise, the three horses that they had met earlier now seemed extremely small as they rode away from her. She assumed she would be following a similar track with Kee—if he returned, that was.

"Right, Tam, are you ready for this?" came the voice of Kee as he made his way up to her side.

Tam nodded back with outward enthusiasm but inward trepidation.

Kee guided her along the grass verge bedecked with seasonal buttercups and daisies before descending down to a steep pebble bank, one that would give them access to the sand. Leading the way, he carefully clambered down at a sideward angle, as the oval grey rocks and pebbles gently gave way under his feet with a gentle clacking noise.

After a couple of steps, he offered up his hand. Tam accepted as she tentatively stepped on the shifting pebbles.

"Reminds me of doing the very same thing when my children were young," Tam stated as she carefully edged down the acute angle of descent.

"Me too... Steady now, Tam."

Her fingers clasped his tightly as she braced herself against the movement of the stones, before finally being delivered onto a patch of bare sand. The sensuality of their contact hadn't gone unnoticed as Tam released herself from Kee's grip and took a single step away.

She smiled. "Thank you... That was nice of you."

"No problem," said Kee before kicking off his shoes and tucking them into the webbing of his rucksack. "It's a fair walk. I usually use the top path, or the Warden's Path as I call it, and cut through the dunes further along, but there's no rush, is there?"

"None whatsoever," agreed Tam, trying to come to terms with what she was truly getting herself into. All the things she ever said to her children about never going with strangers, she was now going against herself. Despite wanting the security of being with Kee, she couldn't decide whether she should stay with him or find her own space when they finally reached wherever he might be taking her. She had to know more about him and, more to the point, find out what specifically drove him to visit this particular spot.

"OK, so apart from the obvious joys of the beach, what are you really doing here, Kee?" she asked.

Kee looked at her intently, his deep brown eyes connecting with hers once more, seemingly unable or unwilling to answer her question.

Tam persisted. "Come on, be honest. It isn't just sun-seeking, is it? You could do that at home. Now, I grant you that this is probably a very different environment from your home, but nor are you seeking the social scene either, given the lack of people... or are you, perhaps?" she added, having caught a flicker of reaction to that last statement.

"Why do you say that, then, Tam? Oh, if you mean the likes of Omni, then 'no' is the emphatic answer to that. Listen, I don't come here to meet people; it's because I want to be here and I can be here. Modern life can get too busy for me now. I'm not as fit as I was, or able to cope with the stresses that still come my way. This place, this activity, is the calm that is hard to find anywhere else."

Tam loved his answer. His softening tones told her that was a deep thinker. She felt privileged that he was willing to reveal this to her so intimately.

She now felt confident to ask about his philosophy when it came to being naked.

"So, would you say you are a nudist or a naturist?" asked Tam, as they strolled along.

"Naturist," came his single-word reply.

"What's the difference, then?"

"I don't choose to go around naked all day, irrespective of where I am. Some do, I don't. Naturist camps and suchlike are not for me. However, being at one with nature at the right time and in the right place, where it doesn't concern or involve others, present company excepted, is what I seek."

Feeling that the real Kee was starting to emerge, Tam offered her genuine appreciation. "Thank you for letting me in today. You could have just walked past and found your own way."

"Yes, it is what I'd intended to do, but you gave yourself away. It was clear to me what you were about. A single woman stopping to talk to golfers en route to this beach, the rucksack, the outfit that you have on and even your hand gestures told me everything I needed to know. The fact is, I didn't want you asking the wrong person, plus I was heading in that direction anyway. So, Tam, please don't consider me to be a Good Samaritan, but a fairly safe one. Let me also say, here and now, that you are welcome to branch off at any point and do your own thing, once we are in the 'Un-Textile Zone', shall we call it."

This guy was completely in control, and it touched her very soul like no man had ever done before.

Feeling reassured by his answers, she asked, "Would it be OK for me to stay close to you when we get to where we are going, please? I honestly have never done anything like this before and I am a little scared, to be frank."

"Of course, yes, you can. Listen, Tam, here is the scene. You will see more men than women today. The few women you see will almost definitely be with a man, but most men will be alone. I don't speculate about their motives, that is their business. You can read into that whatever you like, but that's my interpretation of how it goes down here. The fact that you were prepared to go solo impresses me greatly. It says much about you."

Tam could feel the goosebumps rising up on her skin and a glow inside. She couldn't remember the last time anyone had paid her a compliment of such magnitude. It took her a moment to recompose herself.

"Sorry to ask, Kee, but does anyone ever want to stop to chat? I wouldn't really want that."

"That's a reasonable question. Sometimes they do, yes, and if so, just be as polite as you would be fully clothed. You will suss them out quickly enough, but most are fine. Worst that happens is you put your clothes back on, isn't it?"

Tam had to think about that situation a little more. Being topless was one thing, but being publicly naked and fully exposed was something else, be it with Kee or any other relative stranger.

"Hey, you've gone quiet now. Please, don't worry about it, just see what happens. I promise I will intervene if need be," Kee said, assuaging her worries a little.

As they reached the bend in the beach, Tam could now see the elevated strandline to her right, punctuated with the debris of logs and tree trunks the outgoing tide had left behind. The timbers lay at various angles, some resting upon the very edges of the small bank of paler sand that ran along the front of the steeply faced dunes, the very dunes where she assumed they would be seeking solace.

The reality of the situation now became more apparent, especially when Kee briefly stopped to remove his shirt before tying it around his waist and walking on. He was halfway to being naked. She observed his slim, lightly tanned physique from behind.

If she was going to see this through, she ought to do something reciprocal at least.

"Could you wait a moment, please?" Tam asked.

Kee stopped and turned around to face her.

"Would you mind holding my bag for a second? I could do with taking my shirt off too, this bag has made my back a little sticky," she explained, handing the bag to Kee.

She unbuttoned her blouse, noticing that he looked away while she removed it, only looking back at her once she had completed knotting it around her waist, mimicking his action, but retaining her bikini top.

"Better?" he asked.

"Much," she replied, gesturing for her bag to be returned.

"Don't worry, I can take your bag for you, if you will allow me. You enjoy the benefit of the breeze on your skin. There's nothing quite like it, is there?" he said suggestively.

A flutter went through Tam's tummy at his implication, and she accepted his offer.

If she had any thoughts of not going through with this, then she would have to act now or not at all. Tam knew it was probably too late; Kee's charm offensive was already working its spell on her.

"What is that, in the sand? Is it a wreck of some type?" she asked, pointing at the rotting wooden struts of an old boat that lay sunken in the middle of the beach.

"Yes, it's called the *Caswell*," Kee informed her. "It ran aground here around 1960."

"Washed up on the beach like me, but I have more fat on my ribs," Tam said, half joking.

"Good metaphor, Tam, but why do you self-deprecate?" Kee shook his head. "Anyway, its real significance is that we're here. We've arrived, if you hadn't noticed... the 'Un-Textile Zone', clothes optional, call it what you like."

Tam didn't notice anything significant, until she turned to face the dunes to her right.

There was someone there. A naked man. She averted her gaze quickly, causing Kee to laugh.

"Best we get you out of sight," he said to Tam, whilst waving to the man.

"Do you know him?"

"Probably not, but like I said, it doesn't hurt to be friendly, does it?"

"Shouldn't there be some sort of sign?"

"No, it's an unofficial nudist part of the beach where clothed people, a.k.a. 'textiles', and naturists should be able to co-exist. Right, let's head across to a little place in the dune over there, away from that gentleman, as it's sheltered from view and, more importantly, unoccupied. You can go to the part on the left and I will go on the right."

There really was no turning back now.

"What I mean, Tam, is that you can see me, if you want, but I won't be able to see you," he clarified. "At least, in that arrangement, you will know that I am near, in case something or someone bothers you... How does that sound?"

His clinical delivery provided some assurance, at least.

Tam agreed to his suggestion with an unconvincing smile as they made their way up the sandy bank toward the dune. As she reached the top of the strandline, Tam called Kee back, inviting him to sit down on a large piece of driftwood that conveniently lay there like an impromptu bench.

Discussing her deep emotions with anyone, be it man, woman, work colleague or family member, had been a constant struggle throughout her life. She had always kept them bottled up within. Her chat with young Morgan the previous evening had restored her confidence to a certain degree, yet, whilst he had been receptive and engaging, Tam already knew that she could go way further with Kee. Age mattered, and Kee didn't seem the judgemental type. Confident in his own skin, yes, but probably with his own tale of woe to tell. She had to take a chance on this "open-air confessional" or remain condemned to introversion for the rest of her days on the planet.

"Listen, Kee, I need to tell you something, before we go any further. Something is bothering me," she said, plucking up the courage to be so forward.

"Is it 'women's problems' at all?"

"No, it's a problem with a woman, there's a difference."

"Can I just say something, from my general experience with women?"

"Sounds like you are going to anyway, Kee."

"'Sisters or bitches.' There you go, I have said it. You women either love each other or you hate each other. It's perplexing for us dull males. At least with blokes, they sort out such issues one way or another. We move on. I have," was his impassioned statement, causing Tam to snort at his vehemence.

"As interesting as your philosophy is, you might not want my company after you hear what I have to say. You might consider me to be a bitch, too."

"Well, I very much doubt it. I'm a good listener and, no pun intended, there is clearly something you want to get off your chest. I can see you are married, so go on, shock me," he challenged her.

Tam smirked. What she had to say would test his mettle and truly confirm him as a reliable confidant or a complete waste of time.

She proceeded to tell him an abridged version of the events surrounding Felton, Brig, Majorca and Grant, as she had done to Amey the previous evening.

Over twenty-five minutes later, Kee had proved himself right: he was a good listener but an even better motivator.

"Tam, who looks out for you in your life, day in and day out? Who, in truth, really cares for you? In my own experience, and by my own observations, not many people actually do. The fact of the matter is that you have to do it for yourself. You have obviously been doing that for your kids, and it sounds like you have done a great job but sacrificed yourself, as a result, along the way. Subliminally, or otherwise, you have figured out it's your time to reward yourself for all that input."

"Norm and Amey look out for me," was her timid response.

"But, as you said yourself, they were miles away from you in Sussex, and now that they're here in Skerrid Mawr, they're even further away! That's what your coercive husband probably relied upon: your isolation. If they had lived around the corner from you, it may have been different."

His intuition was hitting the spot.

"So, how often did you visit them?" he asked. "On your own, I mean."

"I can't remember exactly, but no more than a handful of occasions," Tam admitted.

"Exactly. I guess you are staying with them right now as some type of bolt-hole from this Brig girl. I don't know you... yet, but that's the way it looks to me: namely, you have given yourself permission to do what you are doing here, right now."

"I would normally agree with you, but I did something stupid which tipped the balance," she said, referring to the Grant incident.

"You crossed the line once, just once. It's not a hanging offence, is it?" Kee shrugged.

"Yet it's me who gets all the crap, whilst others like Felton and Brig get away with it. Why?"

"Some pay heavily for their mistakes, Tam."

"That's not what I want to hear."

"Felton and this Brig girl, I meant, not you."

"How on earth has Felton paid for his mistakes, then, Kee?"

"Because he has lost you, hasn't he?"

Tam was dumbfounded and flattered in equal measure. He was right; Kee was absolutely right.

"You know the best form of defence in such situations, don't you, Tam?" he said with a smile. "Attack!"

CHAPTER NINE — WEAVER BIRDS

Amey Weaver peered through the small side window into the front room, where Norm sat, bolt upright, in his swivel chair, ensconced in technology, probably seeking information, answers and approvals. Virtual meetings, follow-ups and phone calls were usually the order of his morning's work.

His workload was heavy at the best of times, but after the events of yesterday, all other items had been now deferred in favour of defending his sister, family and British justice in the face of severe pressure from the US Government, who demanded substantive proof of wrongdoing by their representative Brig Huddlestone.

Following Tam's call for help, Amey had discussed the ramifications of the situation with Norm. For the first time since their move to the village, she had discovered a genuine state of unease from Norm. For once, finding a solution, diplomatic or otherwise, was going to be a real struggle, and it was seriously preying on his mind.

Norm had revealed to her that he had been on Brig's case for some months but that the incident between Tam and Grant had diluted his argument with his American counterparts, much to his chagrin.

He, usually a creature of habit, had got up earlier than usual this morning, a clear sign that an unsurmountable problem existed.

As Amey stepped in through the side door, Hertz leapt from his bed in the kitchen and raced to meet her, his nails skittering across the tiled floor, bringing a smile to her face.

"Hello, are you OK?" enquired Amey, as she entered Norm's office with an excited dog in tow, his tail thumping against her leg.

"I've had better mornings. The Americans are playing hardball, not just in London but in Washington too. They're refusing to accept our dossier on Brig, Lord knows why."

Amey could see the disappointment and stress written all over his face. Her own heart sank in turn.

"'Insubstantial' is the bloody word they are toting at me. How dare they!"

"*Himmelherrgott*, what do they want, then? Blood?"

"Yes, it seems so, Amey. You know I can't let that happen, not to Tam, not to anyone in my world."

Amey stepped to the back of his chair and ran her slim fingers through his tousled greying hair, working her way down to massage his neck and shoulders. She could feel the drop in tension as she pressed her thumbs into the knots in his broad shoulders.

She reached forward and planted a kiss on his forehead. "Coffee?"

"Please, Amey, thank you."

She reached out to collect the patriotically decorated mug from his desk and kissed him on the head again as he sat looking at one of his three screens.

"Did you see Liz?" he called after her as she headed to the kitchen.

"Yes," she called back. "Tell you more in a moment."

As she returned with mugs in hand, Norm's email alert pinged.

VPN enabled for Group K has been activated to include Tamsin Kendall & Amey Weaver, as requested.

Norm announced this ad verbatim to Amey as he picked up the coaster from his desk and lazily wiped the old stain away with the loose cloth of his shirt. The print on the coaster was still just about visible: *Frankfurt Am Main, 1992, WPC.*

"You know, it is coming up for the anniversary," said Amey as she placed his mug on the coaster.

"Difficult to forget," responded Norm, reaching back from his seat to rub her leg sympathetically.

"I don't want to dwell on it right now, we have too much else to think about." She sat herself down on an easy chair and changed the subject. "Liz was in the surgery this morning. She told me that she is finishing early to sort out the annexe at Sandpiper, just in case it is needed."

"Ah... right, good. Did you get your prescription sorted out?" asked Norm, finally facing her and not his monitors.

"Yes, the consultant told them that he was happy and that I should move down to some weaker tablets, ones that will decrease my dependency."

"Wonderful. You're doing so well. I'm surprised you aren't a case study or something."

"Were it not for my activities and you, Norm, I think I would have given up years ago," came her emotive response.

"I am so sorry, Amey, I really wish things could have been different, but you have been so strong. You live a very fulfilling life and you are a credit to yourself and your roots, in so doing. An inspiration to others. The feedback you get from your writing proves that."

Norm stepped out from his chair and across the room to embrace Amey.

Amey knew her sadness had always muted his ability to fully celebrate his own achievements, sporting or otherwise. Bizarrely, the Pentathlon event in 1992 had been the very thing that had bonded them as a couple, taking them across many divides to find love. It was a precious moment.

"Well, it looks like Hertz is ready to go out," Amey exclaimed, as the dog attempted to get involved in their chair-based cuddle.

"I did ask Tam to take him, but she had another agenda on her mind... shall we say?" Norm said softly into her ear.

"I know—and good for her, I say, you old fool. She can make her own decisions."

"She thinks I don't know where she's heading, but it was fairly obvious. Your bad influence has made her do this, Amey," he mocked as he stood back up.

"Well, it is about time she stepped out and discovered her own potential. In East Germany no one would care about being naked on a beach. You British are such prudes. Our bodies are to be celebrated, not hidden away," she laughed, playfully trying to pinch Norm's side, causing him to squirm away. "Now, finish your coffee before that one goes cold, too. I will get changed and take Hertz out. Given Tam will probably be at the Morfa end of the beach, we will take the Pipit Path, as I call it."

"Pipit Path?" he replied.

"Yes, you know, the one that takes you around the far side of the lake, past the old ruins of Skerrid Castle and through the reedbeds to the beach."

"Oh yes, of course. That's the one with brambles and the marshy section, isn't it? Best wear your old boots, then, Amey, even on a day like this."

"I will indeed. I hope Tam took sun cream with her or she will regret it later," Amey added.

"Well, she smelt of coconut so she's probably OK. She took the sandwich you made for her and the spare caravan keys. Right, I need to get on now, Amey," Norm said, returning to his chair. "Things are shaping up, which is what we need to see. Not only have we received permission to activate the VPN, but I have just received this personal message from the Home Secretary himself. His words are, and I quote, *'It's about bloody time we stopped them riding roughshod over us. This reckless girl needs putting in her place... as soon as possible, Weaver'*."

Amey nodded in approval.

"So, Amey, you will need to take one of these phones, too. I will text you on your normal phone if I want you to activate it, in which case you must switch yours off," said Norm. He noted down the serial number on a yellow post-it note, in his usual efficient style, before passing over an identical phone to the one Tam had taken earlier. "The others already have theirs, of course. Either way, you know the alternative signal."

"Why would you use that medieval method, Norm?"

"Brig, sadly, is no fool. She has her methods, I have mine, as you well know," he said. "Actually, I almost forgot to say that I took a call earlier, ironically regarding the Frankfurt anniversary. We have been missing something all these years, something which, I hope, we will discover more about in the next few days."

"Oh, Norm, this is all quite worrying. Please be careful, Brig is obviously a malicious maniac who will stop at nothing. And where is Felton Kendall in all of this? Hiding away, as usual, like the coward that he is. I hate him," said Amey, now very animated.

"Don't let anyone get at you, Amey. You know I will get it sorted out," said Norm without turning his head from his work. "I'm just sorry that it's taking a little longer than I planned."

"I will go now, Norm, before I get too angry."

Amey realised he hadn't fully registered her last comment. With a tut, she scooped up his mug and deposited it, along with her own, on the first surface she found in the kitchen. She ventured up the creaky staircase to change, with Hertz close behind, as usual.

Having prepared her clothes earlier, she was ready for her walk.

Now donning white pedal pushers and an orange sports shirt, she descended the stairs and could clearly overhear her husband on the phone, busily doing what he did best: sorting out other people's problems to his own detriment.

Amey knew he shouldn't be doing this anymore; he should have fully handed over the reins to someone else by now. Had that someone not been Felton, then he would be out walking with her or riding a horse across the dunes right now. How it frustrated her.

She unhooked her trusty rucksack from the back of the kitchen chair and packed a bottle of mineral water, a small Tupperware tub containing leftover vegetarian sausages and an apple from the fruit bowl. Norm would have to sort out his own lunch today or she would never get out.

Her hiking bag already contained dog-walking essentials such as poo bags, a tennis ball and a treat or two for Hertz, along with her keys and money, so she was almost good to go. Her blue, anodised Nordic walking poles were leaning against the wall in the hallway, wedged into her hiking boots, with her amber sun cap suspended from one of the wrist loops. Long walks without her poles would otherwise make her hip ache, an annoying consequence of her riding accident.

"See you later, Norm," she called out to no response.

Taking the dog lead from the last hook on the wall, she looped it over Hertz's head and made her exit back out into the sunshine, closing the side door firmly behind her.

Amey was kitted out as if she were taking on one of the long ridge walks that had formed part of her youth in Rennsteig, central Germany. This Welsh terrain was somewhat different, dunes as opposed to dense forest, but both afforded her freedom and peace in their own special way.

The edge of the common was only a short distance from their house and as she stepped onto the relatively lush grass, she became aware of several people looking and pointing in her direction. Amey turned to face her house only to see Norm, the old romantic, hoisting up the flag of the former East German Democratic Republic in her honour.

"You lovely fool, you will make me cry!" she called.

Norm blew her a kiss as the black, red and gold tricolour slowly made its way ceremoniously upward. The emblem of the hammer and compass, partially encircled by a wreath of wheat, shone proudly as it reached the top of the tall pole, drawing a ripple of applause from the bemused bystanders.

CHAPTER TEN — OPEN YOUR HEART

Stepping away from their makeshift bench through a sediment of seaweed and shells, Tam, with Kee alongside, approached an incredibly steep-sided dune. She could see a small knoll in the middle of the dune. It denoted a dividing point, the very one that Kee must have been referring to earlier. He turned to face her.

"OK, Tam, this is it, our home for a few hours. If you like, you take the left side and I can take the right. It will give you a bit more cover and, plus, a small bit of shade from the side wall, if you want it. How does that sound?" he offered, in a very calm, matter-of-fact manner.

"Fine, yes, that's fine by me," said Tam, daunted by the realisation that this man with her, whom she still knew very little about, was soon to be naked. There could be no substitute for trust now.

Kee stepped across and placed his bag on the sand. He unknotted his shirt from his midriff and rolled it up into a makeshift cushion or pillow.

"This is the bit when I lose my remaining clothes. You can watch, if you like, or be discreet, your choice."

"I'll look the other way, don't worry," she said, turning away.

"It's not me who is worrying, it's you," he replied.

Tam knew he was right. She remained facing the sea and edged herself leftwards, trying not to look.

She knew this was ridiculous. It wasn't as if she had never seen a naked man in her life. Why couldn't she be like Amey, carefree and nonchalant, right now? It must be British conditioning, she thought, as she managed to successfully get behind the knoll without casting an eye towards Kee.

"Just shout if you want or need anything, Tam, won't you? Even if you want to chat about anything?" Kee called over the sandy wall.

"I will, thank you, Kee."

Here she was, sequestered in a sand dune, able to enjoy the natural delights if she chose—a complete opposite to yesterday's trauma. She placed her bag down on the banked sand and mimicked Kee's actions by untying the blouse from around her waist and placing it to one side.

She looked down at her ill-fitting bikini top and her stomach, which was not as taut as it used to be. If only she had Amey's slim frame, she mightn't care so much. However, there was no escaping that her figure had changed; she couldn't turn the clock back thirty years to when she was slimmer and single.

Sitting with her knees up, in her own little cubbyhole, Tam looked out from her slightly elevated position above the beach and down towards the water. It was beautiful. It could be anywhere in the world; it just happened to be in Wales.

The dulcet tones of Kee's voice had now subsided. Here she was, effectively alone, absorbing the gentle sound of the sea. Little else was in the air on this deserted stretch of beach.

She was starting to come to terms with the last forty minutes. No one, least of all herself, would have imagined her in such a situation, let alone with a naked escort just a glance away.

She edged across to a slim band of shade and reached into her bag, seeking the once-freezing water Amey had kindly provided for her excursion. Releasing the plastic hinge, Tam squeezed the water into her mouth. It was good, but gin would have been better.

She was so close to living the dream she had sought, but not to its full extent. That would mean losing her remaining attire.

It felt ridiculous, but she really wanted to see how it was done, and temptation was now getting the better of her. Were she to appear to Kee, or others, still clad in her bikini top she would feel a fraud, an imposter in this liberated corner of the world. She assumed, based on his demeanour thus far, that Kee wouldn't even bat an eyelid either way.

Placing the water bottle to one side, she reached back and unclipped her top. With a deep breath, she removed it completely and cast it aside.

She had taken the first momentous step, allowing her breasts to be free.

Her heartbeat increased. This was only the first part of the challenge she had set herself. The true test was to reveal herself, to Kee, if no one else. There was no time like the present; it had to be now. Tam grabbed the wispy grass that lined the top of the knoll and hauled herself up one-handed.

She cast her eyes around the immediate vicinity, hoping that they were still alone. They were. There he lay, naked for all to see, without a care in the world.

Tam surveyed him whilst she had the chance. No wedding ring or tattoos on show. He didn't seem the type to have body art, and his smooth, six-foot frame was more than aesthetically pleasing just as it was.

Tam became conscious of her staring. She usually had the knack of doing the wrong thing at the wrong time and it might upset him if he were to catch her gawping at him. She reached down for her water on the pretext of offering Kee a drink, should he look across. He didn't.

Despite seeking his approval, she didn't want to disturb him either, as much as she really wanted him to open his eyes right now. She ducked back down, excited and frustrated in equal measure: excited that she was halfway to realising her dream, yet frustrated that she had failed to get a reaction from her chaperone. Tam simply wanted his lovely eyes to provide her first endorsement, before anyone else's gaze fell upon her less-than-perfect body.

What she contemplated next was dangerous to that desire—making a sketch of him. She could position herself out in the open, remaining topless whilst doing so and making her available to be seen by anyone in the immediate vicinity. It was a thrilling challenge.

Like the statue earlier, she decided to capture this special moment in a way that was personal to her, something she could look back on and rekindle another day. The light was ideal and the opportunity had presented itself—*so take it.*

He lay there, a more-than-perfect example of the male human form. It was natural and beautiful. Tam placed the water bottle back into her bag and extracted the notepad, folding back the sketch of "Our Lady of the Dunes" to reveal a fresh page. She stood, resting her pad against the top of the knoll, and quickly moved her pencil across the page. If only the art class in London could see her now!

Every second that passed elevated the risk of being caught and having to explain her voyeuristic tendencies to Kee. It was exciting.

Tam knew it wasn't worthy of a Turner prize, but as she made the finishing touches to the drawing, the glow of satisfaction it created was priceless. If only Kee knew.

She knelt down, back out of sight, and kissed the picture, her lip salve leaving the faintest of marks on the paper, before carefully tucking the sketchpad away in the pocket from whence it came.

Inspired by Kee, there seemed nothing else left to do but step out of her own previously diffident self. The inevitable moment had arrived.

Tam bravely stood up and brushed the sand from her shorts, placing her watch into a small, zipped back pocket. Opening the front popper, she eased the zip down, allowing her shorts to fall to the floor, closely followed by the lower half of her bikini. Stepping out, she was bare, her only adornment being her silver locket.

Tam desperately wanted Kee to open his eyes, but he remained motionless, unaware of her amazing revelation. Tentatively, she took a couple of paces to the edge of the strandline and away from the protective concealment of the dune. She stood upright, hands behind her back, southward facing in a state of zen-like calm, as befitting "Our Lady of the Dunes".

She was out there and it felt euphoric.

Tam closed her eyes and let her other senses take over. She felt her body sway in the warm breeze as the sound of the sea filled her mind once more. The exhilaration of proffering her body to the elements was found, there and then.

The breeze on her skin, the freedom, the liberation, created a rush of chemicals that pulsed through her veins like nothing she had ever felt before. This wasn't sexual; it was new, heady and wonderful.

If this was mindfulness, then she had truly found it. Her troubles were, for the moment, lost in the stratosphere, and the seconds seemed to last for hours.

A smile, as broad as the beach itself, was indelibly etched across her lightly freckled skin.

She had done it.

Opening her eyes, the newly invigorated Tam lifted her hands high in the air as she made her way back to her enclave, so proud that she wanted to scream her joy loudly to anyone in earshot, were it not for Kee lying there, oblivious. Tam grabbed her towel and emitted a scream into it, thus muffling it from Kee's ears, dancing in her own little joyous way as she did so.

A clothed couple came into view, still a hundred metres or more away. Ordinarily nothing much of interest, but this was new territory, something fascinating to observe. Tam contemplated what they might do. Would they walk on by, would they acknowledge her? Come to think of it, were they even naturists at all or just a couple out for a stroll?

If that was the case, should she now duck down, out of sight, and avoid any contact?

Yes, her body was on show but they, like her, would have seen naked men on the beach by this point and they obviously weren't bothered if they'd got this far. Tam wanted to test her own mettle, and with renewed strength she edged forward slightly in an attempt to make herself more visible. A weird vibrancy took hold of her body. This couple were now her first test as a fledgling naturist.

As they drew closer, she could clearly identify their tell-tale uniform of rucksack and cap. She could now see how Kee had identified her own look earlier; it seemed to go with the territory.

Tam was a people watcher and always had been, but this was a whole new scenario, one which really started to thrill her. She stepped forward again, deliberately into their gaze.

The couple were getting closer, the lady directing the man to change course, toward her! Whether the lady had spotted her, Tam didn't know, neither did she really care right now.

She looked across to the beautiful, outstretched figure of Kee. Without him, his warmth, his reassurances, she never would have dreamt of being so bold.

The man looked up; there was no doubt now that she had definitely been spotted. He said something to the lady, whom Tam assumed to be his wife, who then looked up and waved, acknowledging Tam's presence.

Tam felt a wondrous feeling of belonging as she waved back before sitting down, this time perching on the dune's ledge, still in full view of them. The broadest of smiles could not be removed from Tam's face.

Even from fifty metres away, she could see that they were probably ten years older than her, so why had she worried so much about revealing herself? She was starting to understand a subject that she had thought of as lewd in her younger days.

Tam had never considered herself a voyeur, but she remained transfixed on the couple as they dropped their bags on the sand, removed their caps and took very little time or grace in removing their clothes, tossing them, unfolded, onto the stones at the base of the pebble bank. Tam was full of admiration for them as they revealed their own less-than-perfect physiques. Within a couple of minutes, they were both lying face down on their towels. They obviously didn't care who might pass by or see them like this; they knew what they wanted. Good for them.

They clearly had no body issues or inhibitions, they just got on with it, not even hiding in the dunes like her, but were there on the beach for anyone to see, comfortable with themselves and their relationship. For Tam, they seemed like the epitome of happiness.

Tam brushed any remaining sand from her backside as she looked across at Kee.

He looked so content. Kind Kee; he didn't have to let her into his day at all—he could have done his own thing. Tam wanted to bottle all these moments, these new feelings of hope, in the face of the potential storm ahead with Brig.

Come what may, this would live long in her memory. Inspirational people really did exist.

CHAPTER ELEVEN – ACTIONS SPEAK LOUDER

Part of Tam wanted to wake Kee up. Here she was, naked, wanting to be by his side, just like the older couple that were still in eyeshot.

The lady in question raised herself up and waved in her direction. Tam knew it wasn't her that she was waving at, so wanted to see if someone was planning on inhabiting a neighbouring dune, another couple or a lone man perhaps. Gingerly, she collected her towel, deliberately draping it across her shoulder, should it be the latter.

Tam edged forward and heard footsteps in the sand to her right. Within seconds, a tall female figure came into sight. Of all people, it was Amey, with Hertz by her side!

There was no point running or hiding now. She had been discovered by the best possible person.

Naturism was second nature to Amey, but it still felt weird to be naked before her in this way. Tam fought that feeling and threw her towel down and stood, somewhat indignantly, with hands on hips, as she watched them approach along the top of the sandbank. Hertz dashed forward, briefly running up to her before continuing over to Kee, who awoke with a shock as Hertz's cold, damp nose nuzzled across his body.

"Where the hell did you two come from?" Tam asked.

"The Morfa side of the beach, by the stream. It's a lovely walk if you have hiking boots on, what with the brambles and the marshy ground," Amey said, gesturing to her stained boots. "I promised Norm I would try to find you, just to check you are safe, which, it seems, you are. Anyway... you finally did it, *meine Liebe*! You are naked!" Amey laughed and threw her Nordic walking poles to one side to give Tam a big embrace.

"I never thought I could ever do it, especially right now, of course," Tam replied as Amey squeezed her even tighter.

Amey's grip relented slightly, and Tam could almost feel her peering over her shoulder toward Kee.

"I couldn't have done it without this lovely man, whose name is Kee," she added, anticipating Amey's next question.

"Hello, Kee," said Amey, as Kee sat up with his knees raised to avoid any further embarrassment. "I am Amey and this is Hertz. Sorry, he is very friendly."

"Hi, Amey, and hi, Hertz," he responded, still in a slight state of shock.

"Thank you for looking after Tam. Maybe I join you another day, yes?"

"Ah... no, Amey." Tam declined on his behalf.

"OK, I understand." Amey raised her hands in a playfully submissive fashion. "I will leave you two alone. I saw my friend Tessa waving to me so will head down and say hello to her in a moment. Tessa is one of my walking friends here in Skerrid Mawr. She is also related to Omni—her aunt, I think she said she was. You may get to see her helping out in Omni's Shack or at The Dragon's Tail over the next few days. By the way, Phil, Tessa's husband, is a scream, very funny man."

Amey always had such enthusiasm; it was infectious.

"Are you heading back home, then, Amey?" Tam asked.

"Not immediately, no. After I see Tessa and Phil, I will head back inland via one of the quieter bridleways. They contain fen orchids, which are out now—they are a wonderful sight, you know. Also, Hertz and I will stop off for lunch somewhere secluded. It seems a shame to waste the sunshine with all these heavy clothes on, and Norm doesn't need me back in a hurry, if you understand me," said Amey with a wink.

"Amey, you are incorrigible. Thank you for the food, by the way, very kind of you. I haven't eaten it yet... Too many things on my mind, too, as you can probably tell."

Amey smiled and nodded before taking Tam's arm and pulling her to one side, out of earshot of Kee.

"I shouldn't tell you, as Norm did not want to worry you further, but I think you need to know."

"What, Amey? What do I need to know?"

"Brig is more than she seems. That is all I know."

"It's something to do with Frankfurt, isn't it?"

"Why do you say that, Tam?"

"I overheard Norm on the phone earlier. I haven't worked it all out yet."

"None of us have worked it out yet, Tam. I left Norm on the phone to his contacts. Maybe we will know later. Listen, I will go now," she said, giving Tam a further hug. She then called over to Kee. "Goodbye, Kee! Look after my gorgeous sister-in-law. If you don't, I will find you," she said with a playful wag of her finger.

Kee took it in good heart, gallantly standing to wish her a safe onward journey, moving across to Tam's side in the process. Amey collected her poles and ushered Hertz away toward the beach, where Tam could see Tessa sitting up, now awaiting Amey's visit.

As she headed away, Kee laughed. "Well, Tam, where do I start?"

"No hiding it now, is there?" said Tam, with outstretched arms.

"Can I be the second person to welcome you to 'the club', then?" he cajoled, offering an outstretched hand.

Tam accepted his request, shaking his hand in a mock acceptance ceremony.

"Amey is my sister-in-law. German, as you can probably tell," she explained. "Technically, she is a devout and passionate East German, and very liberal in her thinking."

Kee gave a thumbs up, then his expression turned serious. "I didn't catch the last part of what she said to you, Tam, but I sense something is wrong, other than your estranged husband and his lover?"

Tam loved his intuition. "There is something, and I need to find out exactly what it is, sooner rather than later to be straight with you," she said, and then inspiration struck. "In fact, Kee, would you help me with a little task, once Amey disappears from view?"

"Anything. I am at your disposal."

The mention of Norm and Frankfurt plus her new-found liberation had conspired to form a plan in her mind.

The VPN.

It was time to use the phone to provoke a reaction. Whether that was from Norm or Brig, she didn't know. If it was from Norm, then at least she would know what the relevance of Frankfurt was to him, if nothing else. Should it cause a reaction from Brig, then they'd know if anyone with access to the VPN was helping her. It might be risky, but at least it might bring everything to a head sooner rather than later.

"Get your things together, Kee, we are going for a paddle," stated Tam, quickly gathering her possessions together and stuffing them into her rucksack, keeping the phone to one side.

"Skinny-dipping you mean?" he asked.

"If you like, yep."

"You have become bold all of a sudden, haven't you?"

"Thanks to you, and Amey, I have, yes... Anyway, hurry yourself along, will you?" she commanded, like an impatient mother might to a young child.

Tam watched as Amey and Hertz departed the beach, heading away up one of the pebble banks. Kee shook the sand from his towel and threaded it through the loops on his bag as best he could.

"It might be wise to put some footwear on, Tam," he called, slipping into his own. "Those pebbles will be hot and some of the debris can be sharp."

His words fell on deaf ears as Tam moved ahead barefoot.

The pebbles shifted underfoot, and she started to slip. She was sure she would be looking somewhat ungainly to her male follower—not really the impression she wanted to leave.

"Told you!" he shouted, clearly enjoying the sight.

Tam ignored him, concentrating on her uneasy path until she touched the soft, pebble-free sand.

She looked across to Tessa and Phil, who both waved in unison. Tam responded with a wave and continued ahead, not waiting for Kee.

She felt alive. Naked and alive.

She heard the patter of his footsteps rapidly catching up with her and extended her hand outward. The touch of his warm hand joining with hers told Tam that the invitation had truly been accepted. Their pact was sealed there and then.

No words were exchanged as they walked at pace, hand in hand, together to the shoreline.

The softer sand soon gave way to the cooler, firm, hard-packed dampness that lay along the water's edge. Tam stopped and released her hand from his. Her rucksack slipped from her shoulder and was handed to the servile Kee. Without question or comment, he added it to his right shoulder, awaiting further instructions.

Tam turned her attention to the phone. She turned it on, put it into camera mode and handed it to Kee.

"I will walk into the water. You follow me, and when I shout 'NOW', hit the red button."

"Sure," Kee replied, understanding that her mood had now changed into a very serious, purposeful one.

Tam made her first steps into the cold shallows. The sudden change in temperature on her skin hardly bothered her as her shins pushed on through the salty waves. Kee stayed in close attendance, striding to keep up with her.

"Ready?" she called.

"Ready," he replied.

With her back to the phone, she quickly swivelled her torso into a pose that would expose both her backside and breasts.

"NOW."

As the camera snapped, her fate was sealed. A confrontation with someone somewhere was inevitable.

CHAPTER TWELVE – A PERSIAN PRINCESS

In a nondescript third-bedroom-cum-office, Parv worked online. With only a local BBC radio station for company, she methodically dealt with her electronic folder of tasks for the day.

Her room afforded her a superb view across to the busy Cheltenham Racecourse, less than half a mile away. Looking at the crowds in the distance, she wished it could have been a day outside in the sun for her, too, watching the thoroughbreds compete, rather than matters of state. The thrill of mingling with the thousands of punters, enjoying Pimm's, dressed in her native finery, always excited her.

Parv always stood out from the crowd, with Ladies Day being her absolute favourite occasion, whether at Cheltenham, Chepstow or even Ascot. A fascinator, high heels and a beautiful Persian-style outfit were often enough to secure her prizes from sponsors, which brought invitations from corporate hosts to join them in exclusive private boxes. She was always immaculate; it matched perfectly with her beautiful face and sweet disposition.

Today, however, she had orders to work from home, despite her main office being a relatively short cycle ride away.

Her work folder only contained non-confidential, low-security data on the Government's Virtual Private Network, so any form of cyber-attack was unlikely. Working from home had its benefits, of course, but Parv enjoyed the social interaction of the workplace, as she lived alone.

Snapping out of her daydream, she pushed her typist-style chair away from the narrow desk using her bare feet and stretched out her slim, tanned legs before giving in to the temptation of an early lunch. Boredom had set in, a common danger of working from home, and food was always a good distraction. A quinoa and halloumi salad would be the ideal lunch to take into her small back garden on such a fine day.

No sooner had Parv opened the fridge door than her computer decided to send out an audio alert. Typical. She had been waiting all morning for that, and the very moment she stepped out, the "call to arms" was received! She knew she had no choice but to react to its urgent demands. After all, this was her *raison d'être* for working at home.

The fridge door swung shut and Parv returned upstairs, plate in hand, to her desk. An icon flashed impatiently in the bottom corner of her screen.

She clicked on it.

Status Alert: Activated
Unit: Handset Six (Tamsin Kendall)
Position Postcode: SF33 4ME
Attachment: Jpeg_1032

This was a surprise to Parv, as Norm Weaver had only registered Tamsin's handset into the group the day before. What was a bigger surprise was the naked body of his sister appearing in the attachment.

The project that Norm had side-tracked her onto was well and truly live in every respect. She had expected something to happen at some point, but not so quickly and certainly not like this. This wouldn't have been in Norm's plan, for sure.

Tam Kendall could be doing this for no reason other than to send out some type of visual alert, given as such Government VPN devices were not utilised for personal or domestic purposes.

Parv knew the reason Tam had been allocated the device and Brig Huddlestone's likely involvement, given the recent worsening in Anglo-American communications. The problem was that Parv hadn't expected the alert to have taken such a graphic form. A text message, yes; a naked photo, no.

Norm would become aware of it soon. Any decision she made now would have to be based upon her own close relationship with Brig, and it was a decision she needed to make quickly and one she hoped Norm would validate later. She figured that if she could change this unpleasant situation into a satisfactory outcome, then that was what she was being paid to do. Likewise, she knew that Norm trusted her judgement implicitly.

It was time to pay back his faith in her, a refugee who had escaped tyranny, who he had picked up and offered an amazing opportunity to serve her new country. Now was the time to act decisively on the information in front of her and, hopefully, draw Brig under the group's control. The opportunity was too good to miss.

Picking up her private phone, she took a photo of Tam's naked image.

It would be needed to convince Brig that she was on her side.

She attached it to a message: *SF33 4ME – phone me.*

***

In Ealing, West London, Brig Huddlestone paced around her small room.

She had been on tenterhooks all morning, knowing the significance of damaging Tam's house. Had Tam told Felton, and would he now recommence the payments that he had stopped? If either answer was negative, then she would need to step up her offensive. Only time would tell.

Furthermore, she should have been away with her housemate, Grant, on a short break to the south coast, but annoyingly, he had been called away to work at the last minute. For Grant, when duty called duty came first, much to Brig's frustration. She needed him on her side, to cover for her, if push came to shove, but the chance to patch up their differences had, temporarily at least, fallen by the wayside.

As she contemplated her next move, she received a text notification from her most special of friends in the Civil Service, Parv.

Oh, Parv wants me now, after all this time, does she? Brig thought. *Hasn't spoken to me for at least a week—what can she possibly want?*

Her jaw dropped down and a toothy grin filled the void.

"Yes, yes, yes... Parv, you absolute beauty. I always knew you would come up trumps one day, you sexy tramp."

There was the picture of Tam Kendall, knee-deep in seawater and naked as the day she was born.

Without hesitation, Brig called Parv on FaceTime.

***

Parv gulped as the phone rang, knowing the danger she had created.

"Hey, sister," she answered valiantly, masking her real emotion as best she could.

"Hey, bitch... How on this planet did you get this picture?"

"By tracking her phone, of course. It's part of my job, isn't it? Anyway, I knew you would be interested. When are you and Grant going away?"

"We're not now... He got called away with bloody work again. So, as you can see, I'm home alone," said Brig, waving her phone around to prove no one else was there.

"Well, what I find to be a coincidence, Brig, is that particular postcode is somewhere I have been before, with work in fact. So, tell me, what is the connection, do you think?"

"I don't frigging well know. I don't play games, just tell me."

"It's Skerrid Mawr, in South Wales, where Tam's brother, Norman, lives. A gang of us from Cheltenham and Whitehall went there last year, just after he had moved down from Sussex. So, I'm guessing that Tam must be staying at his house, too."

"How interesting. Perhaps I could make a personal visit, 'for tea'," said Brig, mimicking Norm's British accent.

"You could do. I can't see that you would be welcome, given your history with Felton." Parv laughed.

"No, I'm serious—I ain't got nothing else better to do. Could take my bike down there. Where did you stay, a hotel?"

"No, it's a small OpenBnB. I can find the details if you really want me to."

"Yes, why not? Hey, why don't you come with me?"

"Actually, I probably could, but not today. Tomorrow morning perhaps, after my shift ends. So, shall I phone Liz at the OpenBnB—it's called Sandpiper—and ask?"

"Yes. Maybe we don't even have to see the Weavers. Might be fun if we did, though—imagine their faces seeing me and you together, in their own backyard!"

"It's a lovely place. I will see if Sandpiper is free and text you back—I have to log back into work before they notice I'm offline," said Parv, not responding to Brig's previous suggestion.

"Make it happen, girl," replied Brig, as Parv quickly ended the call.

Parv had much to do if she stood any chance of manipulating Brig without arousing suspicion.

Ten minutes elapsed before she was able to ping Brig's phone once more:

Spoke to Liz and it's free. You know the postcode.
In a place called Mawdsridge.
Easy to find. Turn left after The Meadow Pipit and look
for the Sandpiper sign.
Let me know when you get there.
I know you love being spoilt, so this is my gift to you.
XXX

***

Brig excitedly ran into her bedroom and, with two hands, lifted the case she'd been going to take on her trip with Grant, depositing it onto her double bed. It was to be a different trip with very different needs to the one she'd had planned. Grant no longer mattered.

Ironically, the case still bore the airport tags from the last trip that she and Parv had taken together to the Canary Islands earlier that year. The long weekend had been amazing. The nightlife, the gay scene and being with Parv were good memories. Ultimately, Brig didn't really care who she was with, as long as she had fun.

She unzipped the black case, knowing that the panniers on her motorbike could accommodate much of what she needed. The weather forecast was good right across the country, so only an additional rucksack would be required for her journey down. She withdrew the panniers for the bike from under the bed, before stretching even further underneath to retrieve a long, slimline plastic storage box.

Based on Parv's information, there was one important piece of equipment she needed in her possession, were the trip to be worth its while to her.

Unclipping the blue lid from the box revealed a mixture of footwear, thick winter socks and a small white towel. Reaching in, she lifted the towel carefully onto the bed and unrolled it slowly.

The shiny metal of a handgun glinted in the summer sunshine. On her bedside cabinet stood a picture of her mother when she was much younger. Brig turned as if to show her the gun.

"The time has arrived, Mama."

CHAPTER THIRTEEN — INEVITABLY OMNI

Leaving Tam to splash in the shallow water, Kee dutifully returned to the shore. He carefully balanced Tam's phone on top of her bag, before chivalrously extracting his own towel to present to her.

As Tam stepped from the water, she thanked Kee for taking the photo and for the plush towel he had wrapped around her shoulders. As she buried her face into the soft Egyptian cotton, the enormity of what she had just done hit her. Now only time would tell what, if any, impact it would have on her life.

"I am not sure what all that was about and I am not going to ask you to explain," Kee said, as she reappeared from behind the towel. "C'mon..." He beckoned her. "Let's head back to base camp. You can dry off as you walk. I don't want to attract an audience."

Tam got the feeling he had a certain shyness about his naturism, which she found pleasing.

However, it wasn't an audience that they attracted, but rather the attentions of someone racing toward them on a large quad bike. Tam realised it was too late to even consider putting clothes on, so quickly wrapped the towel around her body as best she could.

"Tam, prepare to meet the fabled Omni Gayle," Kee proclaimed as the quad bike slid to a halt close to his toes.

Tam watched as Omni dismounted. She wasn't exactly what she had been led to expect.

Denim shorts and a large sleeveless white tee-shirt clad her curvaceous body. As she removed her sunglasses from under her sky-blue bandana, Tam could see her face much clearer. Her strong cheekbones bore witness to her attractiveness.

"Recognised you a mile away, Kee. Now, I wonder why that is, then, eh?" she said with a wink, looking down before continuing unabated. "So, who is this week's model, then, mun?" she asked, turning her gaze to Tam, who turned her gaze toward Kee, very interested in what his reply might be to such a pointed question.

"Which do you want me to answer first, Omni?" he responded coolly.

"He's a swine, isn't he?" Omni remarked to Tam, before adding, "Hold on... hold on... you look a little bit like the knight of this town. Well, facially, I mean, obviously."

Tam shrugged, not knowing what she was getting at.

"Does she speak, Kee?"

"Yes, Tam speaks."

"Oh, Tam does, does she? Norman Weaver, I mean, that's who."

"Yes, he's my brother," Tam explained. "And he's an MBE, not a KBE."

Omni laughed. "Is he now? Well, we must talk again, Tam. I need to know more. Anyway, Kee knows where to find me in the day, or night, for a chat—don't you, my sweet?"

"What do you want?" Kee asked bluntly.

"Help, I suppose. I've got a horse to catch."

Tam was confused; she couldn't see a horse.

"My Aunt Tessa phoned me. She's sat just below the pebble bank—look she's waving now."

Tam could indeed see a figure over there, criss-crossing her arms above her head.

"She said a riderless horse was heading down to the stream at Morfa. She couldn't see the rider anywhere so phoned me, the 'Skerrid Emergency Service', to see if I could catch it. Not sure that I could, but willing to give it a go, before I see this one, standing here," Omni explained, hardly coming up for air.

"Where is the horse now, then?" asked Kee.

"Down the end, there. Look, by the base of the last dune." Omni pointed over their heads.

They turned to see it, stood still, some way away, near the stream that flowed through the sand.

"A girl fell off by the *Caswell*. Apparently, it lost its footing somehow and then bolted off, leaving the poor kid on the sand. Luckily, the stream is there which stopped it, or it could have ended up anywhere."

"Is the horse's rider alright?" Tam asked empathetically.

"Yeah, she's OK, a bit of dented pride. We know that feeling don't we, Kee?"

Kee raised his eyes to the heavens, adding a loud tut.

"So, not coming to help me, then?" Omni patted the vinyl seat between her legs.

Kee shook his head, declining her offer.

"Didn't think so, you lightweight. I could do with your Amey to help really, Tam."

"But I can ride horses," Tam responded quickly, keen to help.

"What, naked? Forgive me, love, but your, you know... whatsit, won't thank you any." Omni gestured to her nether regions.

"The horse has a saddle, and I have my top and shorts in here," Tam replied, pointing to her own rucksack. "Lend me your shoes, and I will do it."

"Love a girl with balls, me... if you know what I mean. Yes, here you go—they do stink mind," said Omni, flinging them over to Tam.

Kee stood there smiling in admiration at the newly formed duo, and Omni added, "See, Kee, tomboys like us have balls at least, even if you don't. Now, Tam, are you really sure about this?"

Tam confirmed that she was and pulled her creased clothes out from her rucksack, remembering to switch the phone off and tuck it deeply into her bag.

"Ordinarily, I would help you hold your towel up—you know, for modesty's sake—but there doesn't seem much point really, does there?" said Omni.

"True, I suppose." Tam cast an eye at Kee as she threw his towel back to him.

Omni watched Kee as Kee, in turn, watched Tam unceremoniously get dressed, neither speaking.

Finally, Tam stepped into Omni's warm, slightly tacky, plastic beach shoes.

"I'm ready now. See you soon back at basecamp, then, Kee," said Tam with a newly found confidence. "Omni will drop me back here—won't you, Omni?"

"Not a chance, babe. You can stay with me at my shack. He can walk back; it'll do him good." Omni laughed. "Now, get on, girl—let's get this bit done first."

Tam duly did so, placing her hands around Omni's hips for balance.

"See you soon, I promise," she called across to Kee, and they sped off on the camouflage-green quad, toward the stream where she could now clearly see the riderless horse. It wasn't one of the trio she and Kee had met earlier; this was a large Liver Chestnut, cob-type horse.

As they drove, Tam felt the need to make small talk with this powerhouse of a woman.

"Why do you keep saying *mun*? What does it mean?"

"*Mun* is the Welsh for 'man'. You would probably say 'mate' or 'darling', up there in posh London Town," Omni replied, mimicking Tam's accent. "I suppose I don't even know I am saying it half the time... *mun*!"

Tam grinned, knowing Omni had eased what could have been an awkward transit.

"Anyway, Tam, given your state of undress with Mr Lovely, you're lucky I'm not from the Rhondda, because I would have called you 'butt'."

Tam laughed politely, not really understanding what that meant either, but she *did* understand what "Mr Lovely" meant, and what Omni was implying about Kee.

By now, the horse had decided to aimlessly wander away from the stream and was standing still, almost bewildered, as they arrived, with its lead reins hanging down on the damp sand.

Tam stepped off the quad bike and calmly but decisively approached the cob. It seemed unfazed by their arrival, possibly tired from its exertions. With a low-angled, outstretched arm, Tam offered the back of her hand for the mare to smell. Its nostrils released its warm breath on her skin, content with her intent. Tam slowly took hold of its leather cheek strap in her right hand while collecting and then carefully guiding the trailing reins over its ears with her left hand.

"Good girl... that's right... nice and easy," Tam said softly, as she looked into the horse's large brown eyes, switching control of the reins to her right hand a few inches below its jawline. She felt assured that she had gained the mare's confidence, and thus control.

Looking down at the mare's sand-splattered hocks, she checked for any cuts or abrasions as best she could before lightly running her hand down each leg for further confirmation that it was fit to ride.

"Is it OK?" asked Omni.

"She seems so," replied Tam, now walking the mare in a slow, tight circle, making her final assessment as to whether she would walk or ride it back to its owner.

"Are you going to ride her, then?" Omni asked.

"Yes, she looks sound. Let's do it."

With the gathered reins in her left hand, Tam grasped the front of the large brown saddle and raised her plastic-clad left foot into the stirrup. She bent her right knee and pushed upward, swinging her leg across its broad back and herself onto the saddle, bringing a cheer from Omni.

"Very impressive. If only I could swing my legs as wide as that!"

Tam pretended not to hear her as she placed her right foot into its stirrup and patted the mare's neck in praise of its calm temperament.

Immediately, she noticed that the stirrup leathers were way too short; her knees sat too high to be able to competently ride. She removed her right foot from the stirrup and stretched her leg forward, resting on the horse's withers as she drew the inch-wide leather strap upward to release the buckle down by a couple of notches. It now felt much more comfortable when she stepped back into the metal stirrup, repeating the process on the other side whilst the horse stood easy.

"Omni, you can go on ahead and let the girl know all is well. I won't be too far behind you," Tam said.

Omni responded with a thumbs up and took off in her own inimitable style, the quad bike's chunky tyres leaving a distinct pattern on the smooth, hard-packed sand.

As peace descended once more, Tam was happy that she was safe to go and encouraged the mare to walk on with the merest of taps on its flank with Omni's plastic shoe. Tam kept a gentle hold on the reins to avoid pulling on the bit in the horse's mouth, confident that it would respond to the lightest of encouragement. With a few clicks of her tongue, the horse's ears pricked up, its head lifting in anticipation of a further command. It was very responsive and obviously well-trained.

Tam added an additional click and a press of her heel, and the horse broke into a light trot, then shifted into a gentle canter with a second press. It was pure joy, exactly the type of horse Tam loved to ride and so reminiscent of her last horse.

In the near distance, the familiar form of Kee, now dressed, was making his way along the water's edge. Tam guided the powerful equine down toward the shoreline, causing it to splash through the sheen on the sand and toward Kee, who had now stopped, his phone trained on her.

"Wow, you look wonderful up there. At last, I have captured my very own Lady Godiva," he said, lowering his phone.

This guy knew how to say the right thing at the right time. Tam would usually rebuff such compliments, but he made everything so vibrant, so special, that she would happily hear more.

"Except this isn't a white horse and I am no longer naked," she teased.

"What I mean is, like Lady Godiva, you have sacrificed yourself for the good of others. If I were a religious man, I might tentatively say you are God's gift to me."

Tam felt truly touched. It wasn't flannel—flannel wasn't his style—which made his words seem that much sweeter.

"You had best get that mare back to its owner. I'd love to see you gallop back... if you dare."

Now, there was a challenge.

The horse felt fit enough, so perhaps she would take it just past the *Caswell* and then ease it down again. Kee passed her rucksack up, and as she secured it on her back, he raised his phone up once more. Tam blew the camera a kiss, and she was off.

Like an automatic car shifting gears, the horse effortlessly moved from a trot to a canter and a canter to a gallop, sending Tam's thick auburn hair flailing in all directions as it gathered pace along the hard-packed surface, its hooves casting sand into the air.

Liberation. Total ecstasy. The type of moment that Kee had referred to earlier, she had it right here, right now.

Tam's hands lay easy on the tight-braided plaits that ran up the mare's neck as it pounded toward the ribs of the *Caswell*. Never, in her wildest dreams, could she have imagined her life would change so quickly, so exhilaratingly, for the better.

All too soon, a small crowd came into view. Gathering in the reins, she dropped the horse down in stages to a steady trot, then patted the horse's neck in thanks for the momentous ride it had just given her.

There, a short distance ahead, Omni's quad bike, another horse and several people gathered together. Tam eased the mare into a gentle walk with the lightest of squeezes on the reins as she approached the waiting gaggle.

As she brought the snorting horse to a standstill, Omni stepped forward. She held the mare steady in preparation for Tam's dismount, preventing any chance of a second escape.

A girl, clad in ankle-length riding boots, jodhpurs and a Pony Club jacket, approached on foot with a woman, whom Tam assumed to be her mother, in close attendance.

"Thank you for rescuing Biscuit," said the mother. "Maddy, my daughter, has been beside herself. This lady told us how well you have taken care of her." She gestured toward Omni.

"Happy to help. Biscuit is a lovely horse, a pleasure to ride," said Tam, directing her comment to the teenager, bringing an embarrassed smile of relief from her in the process. "She seems fine, no injuries to worry about. It was a shame she stumbled like that. These things happen— don't let it put you off, will you?"

"I won't... Thank you," the girl politely responded, as Tam set about adjusting the stirrups back to their previous position to suit the girl's height.

Tam knew from her own experiences, and those with Elinor, how the girl must be feeling.

"Time to get back on the horse, as they say," she said, invitingly interlocking her fingers to help the girl up.

"Thank you very much," said the girl, lifting herself up with Tam's assistance, back into the saddle.

"If you lot want to come down to The Shack, then you are most welcome," offered Omni. "Including you as well, Tam. Come on, jump aboard, I'll give you a lift. Kee will know where you'll be, and we can have a good chat first, eh?"

Tam had little choice but to accept Omni's dubious offer. It wasn't too much further to The Shack, and it seemed the polite thing to do. And, after all, Omni might be able to reveal further information about Kee. In fact, she wondered, with more than a hint of jealousy, how much had Kee previously revealed to Omni, for her to be so smitten with him, too?

CHAPTER FOURTEEN – GIRLS' TALK

Tam was pleased to return the plastic footwear to Omni. She kicked them off as they alighted from the quad bike at the bottom of the bank and, holding them between thumb and forefinger, handed them back, conveying her thanks as she did so.

As Omni led the way into The Shack, Tam couldn't help but notice the faded bunting that looped its way across the corrugated metal. A couple of netting bags contained beach essentials such as footballs, cricket sets and the obligatory buckets and spades.

Inside the dimly lit, modified shipping container, Tam could almost taste its damp mustiness. Hardly surprising, given the wooden boards that lined both the sides and the floor; they would be bound to absorb moisture at any time of year.

A couple of small tables with plastic chairs lay in front of an old shop counter, upon which sat a large stainless steel water urn and a tray containing teabags, coffee sachets and UHT milk, the type usually found in hotel rooms. There, too, sat an honesty box.

Its most modern trait was a coin-operated, refrigerated vending machine offering water and fizzy drinks, which boosted the light level within the container. It was clear that this was more of a public service offering than a money-making business.

Omni inserted a key into the drinks machine and removed a couple of bottles of still water, handing one to Tam.

"I think I've only met your brother once or twice, you know. I guess he isn't really a pub person. Although, in fairness, he has been in for the occasional Sunday roast in the winter. Now, Amey I do see a lot more of, usually with Hertz. She pops in here from time to time. Lovely woman, very funny, never expected that of a German."

"A proud, passionate East German," Tam added, knowing that is what Amey would have replied herself, no doubt.

"Yes, of course, an East German—and a journalist, I understand."

"Indeed. She loves writing her articles, usually very scathing ones about the unified Germany. As a consequence, she has a very large following on social media."

Tam noticed Omni's eyebrows rise. Obviously, she'd not realised the true extent of Amey's capabilities.

"Interesting. You know, we get all sorts of nationalities coming in here, too, as they follow the Wales Coastal Path to and from West Bay. Luckily for me really—lots of steady trade, even in the winter months."

"I like the fact that you've gone green with your solar panels," commented Tam, pointing to the ceiling. "We noticed them on the roof earlier. What a good idea," she said, hoping Omni wouldn't pick up on the "we".

"Thank you, we all have to do our bit. I paid cash for that lot, second hand they were. Sadly, I can't fit any more up there, so I applied for a microturbine instead, but the local council won't let me have one. They say it would spoil the view. You only have to look at those giant ones on top of Talbot Hill to see that can't be true. Bloody men."

Tam was impressed with Omni's spirit and verve. Obviously, she was a woman not afraid to step out and say what she wanted. She was warming to Omni but knew she would have to make an excuse to leave and meet Kee soon. However, Omni wasn't finished with her yet.

"It's the first time I've seen Kee with a woman on the beach. Are you both in a naturist club or something?" she asked, rather directly.

Whilst Tam was glad to hear she wasn't just the latest in a string of women, she now sensed that Omni was fishing for information. It was wholly clear that she had designs on him, judging by the way she had looked at him earlier, and was envious of the chemistry Tam and Kee had developed in such a short space of time. Tam had to defend her new interest with some subtlety.

"Something like that, yes," she said, being as evasive as Kee surely would.

"Have you known each other long?"

"Long enough, I suppose."

"Oh, I see."

"Actually, it's high time I got back to him," said Tam, using that moment to move away from Omni's intrusive line of conversation and to physically stand and step toward the doorway. Outside, she caught sight of Kee in the distance, jogging along the beach in her direction.

"Yes, there he is." She pointed toward him, elated.

Omni, perched against a table, was unable to see Kee from her position.

"In actual fact, I had best get back to Norm's house, too—time's moving on, you know. It's been really lovely to meet you, Omni. I'm sure we will see each other again. Thank you for your hospitality, and the shoes, of course."

"Not at all, Tam, you are most welcome. If you would like to come to the pub later tonight, we could chat some more, perhaps?"

"Tell you what, I'll ask Norm and Amey to see what they say," said Tam, knowing it highly unlikely that they'd agree, whilst also avoiding any mention of Kee.

Deep down, she felt so sad for Omni, a kind-hearted, romantically lonely woman, seeking a partner in the likes of Kee. However, there was no time to dwell on Omni's situation, as she could now see Kee waving his arms and pointing toward a tall post that marked his intended exit point from the beach.

Still barefoot and with her rucksack on her back, Tam deftly made her way along the undulations of the path and down to the marker post he had indicated. She quickly sat herself down, knees up, on the edge of the bank just above the narrow sandy exit gully, awaiting his imminent arrival.

The top of his closely shaved head came into view, his brown brow, and then those eyes.

"Hey!" he called up to her.

"Hey!" she replied.

It was nice to have him back.

"Would you like to join me, take a rest for five minutes perhaps?" she asked, knowing that his journey back in the heat would have been more draining than hers was.

"No, I'm OK, thanks all the same. It would be wise to move away. You never know who might be watching," Kee responded, no doubt making reference to Omni again. "Anyway, everything OK? Horse, rider and you?"

"All good, thanks. I even shared a drink and a chat with Omni at The Shack."

"Come on, tell the truth, Tam. You don't have chats with Omni. She grills you and you defend as best you can, I damn well know," he joked.

"She was very hospitable, shall we say?" Tam tactfully answered.

"She likes you, then. That's another success for you, Tam."

He was right. It was.

CHAPTER FIFTEEN — LOVE AND UNDERSTANDING

Tam took one last look across the beach as Kee offered her his hand and helped her to her feet.

What had started out as a trepidatious solo project had turned into one of the most memorable days she had ever had. If she could play the day back again, she knew she wouldn't change a single thing; it had been truly perfect in every respect.

She let out a sigh, sad to be leaving this beautiful beach. Ultimately, she knew she had to go back to reality at some point, but the day wasn't over quite yet. She needed to discover more about Kee.

However, it was his curiosity about her that initiated the deeper revelations as they slowly ambled away from the roar of an incoming tide and into the relative quiet of the dune system.

"So, Tam, how was it with Omni? Did she drill you for information?" he asked.

"Drilling is a bit harsh. It was interesting—and revealing, to a certain degree," she teasingly replied.

She noticed Kee smiling. He seemed to know she was playing him at his own game.

"Go on, tell me. If it's bad I want to know."

"Should it be bad, then?" Tam responded, playfully eyeballing him.

"No, definitely not. I have nothing to hide," he said, breaking into a guilty laugh.

"Omni has got some kind of a fixation on you, though, hasn't she?"

"I don't know, has she?" he countered, now struggling to reply through his laughter.

Tam put her hands in the flimsy pockets of her shorts, cocking an eyebrow as she did so.

She chose not to respond. It didn't help matters.

"Anyway, Tam, why didn't you ask her that question yourself? It's not as if I live here or see her every day," he dealt back to her. "My observations, if they're worth anything to you, 'Mrs Kendall', are that she is desperately lonely and tries too hard. It's not exclusive to me, you know."

Morgan had inferred the same, but Tam needed further clarification.

"Well, she seems to know all about you, judging by the looks she gave you and the comments she made on the beach."

"Like?"

"Well, she called you 'Mr Lovely' for one."

Kee's self-control became non-existent, and he laughed like a child with a fit of the giggles in a classroom, his face reddening by the second. He held his hand up for mercy, as any verbal response now seemed beyond him.

"I am waiting, Kee. When you're ready," said Tam, smirking defiantly on the spot, arms now folded, making his condition even worse. Had she a bucket of water to hand then he would have got it, full force.

"Yes, OK, I can't deny that I stayed down here one weekend and visited her pub, knowing full well that she was the owner. However, it's a small place with only one other choice of pub. Hers was closer to the car park, it's as simple as that," he said, before starting his manic laugh again.

"Did you stay at the pub?" Tam asked, in her relentless drive for the truth.

"No, but the invitation was there. I turned it, and her, down."

"Where did you stay then... Mr Lovely?" Tam was now laughing herself.

"In my van... alone, before you ask," he spluttered out, his laughter easing slightly as he tried to regain his composure.

Once more, Tam said nothing, maintaining her observation of his body language. Whilst it had been funny to see him this way, she knew that pushing him much further might backfire. She didn't want him to think any less of her for asking such questions, so qualified her interest.

"I'm sorry to ask, but you are an attractive man, and I don't blame her for trying. There, I have said it."

"Listen, Tam, firstly, I don't reckon I am attractive, and secondly, I don't yearn for a female friend that tries as hard as she does. It isn't natural, you either feel something or you don't. I didn't feel anything romantically then and I certainly don't now... for Omni, I mean."

Liking his final addition, Tam immediately softened her tone for her next question, in the hope their day together could be extended.

"Are you intending to stay tonight?"

"To be honest, I don't know. I was thinking of driving to the Afan Valley later, so I can ride my mountain bike up there tomorrow morning. Essentially, it depends on how I feel. Hang on, don't tell me, she has invited you over to the pub?"

Tam was disappointed that Kee might be leaving, but admitted, "Yes, she did. However, I used one of your noncommittal ploys. It wouldn't be tonight anyway, as I know Amey will be cooking for Norm and me. As you can probably imagine, we have much to catch up on, especially with the Brig problem. Ironically, were it not for her savage actions, I wouldn't be here," Tam said, then added, "I have loved my time with you today, I can't deny it, and dearly want us to meet again. If it were my house, then I would invite you over, but perhaps that is jumping the gun."

Kee gave a wry smile. "Perhaps 'jumping the gun' is a bad choice of phrase in the circumstances. Your family are just that, your family. It will be good for you to have time together, to plot your strategy against this bunny boiler," he said earnestly.

She appreciated his thoughtfulness. He wasn't finished on the subject.

"Tam, given what you've told me, I am amazed you did what you did today. That took some guts, let me tell you. I sincerely hope it gave you the chance to escape your predicament, for a while at least. In terms of us meeting up again, I am sure we will sort something out."

Tam felt a rush inside again. He was magical, so easy to talk to and genuinely courteous.

It was now his turn to be inquisitive.

"Seeing as we are on the subject of 'kiss and tell', can I ask you a question, Tam?"

"Of course you can."

"Forgive me for noticing, but I saw a heart etched on your inner thigh. Now, you don't look like the sort of girl who would have a tattoo."

Tam shook her head, effectively agreeing.

"Majorca, by any chance?"

"Nothing gets past you, does it? Am I that transparent?"

"That's what I am trying to find out," he said with a smirk, as they continued to dawdle along the sandy path.

Tam resigned herself to revealing more.

"You're right, Kee, it was another silly mistake. In truth, I was press-ganged into having one and I knew it was daft at the time. A small heart wouldn't hurt much, or so I stupidly thought. My reasoning, would you believe, was that it might appeal to hubby and resurrect his interest in me again. Then again, pigs might fly. The fact of the matter is, having the tattoo did hurt—and I got sunburnt, too, in the areola region."

It was Kee's turn to deliver a deadpan look. Tam already knew where he was going and quickly placed a finger on his lips.

"No, before you say anything comical, the areola is not a region in mainland Spain."

She felt him squeeze her hand. Natural telepathy.

"You know what, I really enjoyed going topless in Majorca," she continued. "It felt rebellious but, being auburn and not applying lotion properly, I ended up with water blisters around my nipples! Imagine me getting home and old 'Mr Misery' having a row with me about going to Majorca without him in the first place, let alone about nipple blisters and a tattoo! He was so horrible, so demeaning. Do you know what he said to me in the bedroom?" she asked, suddenly struggling to retain her composure.

Kee stayed quiet.

"He pointed and said, 'Why did you bring that baggage home with you?' I turned to my bags, when he venomously delivered his punchline: 'No, not those, the ones around your waist.' It hurt me so badly I couldn't even speak. He literally laughed in my face as he upped and left the room."

Tam struggled to keep her emotions down as Kee took hold of her hand.

"I feel so sorry for you, Tam. The man is a complete fool. Thank you for telling me—you are so brave. Just remember, you have a right to enjoy your life, too. You should never live in someone else's life without wanting to. That's not a partnership, it's a sentence for misery. It's why you went away in the first place, isn't it?"

With his wise words, Tam finally let the last of her guard down, allowing Kee to wrap her up in his arms. It had been years since she had found consolation like this, such was Felton's coldness toward her, especially over the latter years of their relationship. Only after the death of her mother did Felton begrudgingly provide such sympathy. That, too, was a sham, laid on in front of the mourners to make him look like a loving family man. Kee, by contrast, knew the value of the act in abundance, his fingers gently easing their way through her sandy hair, making her feel comfortable and safe inside.

As they stood there, bonded together, in the middle of the path, Kee finally broke the silence, whispering into her ear. "I'm sorry, I feel a bit of a fraud now, Tam. I haven't really told you very much about myself, which, all things considered, is unfair, based on all the things you have told me today. I was evasive earlier. It's just a coping mechanism, I suppose."

Tam squeezed his hand. "Only if you really want to, Kee," she said as they stepped apart.

"I do. I really need to talk to someone, other than my kids, who can understand."

He led her off the path toward a bench set into a bank a few yards away. Kee dumped his rucksack to one side and helped Tam with hers. Tam extracted her half-full bottle of water, the one that Omni had given her. It was still cool. She took a sip and offered it to Kee, who gratefully accepted, before returning the bottle to Tam.

The bench afforded them another spectacular view back across the bay. Kee sat back, his arm across the bench as Tam sat upright with legs crossed in his direction, ready to hear what he wanted to say.

"Like you, Tam, I have had a problem with a woman. Unlike your husband, I loved that woman, every single day. Izzy and I had built a life together. House, kids and all that stuff. The issue was that she ended up leaving me... for another woman."

Tam didn't know how to respond, other than by allowing him to continue.

"You see, in our marriage, I gave her the world, but ultimately, it wasn't the exact world she wanted. It has taken a lot of time for me to come to terms with it, a victim of the modern age, you could say.

"There is no hate and I still see her, as do the kids. They are old enough to make up their own minds and fully accepted it, better than I did in reality. Izzy is still their mother, after all. However, it makes you doubt yourself and crushes your self-confidence. You know, the 'What did I do wrong?' stuff and all that malarkey."

"I know only too well," Tam replied, gently rubbing the back of his hand.

His tone changed, a choked edge now evident in his voice. "We were financially stable, but this rocked things. Try as I might, there was no going back, and I had to buy her out of our home to help her set up with her new love. Can you imagine? Anyway, I felt like I had to start life all over again. The home we had together became merely a house again. That's bloody tough to take when you are more than middle-aged."

Tam sat quietly, amazed by his honesty and deeply saddened by his hurt.

"I might not be a 'pipe and slippers' man, but the thought of going out to pubs and clubs looking for women didn't excite me. It never has. You'll never guess what... the kids even set up some online dating accounts in my name, without me knowing. They were vetting women for me. Definitely not my style, and once I found out what was happening, I had to insist they remove them, much to their disdain. 'How are you ever going to meet someone, if you don't go out, Dad?' they would say. They meant well, I suppose."

Tam thought of Anthony and Elinor. She could understand why Kee's children had thought they were doing their best to make their father happy again, but she was glad her two children hadn't resorted to doing that for her—she would have been equally horrified.

"What about Izzy? Where do you and her stand now?"

"Well, she still cares for me, you know. Invites me to parties, like New Year's Eve, Christmas Eve and so forth, but I usually work. The money is too good to turn down and it brings a modicum of social interaction, I suppose."

"So, are you saying you get lots of drunken offers, then?"

"Some, yes."

"And...?"

"What do you think, Tam?"

"I think you turn them down. You are a man of principle, I feel."

"You 'feel' correctly."

In Tam's eyes, his need for companionship over lust was a sign of strength.

Kee continued, "Inevitably we still see each other at family occasions, like the kids' birthdays usually. We talk, more about how the kids are doing, rather than about me on my own. Izzy feels sorry for me, you know. It's probably a sense of guilt. If she could match me up, then she would."

"Would she like me, do you think?"

"No, Tam... she would love you."

Tam looked away in disbelief. How could this man still be available? He was a dream come true.

The way he spoke, his beliefs, his deep disposition all penetrated her soul. There were many ways to be a millionaire, and her winning ticket was, potentially, sat right next to her.

"Working longer hours became the distraction I desperately needed. It kept my mind away from my own demonic thoughts and stopped me from drinking. I called in a few favours and plunged myself into some new projects which, luckily, have turned out well. Believe it or not, my ex-wife and her partner have since worked with me, or rather, for me. It's all been a bit mad, to be honest.

"I invested in a campervan, which I can use for work or pleasure. It was by virtue of touring around the Welsh Coast in the van that I discovered Skerrid Mawr's plentiful bounty a couple of years ago. By chance, I ended up riding my mountain bike along the beach, right where you expertly rode that horse today. I have always enjoyed my freedom—time over money, I say—and noticed this whole natural area one wonderful, sunny summer's day. In fact, it was very much like today."

Tam stared out across the bay, listening to every word he said, on the brink of tears. It was so touching, so relatable.

"The naturists intrigued me. What struck me was they weren't a bunch of unsavoury exhibitionists, they were ordinary people who had found something different, something better if you like, some type of belonging. It gave me that ethereal connection when nothing else like it existed in my new life. That's why I am here today, to escape. Thank God I was, and so were you, Tam."

She noticed a tear rolling down Kee's cheek as his words petered out. Tam felt his emotional burden releasing. No wonder his words to her earlier had been so accurate. He understood her hurt; now she understood his. Kee edged forward on the bench, his elbows resting on his knees and his head in his hands.

As he lightly sobbed, Tam put her arm across his broad shoulders, akin to what Amey had done for her the night before, rubbing and patting him to assuage his sorrow.

"I'm sorry," he mumbled a few minutes later.

"Hey, shh, I feel honoured you let go and told me, you beautiful man," Tam said, planting a kiss on the side of his head. He didn't need to speak anymore.

Knowing now how the sadness in his life mirrored her own, Tam felt immensely proud of him.

"Here, take this," she said, handing him a tissue from her bag.

They sat quietly for several minutes as Kee tried to gather himself together.

"Thank you for today, Tam," he said eventually. "Perhaps I had best get back now."

Tam stood up and, with outstretched hands, hauled Kee up from the bench.

"Look, there are the famous Steps, where we met a few hours ago," she said, hoping to lift his spirits. "I can honestly say, Kee, that I have loved every minute with you."

"Listen, Tam, I need to tell you that, even though I visit here from time to time, I have never experienced with anyone else what we have found here together, today. It's very important to me that you know that."

Tam acknowledged this with a very quiet "Thank you." He'd confirmed what Omni had told her at The Shack. It felt good to know how genuine he was.

They collected their things and meandered on until they reached The Steps.

"It's a great view up there. You really should take a look, while you're here," said Kee.

Tam readily accepted the offer and followed him up the black metal steps to the highest point of the dunes.

"Look back across to where we have just been," Kee said enthusiastically. "Can you see the low-lying patches, in between the dunes?"

"Yes, what are they?"

"They're called the dune slacks. They tend to flood and leave some small lagoons, even in the summer."

"Yes, I can see those, too. Wouldn't have thought that possible."

"It's why we didn't cut across that way earlier on. Horses could probably get through, I suppose."

Tam smiled back at Kee for imparting his local knowledge, his own upset seemingly put to one side. She marvelled at the view, turning to look toward the village, picking out Norm's house in particular.

Her stomach turned over. The flag of East Germany, not the Union Jack, was resting at half-mast.

She quickly descended the steps.

"Things are happening," she said to Kee. "I can't tell you exactly what, but I do not want you involved, you hear? You have been so kind to me, and I do not want you to get hurt. This will get nasty. Do not mention this to anyone, especially Omni."

"OK, OK, I hear you, Tam," he replied, obviously taken aback by her sudden change of demeanour.

"Please don't follow me," she said. "Stay here for at least ten minutes, I implore you, it is for your own safety. I can't even divulge where I am staying—it would bring its own dangers to many people, potentially even you, so promise me. Please, please, promise me."

Inevitably, Kee looked bewildered. Tam knew he wouldn't have seen the flag at half-mast, and even if he had, he wouldn't have known its significance.

"I promise, Tam," he said." Whatever you want."

"Give me your bag," she requested, "and turn around, please."

Within a split second he had complied.

Tam extracted a slip of paper from her own bag and quickly transferred it into his.

"Don't look in your bag for at least thirty minutes. It's really important to me. I hope it makes you smile, the way you have made me smile today. We will see each other soon, Kee, I am sure of that. So, until then, take care, you lovely man."

Tam planted a kiss on his mouth and then walked away at pace, not even looking back.

CHAPTER SIXTEEN – MUTUAL APPRECIATION

Kee, still in a state of shock from Tam's sudden departure, reluctantly took his phone from his pocket and sat on the grass bank next to The Steps. He needed to do something trivial for ten minutes, at least.

Not surprisingly, there was very little to deal with, other than deleting spam from his emails and checking booking enquiries for his business. There were no messages and nothing of any interest on social media; then again, there never was.

He knew it was no use trying to divert his mind away from the last couple of hours. Tam was indelibly stamped on his soul. She was vibrant, bold, sassy yet polite. The very qualities he loved in a woman were there in Tam.

After losing his wife to another, he'd never thought he'd be able to talk with any emotional depth to a woman again, yet nothing felt awkward or taboo with Tam. Finding someone who would actually listen meant the world to him. There was no judgement with Tam, only empathy and the parallels in their lives.

Being naked wasn't an issue, nor should it be. Perhaps the purpose of Tam's photograph had been to prove to herself—or to Amey, whom she had acknowledged was a strong influence on her—that she had a strength inside that was waiting to come out. He didn't truly know. His only hope was that they would meet again soon, but how? He had no way of contacting her, other than finding her brother's house, somehow.

As he struggled to make sense of it all, Kee became aware of movement in his peripheral vision and looked up, only to come face to face with Hertz, for the second time that day.

Reaching out his arm, Kee patted him on his side. "Hertz, my boy. Either I must smell really bad or you must really like me."

"Sorry, Kee," said a flustered Amey, running after him. "Hertz, come away now, you silly thing."

Kee stood and turned toward her with a smile. "I hear you are a passionate East German, Amey, and patriotically proud."

"Of course. Do you know East Germany at all?"

"I know very little sorry, only through sport."

"Equestrian?" Amey enquired.

"No, football. CZ Jena, if you must know."

"Wow, you know CZ, how wonderful! My brother, Sten, now sadly departed, played for them for many years, maybe you saw him in Wales? He played for CZ against Newport Ironsides. They won."

"I did see him, and yes, they won, somewhat undeservedly," bemoaned Kee. "But what a small world it is!"

"*Ja*, definitely. They did very well in the competition and were in the final, of course. However, like the Newport match, the authorities and the Stasi would not let us travel to watch, in case we defected. Not that we wanted to, of course, we were quite happy where we were. Anyway, Kee, I am wondering where Tam is, please?"

"She headed away, must be at least five minutes ago, but asked me to wait here for some strange reason."

Amey looked concerned. "She didn't say why?"

"No."

"Did you argue?"

"No, she went up The Steps to look at the view and then her demeanour changed in a split second into one of panic and worry. It was most peculiar, to be honest, Amey. I couldn't understand it."

Amey stood there, looking perturbed herself.

"Shall we talk as we walk?" Kee suggested, knowing enough time had elapsed by now. "I'm heading back to my van."

"Yes, let's do that," Amey said and fell into step alongside him. "As you say, Kee, it is strange, not like her at all. I can't think why she would ask you to wait." She shook her head. "Sorry, you were asking me about my homeland, East Germany. What did you want to know?"

"Well, I was only going to ask if you considered yourself poor, but you said you were happy. Obviously, you weren't as wealthy as the western side, were you?" he asked as they descended down the soft sandy path, now enclosed by the high banks of scrub alongside.

"No, that is true, but we were happy. However, what we lacked in money we made up for in pride, as Welsh people like you have, I believe. We had, and still have to this day, our culture, music, theatre, sport, of course, and even simple traditions like Skat, our national card game, and even in the darkest times, no one could take that away from us."

Kee found himself nodding empathetically again, not wishing to divulge the fact he was born English but had lived in Wales for most of his life. He considered himself British, not loudly but quietly.

"I know Jena is not close to Berlin, but did you ever visit there, before the Wall fell?"

"I did visit East Berlin a couple of times when I was younger, but it held no inspiration for me. I loved the forests and countryside of Thuringia too much. It was somewhere we could walk freely and ride our horses in the summer. In the winter, we had an abundance of skiing choices, of course, with downhill and my particular favourite, cross country."

Kee nodded, surprised at her quality of life during the Cold War.

"It isn't about money to me, although, I confess, I was lucky to meet Norm. He has done very well for himself. It is why we recently moved here," she concluded.

"Yes, I agree, Skerrid Mawr is a lovely place indeed," said Kee as they walked along together. The car park was now almost in sight.

"I know," said Amey. "We are very privileged to live here now, and everyone is so friendly."

"Tam told me a little about Norm. He sounds like a stoic Englishman. How on earth did you two get together, if you don't mind me asking?" probed Kee.

"We met properly at a Modern Pentathlon event in 1992, two years after the Berlin Wall had fallen. I knew who he was, as I had watched him many times on training video recordings with my coach. Norman was my idol, and still is. To meet him in person went beyond my wildest dreams, and he was there when it mattered. Anyway, Kee, I am talking too much—I need to find Tam to work out what happened earlier."

Kee stopped dead in his tracks. "Why are you going this way, then? Tam took the left track. She is staying with you, I assume, so why this way?"

Amey looked across the car park, toward her home, and then directly at Kee. "You say you don't know why she left so quickly; well, I think I do now. How could I have been so blind? You are correct, I should be going left. It has been lovely to talk, and now I must depart also. Come, Hertz, this way." Abruptly, she ushered the dog to the left with her Nordic pole.

Like Tam before her, Amey did not look back.

"Send Tam my love, won't you?" Kee shouted after her.

Amey raised a pole in acknowledgement and carried on along the left path. Kee knew that pathway would take her toward the nature reserve building, but after that, it was anyone's guess.

First Tam, and now Amey. They must both have met with some type of epiphany; he just couldn't understand what it was or why it had caused this extraordinary reaction.

Making his way to his van, Kee reproached himself for not having asked Amey about Brig Huddlestone. He strongly suspected that Amey's sudden response, like Tam's beforehand, somehow revolved around this bad penny. Until he saw either of them again, he could only spend the evening guessing how this had manifested itself.

CHAPTER SEVENTEEN — FRANKFURT AM MAIN

1992 World Pentathlon Championships

True to form as reigning champion, Tam's older brother, Norman Weaver, continued his winning ways, taking the individual gold plus a bronze medal for Great Britain in the team event. With the men's event having concluded the day before, both he and Tam were free to watch the conclusion of the women's event, which was culminating in the show jumping element, as usual.

They knew the British female competitors well. Naturally, they wanted to support them as much as they could, flitting between the stands of the main arena and the perimeter of the warm-up arena, providing them with all the motivation they could muster.

Norm returned to the main arena for the finale, leaving Tam to watch in the warm-up arena as the last three competitors went through their paces, all trying to bond with their randomly selected horses in the scant twenty minutes allowed for such familiarisation. Currently in the warm-up ring was Tam's close friend and top-ranked British lady, Michelle Devers-Lee, a competitor from Hungary and the third representing Germany.

Tam had a good knowledge of the event, having competed at junior level in the UK and Europe herself.

Family connections, via her brother and supportive parents, had definitely contributed to her inclusion in British squads. Her skill and fitness meant that she too was an accomplished athlete, but the gap between junior and senior grade competition had been too high for her to be considered for Frankfurt. Still, she lived in hope of a future opportunity.

Attending with Norm had given her invaluable insight into the next grade. She considered what it might take to become a future World Championship winner herself at senior level. Observation in the practice area could provide valuable insights she could use in the future.

The German lady, wearing the number sixteen on her bib, sat well in her saddle, her heels pointing down, in complete control of her mount. Every one of the five test jumps was taken effortlessly. She eased her way down to the end of the arena before turning to jump a double combination, again without issue or concern.

Tam checked the scoresheet that contained all the previous days' results, to see that Number 16, Amey Vogler, was lying in first place after the first four rounds. She was just a few points ahead of the Hungarian competitor who was due to jump just before her and was, therefore, her nearest challenger for the title.

However, the Hungarian lady seemed to be having trouble with the horse she had drawn. It had refused the first jump and lurched sideways at the next. Tam had experienced a similar fate herself at an event in the UK and knew that victory was down to the luck of the draw very often, not necessarily the rider's ability.

Her friend, Michelle, was now exiting the warm-up arena and heading away toward the main arena. Tam was torn. She wanted to go and watch Michelle but was fascinated by the contrasting fortunes of the last two women, now unfolding before her.

The Hungarian competitor had stopped for advice from her team manager who was gesticulating with his hands on how to hold the horse's head, seemingly with a softer grip, and to sit well forward. She nodded and the horse trotted away before finally jumping the fence that it previously refused. It wasn't convincing, but at least all was not lost for her.

An official beckoned for the Hungarian to proceed to the exit point to transfer to the main arena. All the while, Tam was listening to the noise of the crowd. Unable to understand the German commentary, she judged Michelle's performance on applause and cheers. Based on the loud response, she had performed well.

All the while, Tam continued her education in horsemanship, transfixed by the skill of the German rider. Smooth, calm and collected. In fact, everything Tam aspired to be as a rider.

Tam decided she couldn't miss this lady jumping in the main arena and left the warm-up area immediately to get a good seat in the main stand in time to watch her start her final round, only to find they had closed off entry to the main viewing stand. Apparently, it had reached capacity. Tam was annoyed and disappointed that she hadn't been able to gain access to a better viewing angle—she would have to watch from ground level now, next to the ungainly crisscross of scaffolding poles that comprised the sub-structure of the main stand.

The Hungarian competitor was now halfway through her routine. She had knocked two poles down already, so was probably likely to drop a place or two. All things considered, she had performed well, and the scoreboard indicated that she was just behind Michelle, who lay in the coveted gold medal position. Only one competitor left.

Tam clapped wildly as Number 16, Amey Vogler, entered the arena to rapturous applause from the partisan home crowd, eager for a German victor to emerge.

"Good luck!" Tam called out as Amey passed her.

Amey heard Tam's call and nodded to her, appreciating her kind wish, as the noise of the crowd dropped down in respect and anticipation of a clear round.

The bell signifying the start of the round sounded.

Just twelve obstacles stood in Amey's way. She gently nudged the horse into a gentle pace and set about the course as if it were the practice arena in her calm, assured and magnificent manner. Tam wondered how she could look so efficient on a horse she barely knew. They looked like a partnership made in Modern Pentathlon heaven.

This was looking like a foregone conclusion; the gold was hers for the taking.

In her peripheral vision, Tam became aware of a figure moving in amongst the scaffolding tubes, several metres away.

Dressed in a long, dark coat, despite the warm conditions, and a wide-brimmed fedora, the figure—female, Tam thought—stood very still with her hands in her pockets. Tam thought it strange for her to be standing there; after all, she couldn't possibly see the arena properly from that obscured position.

As Amey approached the combination double fence, it became clear why the person was there and why they were hiding their appearance.

A loud *pop, pop, pop* noise burst from the stranger's vicinity. Mayhem erupted in the stands above. Amey's horse reared in terror and crashed through the two fences in front of her, leaving Amey lying prone upon the sandy arena floor.

All hell let loose as officials rushed into the arena to intercept the horse before it could trample Amey's motionless body whilst the stewards evacuated the stands.

Tam looked straight back to the stranger. She was purposefully edging away to the far side of the stand, side-stepping through the scaffolding bars. Tam tried to follow, but the angle of the bars was making it difficult to keep pace.

"Stop, Stop!" she shouted, with all her might.

The figure turned. The lack of light under the stand made it difficult for Tam to clearly see her face; her blonde hair, however, was evident.

"Stop, I can see you! Stop!"

Tam knew that she had been seen. As the woman fled, she caught herself on one of the angled bars in her haste to escape. She fell to one side, her hand reaching down onto the grassy surface for balance, before recovering and exiting into the melee of people in the daylight.

Tam's adrenalin took over and she continued the chase, dodging the bars as best she could. At the point of the woman's stumble, Tam herself slipped. She thought she had stood on a metal bar, only to discover it was a pistol, similar to that used in trackside athletics to start races.

She knew she had to recover it, despite losing valuable time in her pursuit of the woman. Gingerly, she lifted it by its barrel and tucked it into the pocket of her GB jacket. She zipped it up as best she could in her agitated state, her hands shaking as she did so.

A glint in the semi-darkness caught her eye.

Reaching down into the grass, her fingers found a silver chain lying there. It had snapped, the heart-shaped locket wedged against the clasp at the one end.

The scaffold bar the woman had caught herself on had a small smear of blood on the end of it. Whoever she was, her neck would have a mark on it, one that would be hard to cover up.

Tam stuffed the necklace into her jeans pocket and took the last few steps into the manical crowd outside. No one had taken notice of the fedora and long coat that were now draped on the outskirts of the stand, the owner clearly having removed them to merge with the crowd.

But Tam remembered the long blonde hair she had seen and picked out a matching woman's head across the way. The woman appeared flustered as she glanced back to check on Tam's progress.

"Stop her, stop her!" Tam cried, but her shouts were either unheard or not understood. Person after person ignored her, many barging past her as they sought their own refuge from what they thought was some type of terrorist attack.

As Tam pushed deeper into the oncoming crowd, something slammed into her, knocking her down. A security officer had tackled her to the ground, winding her in the process. He was quickly joined by two other guards, who lifted her clean off the ground and carried her at speed into an officials' Portakabin-style building nearby. Her head barely missed the doorframe as they did so.

She could hardly catch her breath, let alone protest, whilst the manhandling continued. They located and extracted the gun from her jacket.

A conversation took place in German on their intercom radios, none of which she could understand. Within moments, armed police were there, pushing their way into the already overcrowded room.

A heated discussion broke out between the police, the stewards and security about her and the gun, which had been handed over to the policeman in charge.

"I am Himmelmann, Anton Himmelmann," he introduced himself to her in English. "Are you English?"

Tam nodded, still unable to speak, and now in tears as the pain and shock took over.

"Who is here with you?"

"My brother, he is with the British team... please find him," she panted.

"His name, please."

"Norman Weaver. He won the gold medal here on Tuesday. He was in the main arena. He is probably looking for me."

"You tell us what happened, exactly, please," he demanded.

Tam proceeded to tell them what had taken place, as best she could in her distraught state.

They didn't seem to fully believe her, insinuating that it was she who had wanted to affect the result of the contest by upsetting the German competitor. After all, she had the offending weapon on her and she was British—and Michelle was now the winner. Her protests were falling on deaf ears.

The officials and police then started arguing amongst themselves once more, before the welcome sight of Norm and a British delegation appeared at the packed doorway.

"Norm, Norm, I'm here!" Tam shouted, above the noise.

Norm forced his way in, despite attempts to prevent him. A scuffle broke out, and the police launched a verbal attack on him, too, this time accusing the whole British contingent of deliberately sabotaging the event, in front of millions of viewers across the world, for their own gain.

Norm asked Himmelmann for proof, if he had any, and the policeman waved the gun at him. Norm countered quickly by asking how anyone, other than a German native, could have one in their possession, or were German border controls still that bad, igniting yet another fracas.

Tam could see that the officials had lost control, but none of this was helping her case as the main suspect.

Norm spouted off again. "You're afraid of the backlash from dignitaries who were present from across the globe. We all know it was an event designed to promote the reunification of Germany after the fall of the Berlin Wall, but it is you that has messed up. Don't you dare use my sister as a scapegoat, you hear?"

Norm was adamant, standing his ground firmly. "I suggest you lot get out there and find whoever did it, rather than bullying us," he shouted as he finally got to Tam.

"What happened, sis? Tell me, ignore these goons," he said pointedly, directing his gaze straight at the police.

A hush descended as Tam, once more, relayed the sequence of events, including how she trod on the starting pistol gun under the stand.

"Long blonde hair, you say?"

Tam nodded.

"I know who it is," proclaimed Norm. "It's Renate Brenzlig. It has to be her, I'm telling you."

Tam knew very little of Renate Brenzlig, having only seen photographs of her in journals, usually of her riding, where her hair would have been tucked away in a hairnet, inside her riding hat.

"But she is German, is she not?" replied Himmelmann.

"Yes, a famous West German. She didn't get picked for your team, though, yet I saw her here, today."

"So why do you think she is responsible?"

"Because she, a West German, thinks that she didn't get picked in favour of an East German, Amey Vogler. Think about it, Amey Vogler is sitting in gold medal position. I can only imagine the ignominy in her mind. She feels humiliated that she wasn't chosen in the first place and, seeing the inevitable outcome, decides to spoil it. I suggest you follow that line of enquiry and let us leave. In addition, you ought to know that I hold a high position within the British government and regularly work with my German counterparts on matters of security—the same people to whom you are accountable. Do you understand now?"

An official reached over to Himmelmann and whispered something in his ear, causing his eyebrows to lift.

"OK, Herr Weaver, we will make more enquiries. For the time being, you will be free to leave here, but not the country. I expect you to surrender your passports to an officer, who will take you to where you are staying. Do you agree, *ja*?"

Tam looked at Norm, who was now looking at her for a decision.

"Yes, on one condition, though," she said.

"Which is?"

"My side hurts, thanks to you and your bloody men," she said, pointing at the security team who had tackled her earlier. "Where can I go to have it checked out? I'm not sure that you haven't damaged my ribs."

"We will take you to Frankfurt Hospital immediately, of course," replied Himmelmann.

He beckoned to an underling to make the appropriate arrangements, and Tam was helped out of her chair, wincing in pain. When she and Norm stepped out from the hot demountable building and into the fresh air, the vicinity was all but deserted.

An ambulance was already there, parked up next to the main arena, whilst a crew attended to Amey Vogler. A stretcher was being taken from the vehicle and into the arena.

Norm and Tam made their way across to the arena to where Amey lay on the ground, now with a neck brace on and covered in a white blanket.

"*Wie geht es dir*, Amey?" asked Norm, in fluent German.

"Hello, Norman. My hip is sore. I go for X-ray, for my spine, yes?" Amey said quietly in pidgin English, clearly in pain.

"We are also going to the hospital. My sister has been injured trying to find out who did this to you," Norm explained, bringing Tam forward.

"Hello, Amey. I am so sorry to see you like this. I saw the woman who did this—she was blonde—"

"Sounds like Renate Brenzlig," interjected Amey.

"That's what I thought, too," said Norm. "I have told the police. She had the motive, after all."

"I was so looking forward to seeing you after the championships, Norm," said Amey. "We could have been 'the golden couple' on the television in Europe tonight. It's been too long since we last saw each other. At least Michelle won, I hear. You will be the golden couple now."

"No, not Michelle. You, Amey, you," he murmured, appearing deeply saddened by her words as much as her injuries.

"*Entschuldigen Sie, bitte,*" said the ambulanceman, as he positioned himself between them.

Tam had never known the depth of Norm's feelings toward Amey. He had never even mentioned her name in such a context before.

She watched as they carefully placed her onto the stretcher, then followed her across to the ambulance. As the ambulancemen made final preparations to lift the trolley, Norm stepped in once more.

"We will be at the hospital shortly, and we will see each other; I promise we will." He bent down and kissed her forehead lightly.

Tam grasped his arm as he stepped away, hardly able to contain his tears as the doors were closed and the ambulance slowly drove away.

They made their way to the hospital in the back of the police car, neither saying a word.

Tam's subsequent X-ray revealed nothing more than very bad bruising. She was allowed to leave the hospital the same evening. Norm made enquiries with the hospital about Amey and was told that he would be unable to see her until the following morning, at the earliest.

True to his word, Norm, with Tam alongside, visited the police station the next morning for a second meeting to clarify the position of the incident. They did not need to surrender their passports as new information had come to light, proving their innocence.

Television camera footage had caught images of Renate Brenzlig emerging from under the stand, just as Tam had described, and also showed Tam's pursuit of Renate just prior to being intercepted herself. The blonde hair had given Renate away, and the clothes were identified as hers.

Tam and Norm were now free to leave whilst Renate, who had been arrested overnight, was being held in a police cell pending a court ruling within the next hour. This would decide if they would press charges and whether she would be eligible for bail if they did.

Norm thanked them for their help and confirmed that he wouldn't take any further action, understanding it was an honest mistake that had led to Tam being a suspect, and that he trusted the German judicial system.

In reciprocation, Himmelmann offered a full written apology to Tam and stated that they would both always be welcome should they wish to visit Frankfurt again.

A police car was made available that evening to take them back to the hospital, where Amey still remained. En route, Norm and Tam were given the update on Renate.

They had news for Amey. Very bad news.

The police had interviewed Renate again that afternoon and immediately released her on bail. It defied all belief. However, the evidence they had was irrefutable. At least Renate would be held to account when she had her trial—not that this would ever get Amey back the gold medal that was cruelly taken from her grasp.

The following day, Norm and Tam had to leave to return home. A few days later, Amey was transferred back to a local hospital in Thuringia. A further week passed before Amey was able to contact Norm by telephone, having finally been allowed home. Himmelmann had phoned her in Thuringia to say that Renate's bail had been paid for by an American diplomat whom she had admitted she was in a covert relationship with. Worse still, they had left Germany altogether, to seek permanent residence in New York, thereby avoiding a trial and any further adverse publicity for all concerned.

Off the record, Himmelmann stated that strings had clearly been pulled from within, without his prior knowledge. The very next day the police hierarchy publicly stated on German television that the culprit was never identified and the case was being closed. It was a cover-up of the worst order.

Subsequently, Norm arranged the first of many visits to Germany to see Amey. Using what free time he had, mostly on weekends and holidays, he travelled to Thuringia, before she agreed to move to Britain and become his wife. Tam was bridesmaid, of course.

Sadly, fate dictated that they could never have children, but their new life was spent in the countryside, surrounded by horses and dogs, whilst Norm commuted to Central London from West Sussex on a daily basis and Amey pursued her journalistic career during her ongoing rehabilitation.

For her part, Tam retained the necklace, unbeknownst to anyone. Originally meant to prove her innocence, she kept it as a memento of her traumatic experience that fateful day, a day she could never forget.

CHAPTER EIGHTEEN – REFUGE

Approaching the now familiar nature reserve building, Tam stopped briefly to check that no one, least of all Kee, had followed her to this point. Being alone once more was a strange feeling, especially somewhere that was still new to her.

She thanked her lucky stars that she had already checked out the route to salvation, namely the Sker Lake Caravan Park. Daresay Norm would have something derogatory to say to her when she got there, for using his special phone in the way she had—if, indeed, that was the reason for the half-mast flag. For all she knew it could be something else that had occurred. Unlikely, but nonetheless possible.

She had no idea how things would pan out from there, but it would surely be revealed when she saw Norm or Amey. Then, at least, she might know the full ramifications of her actions.

Hannah reappeared, drawing the metal shutters down, one by one, all along the side of the building, using a hook on a long pole and then applying a padlock to a fixing point on the concrete surround. Knowing now was not the time to stop for a second chat, Tam stepped away swiftly so she wouldn't be seen, making her way behind the building and up to the carving that had emotionally moved her earlier that morning. She stopped, knowing it would have to be brief.

"Well, I think I may have a lot to thank you for," she said to the southward-facing figure. "You gave me strength today. I hope I can retain it—I feel I am going to need it."

Deep down, Tam wasn't sure whether to be elated or deeply worried. After all, the inspiration she had gained from the statue and the lovely Kee had given her one of the best days of her life. Being naked with a stranger and riding a horse along the beach, both impossible dreams, had amazingly come true.

Tam felt that this new wave of inspiration was overriding her immediate worries surrounding Brig as she made her way along the bracken-lined path toward the kissing gate into the caravan park ahead.

If Brig Huddlestone was on her way to find her, then bring it on. It had to happen one day, so why not here in Skerrid Mawr, where the odds must now be in her favour by virtue of having Norm and his renowned power on her side?

Passing through the narrow gate, she noticed a small shop across the tarmac road. A sign ebulliently stated "Essentials Here" above its door, and a large, outdated CCTV camera stared bluntly down at anyone who entered.

She would make it brief. She knew who had the authority to access that footage—her brother, Norm! Just as long as Brig Huddlestone wasn't another, she mused, covering her face with her hand as a precaution.

Stepping out of the sunshine and into the shop, Tam had to remove her sunglasses to allow her eyes to adjust to the dim light. It was almost darker than Omni's Shack!

Bottled gas and binoculars, however, were not on Tam's shopping list, nor was bird feed.

"Linda", as her badge showed, appeared from the back room and was very pleasant and chatty. Judging by the puzzle book and pen lying upon the grey lino-covered counter, she was probably bored witless by the job. She asked open-ended questions which, no doubt, she had asked many times before to all and sundry:

"Are you on holiday?"

"That's not a local accent, is it?"

"Oh, I went there once" type of patter.

It was unnerving being watched so intently as she scoured the shelves.

Tam felt churlish with herself for thinking that way. She wasn't used to nice people, just impatient ones who usually wanted to get back onto their phones at the first opportunity, rather than talking to another lonely human being, like her.

"Would you like a bag?" Linda called, trying to maintain the small talk.

"Please," was Tam's single-word reply.

Gathering her items into the crook of her arm, Tam took them to the counter to allow Linda to scan them, albeit slowly, and put them into the flimsy bag.

"Sorry, we have to charge ten pence for bags—it's the Welsh Office, you see," Linda explained.

Tam nodded in acceptance as the till displayed the amount. Linda proffered the card machine. Tam thought better of it. She had watched programmes on TV where card activity had given locations away, so opted for cash instead, tendering a brand-new, slippery £20 note to Linda.

"Fresh out of the machine, is it?" she asked in yet another small talk cliché.

Tam said she didn't know, not really getting the inference from Linda that it might be a forgery.

"We get people in here trying to pay with euros and dollars, you know."

Tam didn't want to hear about dollars.

A quick check under the UV machine confirmed the note's validity and Tam duly exited with her change in one hand and the white plastic bag of "essentials" in the other, namely peanuts, crisps, red wine and chocolate.

She knew Norm's caravan was somewhere near the bottom of the park, with a view across the lake, so proceeded down the shiny tarmac road until she was outside "Burgess". A bespoke weathervane sat plum middle of the roof. She recalled Amey telling her last year that she'd had a local blacksmith make it for her. Along with the N for north and S for south, the silhouette of a naked female form represented west and the letters DDR signalled east. Unique, if nothing else.

The maintenance team were out, one painting brilliant white gloss onto the large stone boulders along the grass line, whilst another was trimming the grass, his ride-on mower now working around the caravan next door to Burgess. As Tam arrived at the uPVC gate to the decked entrance, the driver cut the mower engine. It seemed very quiet all of a sudden. Tam stopped to remove the keys from her bag and, upon doing so, became aware of the driver looking in her direction, almost blatantly so, making her feel extremely uncomfortable.

She covertly glanced at him a second time, but he remained intent on staring at her.

Tam put the carrier bag down and started towards him, in no mood to be ogled in this way. It clearly showed, as the man restarted the engine. Tam stood in front of the mower, preventing him from escaping without either an explanation or an apology.

"Do you make a habit of staring at women generally or do you keep it for unfamiliar visitors?"

"No," came his brief answer.

"Well, why did you stop your motor and watch me, then?"

"I was going to check the blade—not cutting properly, see?" he explained, in an accent not too dissimilar from Morgan's.

"Do you honestly expect me to believe that? Perhaps I'll go and ask your wife in the shop, then, shall I, yeah?"

"Hold on a minute. She isn't my wife, she's my auntie—and I can do what I want. I don't need to explain myself to anyone, least of all you."

"So, who am I, then?" demanded Tam.

"I don't know, that's why I stopped to look. You could have been breaking in. I know Burgess isn't yours, so who owns that caravan, then?" he threw back at her.

"My brother, Norman Weaver."

"Oh yes, come to think of it, I can see a likeness now," he said, clearly changing his tune. "He's a good man, is Norman. We see Amey down here usually, either on her own or with people from one of her charity things, nice touch that. Lovely lady, always very polite."

"Meaning I'm not?"

"I didn't say that."

"You didn't have to."

A face appeared in the window of the adjacent caravan, looking out to see what was causing the raised voices, as the mower man's stone-painting colleague put his brush to one side.

"You're attracting attention," said the man on the mower.

"I am attracting attention?" replied Tam, her blood now boiling with this buffoon.

"Right, I had better get on," he said, trying to ignore her. "Enjoy your stay, won't you?"

"Don't you dare belittle me. Do you speak to all women like this or just me?"

"Only the good-looking ones, if I'm telling the truth."

With that bullish statement, he pulled his ear defenders down, put his safety goggles back on and proceeded with his task with no hint of compunction.

Tam was furious. This was the type of man her mother would have warned her about, and most certainly not someone to be let loose in a caravan park with that attitude. Were she not so hot and angry, she may well have marched back to the shop, but felt Linda might bore her to death if she did.

Tam returned to the caravan and unlocked the door. She lifted the shopping bag up and placed it onto the first surface she could find.

The living room was light, if a little musty. Not quite to the levels of damp in Omni's Shack, but musty nevertheless. The presence of a dehumidifier in the corner indicated that condensation must still be a problem in such a thin plywood construction.

It was a smell Tam always associated with holidays, particularly when she was a child and they had stayed near Weymouth in a caravan belonging to her late Uncle Reg. Then, it was the weird, sweet smell of the bottled gas fumes that emanated from the cooker which had created condensation on the walls and the windows the very next morning.

At least Amey had an electric kettle, unlike Uncle Reg. She filled it up with water from the low-pressure tap, hoping that there would be teabags in a cupboard somewhere. If not, then the wine would have to be opened earlier than intended.

As the kettle started to boil, Tam made her way to the window in the lounge area, drawing back the outdated net curtain to take in the view.

If there was a highlight to the caravan, then it had to be the spectacular view across the lake. The sun glared off its surface, making her shield her eyes with her hand, even though she still had her cap in place. She could see various flocks of birds on or around the lake, including ducks, swans and others she was unable to identify—daresay Hannah could help her there. A telescopic device sat upon a tripod, the type of thing that Norm would probably have bought for Amey as a birthday present. Tam knelt down and peered through, trying to spot what she could with this new toy. Panning across the lake she arrived at the ruins of an old castle, rising out from the still water. She angled the barrel of the telescope until she could see the tips of the dunes that bordered the beach, the very place she must have been with Kee.

She liked this view, very much.

CHAPTER NINETEEN — FACE THE MUSIC

Norm paced back and forth in his office, peering out of the window momentarily before repeating himself, like a bear trapped in a cage.

He was angry. He hadn't given Tam a VPN phone for her to do that with it; it was meant to be for emergencies only. Now his plans had been thrown up into the air, by his own sister! All the arrangements and timings that he had agreed with the powers that be were now in tatters. Backpedalling and apologies were not in his armoury.

He was the control hub. The glue.

What had possessed her to do this without his consent? How could he possibly justify her actions now?

The embarrassment.

It was only a matter of time before the Americans would make contact, asking for explanations he wasn't able to give. The corridors of Whitehall knew already; therefore, the Home Secretary would inevitably be onto him again, too. He knew he wasn't the most popular person with either side even before all this furore, so he would need to think quickly to justify his position before they stepped in and bulldozed his whole plan.

The ignominy. He just hoped that Felton wasn't in the loop, gloating somewhere.

His phone started ringing but he killed it without even looking at who the caller might be. If it was something of importance, then they would phone back or contact him some other way. He needed time to think, away from inane distractions.

Certainties. He had to work on certainties.

Norm had dealt with many a crisis in his time but none that were as much about his own family's security as they were about international importance. Had he been given a bigger budget by the Home Secretary to manage this particular problem then he may well have been able to apply greater resources and provide him with a solution sooner. Cutbacks and diminishing influence hadn't helped his cause, leaving him fewer options than he was used to enjoying.

Irrespective of that, it was time to deploy the small, loyal band of troops he had now come to rely on and then get across to the caravan where both Tam and Amey must now be—judging by their absence at the house. At least, he surmised, the flag lowering had worked.

Tam had some serious questions to answer. Perhaps Amey would support him and be the voice of reason he needed.

The phone rang once more. It was Parv, delivering a certainty.

"It looks like your sister may well have done us all a favour, Norm. Brig will be with you in the next couple of hours," she said bluntly.

"At Sandpiper?" Norm asked in astonishment.

"Yes, at Sandpiper. I spoke to Liz earlier to set up the necessary arrangements. Brig called me to say she was just leaving West London—that would have been at least half an hour ago. She is on her motorbike, so at least you know how much time you have to play with now."

"Thank you, Parv, that is good to know. I can work with that. When are you leaving Cheltenham?"

"Well, I have told Brig that I will get there in the morning, so I will continue liaising with everyone as you have asked. It will be easier for me to do that from here and travel down in the morning. I am keeping an eye on her phone for movements and will speak to her later, no doubt. If not, Liz will inform us all when she arrives and apply a tracking device at the first possible opportunity," expounded Parv. "Brig isn't stupid—if she suspects anything, she will turn her phone off. If that happens, then I am out of the game, as my cover will have been blown."

"Got it. One quick thought, Parv—do you think she is working alone?"

"She has less friends than you think, Norm, so my answer is a categorical yes."

"Excellent. Should there be any developments from my side of things then I will let you know. Outstanding work again, Parv, thank you," confirmed Norm as he concluded the call.

Norm knew he had to visit the caravan to update Tam and Amey before Brig arrived in the village, and get himself back home in that time, too. For safety's sake, he felt that only he could remain in the house. Amey and Tam would need to be, in his parlance, "confined to barracks"—it wasn't safe for them to roam free or return home just yet. Consequentially, he would need to provide additional provisions for them, like clean clothes and food. Even the caravan park shop would have to be made out of bounds.

It was just part of his detailed thinking, born from his many years of army training.

CHAPTER TWENTY – TONIC

Tam headed back to the kettle and picked up one of the mugs on the small draining board with the intent of making herself a black coffee to go with her snacks. Noticing the aged tannin stains etched upon the mug's walls, she decided to re-wash it before using it, if she could find anything suitable to do the job. Looking for a scouring pad, she opened the minuscule cupboard above the sink, only to find a bottle of washing-up liquid and toilet bleach on hand.

Keeping herself busy during a personal crisis had become a regular therapy session for Tam, and cleaning was something that she had come to rely on when in London, especially under the more recent stress of Felton's actions.

Upon further inspection, she found that all the mugs seemed in need of a good soak. Using the hot kettle water, she filled the small sink up as best she could. She squirted the detergent over the mugs, allowing them to sit there for a moment as she looked out of the side window.

Why Norm and Amey had kept this caravan, she didn't really understand. She knew it had been part of the house purchase, a job lot from an old colleague of Norm's, but it had seen better days and needed upgrading or selling, if truth be told. Given they had such a large house no more than a five-minute walk away, it seemed somewhat surplus to requirements. The annual ground rent couldn't be cheap either.

When they bought it, Amey had told Tam she intended to use it as a bolt-hole for when Norm had his cronies over at the house, if she wanted some solace either to read or write up her journals. Today, however, it had become a bolt-hole for Tam, so she should be grateful for its existence, really.

A loud knock on the door startled Tam from her daydream, and in a moment of instant horror, she dropped the damp mug from her hand. It bounced across the wooden flooring.

She froze, praying she hadn't given her presence away to whoever was there.

"Tam... it's me," came the voice. It was Amey.

Tam let out a gasping groan. "My God, Amey, you frightened the life out of me!" She approached the door, where Amey's tall profile could be seen behind the bevelled glass. "Are you alone?"

"*Ja*, only me, and Hertz, of course."

Tam unlocked the door and allowed them in, quickly locking the door behind them.

"How did you find out?" she asked.

"Probably the same as you, the flag at half-mast. Norm was clever to do that, wasn't he?"

"Yes, he was, but I was worried you would not see it and go back to your house."

"Well, your gentleman friend was sat by The Steps. Hertz ran across to him."

The mention of Kee lifted Tam's spirits immediately. "What did he say? Did he realise about the flag?" she asked.

"No, he said that you seemed to have some type of 'funny turn' and had asked him to wait there for ten minutes, which is what he was doing when we arrived, just waiting. Hertz and I must have just missed you, Tam. Tell me, why did you ask him to wait?"

"Because I didn't want him involved. If he saw me coming here, to the caravan, he might have followed me."

"He obviously respects you. It's just as well that he is unaware of the significance of the flag or what is happening, which is good—no need for him to get involved, as you say. Actually, it gave me a chance to talk with him. We have much in common, you know."

Amey proceeded to expand upon the conversation she had with Kee, much to Tam's delight.

"It was good to find someone who knew, and was interested in, East Germany—and in sport, generally. If I didn't have Norm, I might be tempted myself, Tam!" she said, causing Tam to give her a friendly slap on the arm. Amey took it in good spirit. "In fact, it was only when we were nearing the car park that he pointed out that he had seen you branching left. The penny dropped. It was only then that I looked up, realising that you must have seen the flag at half-mast, too. How I didn't twig earlier I will never know. Anyway, I made my excuses and took the path in front of the nature reserve building, checking out which vehicle was his. For your information it is a silver campervan. I even got his registration number for you."

Tam was pleased. Norm could trace that for her, to get a telephone number or home address at least.

Amey was already ahead of her. "I messaged Norm immediately on my VPN phone, knowing at that point that you must have seen the flag—thanks to Kee, of course—and be heading here. Norm will trace him, no doubt. Just for security, you understand."

At that precise moment, Amey's phone buzzed.

"Oh, Norm has messaged me back to say he will get over here as soon as he can. He is just arranging cover for the house whilst he gets some clothes and provisions for us. Be prepared, though, Tam—he isn't happy with you."

"Tough. Why do you think I bought this red wine, Amey? I have seen his temper before and I daresay you have, too. In fact, forget the tea; let's have a glass of 'Chateau Linda' and a game of cards or something, like we used to years ago, or I might say something I will regret."

Amey headed for the boiler cupboard and took the old biscuit tin from the shelf.

"I saw your photo, Tam," she said, prising the lid off to check the cards were there. "What possessed you to do such a thing?"

Tam unscrewed the top from the bottle and poured them each a child-sized beaker of wine.

"If you really want to know, it was because both you and Kee opened my eyes to a world of possibilities, the potential to actually enjoy myself for once. Why should I feel repressed and be hiding away in fear of an attack by a psychotic freak like Brig Huddlestone? I can't live like that anymore, Amey, it hurts too much in my own head, do you see?"

Amey stood there, looking slightly taken aback.

"Listen, Amey, I am sorry to be like this and it isn't your fault in any way, shape or form, but I'm not so sure that everyone on Norm's team is truly trustworthy. Someone is feeding Brig information. Grant told me on that awful night that Parv and Brig were having some type of liaison, if you must know. That's why I did it—I knew deep down inside that this whole mess had best be sorted out sooner rather than later. Surely, the fact that the flag was at half-mast proves it worked, does it not?"

Amey took a sip of wine and sat beside Tam on the narrow-cushioned bench seat. "I hear what you're saying, Tam. This is why Norm wants it sorted out, too."

"I get it, Amey. But if someone's undermining him, then they're undermining all of us, aren't they? I'm not convinced we're safe here in this caravan either."

Tam noticed Amey looking down, her fingers running around the edge of her cup. Tam picked up the bottle of wine and topped up her own beaker before offering it to Amey, who declined.

"If I am going to die at her hands then I want to have a say in it, not just leave it to big brother," Tam stated vehemently.

"I have never heard you speak this way. It is very sad."

"Maybe it is, but I have taken way too long to climb out of my shell. The time has to be now."

As she spoke, another thought came to mind. Surely, switching on her own phone, not the VPN one, would make no difference now? The VPN had served its purpose and a reaction had occurred. Ordinarily, she'd use her phone to receive messages, usually from Elinor or Anthony, more than send them. If she was to be based in this old caravan for a few days then having it on might provide some comfort—no disrespect to Amey. She took it out of her bag and laid it on the table.

"Don't, Tam. Switching on your own phone won't help us now, will it?" said Amey, as if she had read her mind.

On second thoughts, she realised Amey had a valid point. Tam decided she would wait for Norm to arrive and ask his permission. He deserved that from her at least, given the way he had looked after her following yesterday's frightening attack.

A hush fell. Tam felt a little awkward for overreacting to Amey's comments.

"Sorry, Amey," she said, planting her empty cup next to the wine bottle. "It's the stress of it all. I feel awful that I have brought my problems to your idyllic world. You don't deserve it, any of it."

Amey put her arm around her shoulder. "Once this is all over, why don't you make Skerrid Mawr your idyllic world, too? We would love for you to be closer to us again. In fact, why don't you pack it all in? Take voluntary redundancy if you can. Nice lump sum to spend."

"Then what do I do? Nothing?"

"Find something new and exciting, where the likes of Felton have no say anymore. You already know there's plenty to do down here, so be free and spoil yourself for once, In fact, you can move in with us—we have space," she kindly offered.

As lovely as Amey and Norm were, Tam knew she needed her own space somewhere else. "I suppose for only half the value of the London house, I could buy something equally as big down here. Well, probably."

"Exactly. We could see Ant and El more often, too. Now you are thinking, Tam. Go the whole way and buy another horse, get another dog, then the kids might want to spend more time with us again."

"Maybe," said Tam, imagining it herself. Amey's enthusiasm was getting infectious.

"It could be their new home, too, you know," she suggested. "Yes, they have their own lives and their own friends, but you could probably buy a flat somewhere on the outskirts of London for them, once you have taken Felton for everything that you can. That way, they could use it to live in and, if you need to go back that way at any time to see friends, you can stay there, too. Sounds like a win-win to me."

"You know what, Amey, you may well have a point. All this nonsense will surely force Felton to complete the divorce quickly, especially when Argent gets hold of him. Workwise, Felton knows he will get moved sideways after all this comes out, if not completely out of the Service, so he needs to be compliant. Ironically, Norm's influence will have a direct bearing on the outcome, of course."

"He will do the best deal for you, not that puffed-up toad," added Amey, picking up the playing cards.

"I am sure he will," replied Tam, her spirits definitely lifted.

CHAPTER TWENTY-ONE — SEEK AND YOU WILL FIND

Kee drew back the side door of his German-built campervan, allowing the heat inside to escape before placing his rucksack just behind the front passenger seats. He wiped his sweating forehead with his shirt sleeve. It still had Tam's smell on it.

The Tam effect was still resonating in his head, caused by her kiss, her kindness and her compassion.

Opening the small fridge, he extracted a cold bottle of water before flicking the switch of his travel kettle into the "on" position and plugging in his phone to recharge. He knew it was too hot for tea, but his need for caffeine overrode everything.

Taking a drink from the bottle of water, he remembered that Tam had put something in his bag. His curiosity got the better of him, and he unzipped the outer pocket. A small slip of paper fell out and he caught it. Turning it over, he saw the sketch Tam had made of him.

"Interesting," he said to himself. "A girl of many talents, and beautiful, too."

Kee proudly propped it up against a spare mug on the sideboard, using his van keys to hold it in place in case it blew away. It was a lovely keepsake and a gift that touched him deeply. He lay back on the cushioned bench, staring at the picture with a smile before closing his eyes. By the time the kettle had boiled, he had drifted into a deep slumber.

An hour or so had passed before Kee awoke to the distant sound of a dog barking.

It took him a moment to realise where he was, and he momentarily panicked, having realised he had left the van's side door wide open. He sat up. Outside, there were very few vehicles left in the car park. The lure of teatime was evident in their departure, no doubt.

Sod it, he thought. He couldn't be bothered to drive anywhere else now. The campervan was, after all, designed for overnight stays, so he would sleep here, in Skerrid Mawr, tonight.

He knew that provisions in the van's store cupboard were low, so opted for a walk to one of the two hostelries for a good meal. The issue was which one: The Meadow Pipit or The Dragon's Tail?

Ordinarily, he'd take a quick wash in the nature reserve toilets, but it was too late now; the centre would be closed. Pity they didn't have an outdoor shower or standpipe he could use.

He stepped around to the back door of the van, lifted it open and removed the small cover where the spare wheel was sited. A large bottle of water lay there. It was warm and would have to serve his immediate need for cleanliness. Then there was the added problem of clean clothes.

Essentially, this would come down to whatever he could find secreted about the van, however creased it might be. His main concern was appearing clean, in case he was fortunate enough to bump into the beautiful Tam again. Perhaps she'd be in The Dragon's Tail at some point, the pub having cropped up in their earlier conversation.

Twenty minutes later, Kee had managed to wash and change and was leaving the car park on foot. As he walked along the West Bay Road, he looked over the random array of unique houses in Skerrid Mawr, wondering which, if any, he would buy, given the choice. A sea view with a balcony was a must; the only problem was that it would probably mean living very close to Omni, almost a fate worse than death.

Walking past The Dragon's Tail, he stopped and peered in through a small side window. He felt somewhat conspicuous, given he was now dressed in an old pair of navy tradesman shorts coupled up with a bright orange cycling top, one that he only tended to use when mountain biking. The combination actually matched, more by luck than judgement. However, it wouldn't take much to signal his presence to Omni, let alone by wearing this bright orange top. This needed a quick decision.

The pub looked packed both inside and out with afternoon revellers. With Tam nowhere to be seen, he opted to briskly continue up to The Meadow Pipit. At least The Meadow Pipit was an Omni-free zone.

A wide patio area lay before the large, double-fronted, whitewashed pub. Kee knew it afforded a spectacular early evening view across to Swansea Bay. It was an easy choice to sit outside with his pint of Irish stout, having also ordered a simple pub meal of vegetable lasagne with a side salad. He wasn't a vegetarian as such but knew it was a speciality of the house and one he had enjoyed there before. Like The Dragon's Tail, The Pipit was fairly busy, but the wait was a welcome chance to catch up with the wider world via his phone and start his investigations.

Norman Weaver, he keyed in, searching through all the main social media channels, but succeeding only in finding people who were clearly not Tam's brother.

This frustrated Kee. His route to Tam was now effectively stymied.

He tried *Tam Kendall* and *Tam Weaver* and all such derivatives, again without success.

"Damn," he called out, louder than he'd thought, causing other customers to stop and stare in his direction.

"Sorry," he apologised, holding his hand up. "Actually, does anybody know a Norman Weaver who lives around here?"

A few mumbled "no"s were thrown back in his direction.

His frustrations grew as a message appeared on his phone.

Hi Dad,
Have you arranged our passes for the festival yet?
Me and Ellie can't go now—we have a wedding party to go to that weekend, sorry.
And I think Sparky is away with Mum too.
Hope you can find replacements.
Jem

"Aw, thanks, kids. All of you!" he blurted out. "The one weekend in the year you know I need you." He dropped his phone onto the table in frustration.

"Problems?" said a young lady behind him as she placed a tray laden with his food, cutlery and condiments beside the discarded phone.

"Nothing I can't sort out, I suppose," Kee replied, remembering his manners.

"Can I get you another drink, to go with your food?" she kindly offered.

"Just a half, then, please—and here, have one yourself," he said presenting her with a ten-pound note.

"Thank you, very kind of you. I'll be right back," she said, waving the note as she departed.

True to her word, she was back quickly, complete with his drink and change, which she placed onto his tray. This efficient girl was the sort of person he needed on his work team: friendly, dynamic and reliable.

At that very moment, a touring-style motorcycle, complete with panniers, roared past, making everyone look up as it needlessly revved louder. The rider—a woman, Kee noted—looked toward the unwilling audience, making some form of arrogant statement of intent, before turning left between the pub and the adjacent All Angels' Church, disappearing from sight down into the neighbouring hamlet of Mawdsridge. Kee chose to ignore the juvenile action and turned to the girl once more.

"Do you happen to know a Norman Weaver at all?" he asked.

"Yes, actually, I do... He lives by the golf course, just past The Dragon's Tail, but I don't know him personally. His wife is German—Amey, I think she is. I often see her walking her dog or riding her horse of a morning. The house has a flagpole outside, if that helps at all?"

"Wow, it really does. Thank you so much for that."

"You're welcome. Enjoy your meal."

Maybe now he could locate Tam. How he would have loved to see her pretty face opposite his right now.

CHAPTER TWENTY-TWO – SANDPIPER

Liz Jenkins heard the throaty rumble of a motorbike arriving outside the house. She knew there was only one guest due in today: Brig Huddlestone.

She closed her laptop and placed it to one side, then pressed the button below the arm of her chair to gently elevate her into a position to enable her to stand. Liz was only twenty-five years old, her life damaged by a car crash that had killed her parents just two years previously.

"I think she's here," came the excited voice of her brother, Rich, from upstairs. "Shall I get the door?"

"No, Rich, please leave this one to me." Liz reached across for her walking stick and used it to support her exit from the chair. Her rehabilitation had been slow, but she was a fighter.

She cast an eye out of the lounge window at the paved drive, upon which stood a steel-blue, touring-style motorcycle, the rider now dismounting.

Liz slowly made her way to the smooth parquet flooring of the hallway and waited there for the bell to ring. Catching a glimpse of herself in the mirror on the opposing wall, she feathered her distinctive page-boy haircut with her fingers to stir up her curls. Through the bevelled glass of the front door, she could see the figure approaching and waited for the shrill ring of the bell before easing her way to the door and opening it with her professional smile.

There in front of her was the svelte form of Brig Huddlestone, clad in black leather and fancy blue boots that matched the hue of both her bike and her eyes, holding her white helmet.

"*Croeso*, Brig," welcomed Liz, in a soft Welsh lilt. "I'm Liz, please come in."

Liz turned away and stepped slowly but surely toward a small desk that housed a small occasional table lamp and a visitor book. She could sense Brig very close behind her.

"Good journey?" asked Liz as she arrived at the side of the desk.

"It was OK, I suppose," was the mundane reply from Brig in what Liz thought was a New York accent.

Liz decided not to ask anything further, instead inviting Brig to sign the visitor book.

"If you could just sign in for me, please, just for health and safety purposes."

"Sure," said Brig, picking up the pen.

Liz watched as bejewelled fingers quickly scribbled down a name. Brig then licked her thumb to scroll back through the book.

Liz was a little dumbfounded. "Sorry, are you looking for something specific?" she asked politely.

"Just satisfying my curiosity, if you must know."

"Oh, if you looking for Parv's name then it will be August, last year," Liz said, guessing the only logical explanation for Brig flicking back through the pages. "Would you like me to find—"

Her offer was curtailed. "No, I am quite capable, thank you."

As Brig stooped over the book, Liz stared at the back of her head, observing Brig's closely cropped fair hair, her shaven neck below and a trio of studs along the helix of her ear, dearly wishing she had the courage to slap her for her ill-mannered impertinence.

Finally, as Liz had suggested, Brig found Parv's name in the August of the previous year.

"Wasn't she here with a guy called Grant? A stocky, good-looking English guy?" asked Brig nonchalantly, checking other signatures up and down that very page.

"She was definitely here on her own. Every adult that stays here has to sign the book, and, as you can see, this Grant person isn't there. I remember Parv, though, beautiful-looking girl."

"Is she?" said Brig, looking at Liz.

"Well, I thought she was and so did my brother Rich. Stunning is the word he used. I thought you knew her well?"

"I thought I did, too, but that's another story."

Liz knew she had to change the subject.

"Staying for a few days I see from the booking form Parv sent me earlier?" She reached across Brig and closed the duly signed visitor book. "Is there anything you want to specifically do down here, walking or...?"

"None of your business," came yet another blunt reply.

"Oh, sorry, thought we could give you some local information that might help you enjoy your stay."

"Most, if not all, of the information I need I already have, OK? Now, rest assured, Liz, you will be the first person I will ask if I need further information. Is that good enough for you?"

"OK, right you are," replied a condescending Liz, unhooking the key for the annexe and immediately offering it to Brig between thumb and forefinger.

There was an awkward silence.

"That way." Liz gestured toward the annexe, giving Brig short shrift as the key was snatched away. "This is going to be fun," she muttered under her breath as Brig headed for the door.

Brig looked back momentarily. Liz knew that if looks could kill then she was more than dead.

Liz followed a few steps behind and shut the door firmly, lifting the handle to activate the locking device, so Brig would be unable to return without ringing the bell again.

"What's she like?" called Rich, as he swiftly descended the stairs.

"Definitely trouble, brother," Liz replied loudly, hoping Brig could hear her.

"It sounded a little fractious," said Rich. "I was going to come down but thought better of it. Bit of a bunny boiler that one, if you ask me."

"Can't disagree with you there. In fact, there is something that needs to be done right now. Can you watch her, and when you think she has gone in, give me a shout?"

"Gladly."

With that, Rich headed into the lounge to observe the new arrival as covertly as he could.

Liz made her way into the utility room, stopping at the washing machine to collect a small magnetic disk that she had left stuck to it, in readiness of such an opportunity. She proceeded to the side door, waiting for the all-clear from Rich.

"Wait a minute, she's just gathering her things," he called, peeking from behind the long, blue silk curtains.

Rich observed intently as Brig unfastened the panniers from her bike. He ducked back behind the protection of the curtain as she passed close to the window and out of sight. He listened intently for any confirmation that she'd gone inside, but nothing was forthcoming.

"Ready yet?" called Liz.

"No, not yet. She isn't exactly rushing."

"Wish I hadn't cleaned the annexe so thoroughly for the nasty little cow now," Liz shouted back.

Rich moved himself across to the other side of the window to get a better angle. However, in his haste, he was caught by Brig making her way back to the bike.

He opened the window to cover his actions. "Hello, I'm Rich. Let me know if you need anything. It should all be ready for you," he gushed.

Brig gave a begrudging smile and unlocked the boot box at the back of the bike, removing a plastic carrier bag from it before heading back to the annexe. She slammed the door shut behind her.

"The coast is clear now, Liz, I hope," confirmed Rich.

"Thanks. Can you message the group, please, and say that the rude bitch has arrived? Also confirm that, from here on out, her bike is being tracked by me... personally."

CHAPTER TWENTY-THREE —
THE SPIDER AND THE FLY

In Cheltenham, Parv's private phone rang. It was Brig.

"*Salaam*, Brig. How are you?" Parv answered in her soft Farsi accent.

"Hey, sister, I'm here. Say, this is a nice little place. Not sure about that Liz woman, though—she's a kooky one for sure, and her goofy brother is a bit weird, too. Anyways, you never told me it had a double bed."

"How is that important?" asked Parv, a little mystified by such a remark.

"Well, seeing as you stayed here before, I was wondering with whom you shared it?"

"Oh, you're a jealous one. No one actually, it was just me."

"OK, but I am sure Grant was down this neck of the woods one time, too. Perhaps it was the same event he came to, thinking about it?"

"No, he wasn't at that event, Brig. You, of all people, know that I have never met him. Plus, he isn't really my type, is he?"

"Dunno, do I?"

"Brig, what is it with you? I suggest a nice place for us to stay and all you do is cast doubt on my integrity? Tell you what, I will stay here in Cheltenham and you deal with it all yourself."

"No, no, Parv, I'm only teasing you, babe. You know I wanna see ya," she said in a fake, New-York-style gangster accent.

Parv was not impressed with her accents or her inferences.

"Look, Brig, I have to go, work is calling again, OK?" she said and abruptly killed the call.

She knew that ringing off like that would rankle with Brig, who usually liked to be the one in control. Not anymore.

Parv could well imagine Brig's response. She was probably seething with anger and, more than likely, sourcing an object to throw at a wall. It was the type of response she had witnessed first-hand on several occasions, including at a Civil Service cricket match they had played together when Brig first came to the country. The match, organised by a social committee, was meant to foster relations between different departments and associates, such as the American Embassy staff, and was intended to be light-hearted, not overly competitive.

Brig had only ever played cricket once before, yet expected to be the captain and first to bat or bowl. She didn't understand the etiquette, treating it like a schoolyard game where she had brought along the bat and ball herself. Inevitably, it caused instant consternation from the hardy annuals, who reluctantly relented for the sake of peace, allowing her to bat first, with one proviso—namely that her batting partner was changed to a former Surrey ladies player.

Parv initially couldn't understand this logic, until the third delivery took place. The lady called for a run to be made by Brig when, even to Parv's untrained eyes, it seemed suicidal to do so. As a result, Brig was left halfway down the pitch when the ball was quickly fielded and thrown against the stumps at the end Brig was heading for. Brig refused to accept the decision that she was out, kicking the stumps and directing abuse at the umpire. Needless to say, she did not stick around to take any further part in the match and the very next day attempted to file a complaint against the organisers.

Hardly the way to win friends and influence people. She'd also left Parv with no way of getting home, as Brig had driven her there!

Parv knew that she shouldn't have got involved with Brig, but Brig was relentless in her chase to be more than a friend, phoning her a few days later as if nothing had happened. Consequently, their intimate relationship continued on the basis that they were two lonely outsiders, now based in Britain for work. They began meeting on a more regular basis at weekends until Parv discovered, purely by chance, Brig's true sexuality and infidelity when her name cropped up in regard to a blackmail case involving Felton Kendall, which Parv was investigating on a secret team headed by Norman Weaver.

As she put the evidence together, she had asked Norm, in confidence, about any possible association between Brig and Grant, knowing that he was another member of his team. Apparently, Brig had let slip about Grant, when intoxicated one weekend, to another mutual friend.

When Norm confirmed the truth about Brig and Grant, Parv felt betrayed, biding her time to deliver a sucker punch of her own when the opportunity arose. That time had now arrived.

Having used her initiative to sway the whole Brig Huddlestone mess back in Britain's favour, Parv decided that now would be a good time to take a brief time-out from her computer and prepare for her impending trip to Skerrid Mawr in the morning, given that Liz was now monitoring Brig for the group. Disconnecting her headset, she switched her computer back onto loudspeaker alert mode.

As she opened her dresser, she had a smug feeling of contentment knowing that the plan was advancing faster than envisaged. The downfall of her ex-lover couldn't come quick enough. The American "daddy's girl" who thought she could use her guile and cunning to get what she wanted was going to get taught a lesson in diplomacy that her parents obviously hadn't bargained for.

Picking up her peach hijab, Parv regretted that she had been lured into Brig's world. For a while, it had been exciting and carefree, particularly the radical social activities and sexual liberation that were very different from the Middle Eastern world she had been born into. Deep down, she knew it wasn't her style and that she had been rash to act that way.

Parv pulled her travel case from the wardrobe and laid it open on the laminate floorboards. It still retained the Las Palmas baggage ticket from the Gran Canaria trip they had made together in February, another event with mixed memories, including being ignored or belittled in front of others whom Brig obviously found more entertaining than her.

Nothing was ever straightforward with Brig. Perhaps that was the initial fascination: she was dangerous and exciting, unlike any other woman Parv had met before.

The phone started to ring. It was Brig.

"Hey, sorry about earlier, Parv. I didn't mean to take it out on you," an apologetic Brig explained.

"You're probably just tired after your trip. I know your head must be racing right now," said Parv with feigned sympathy.

"It is, babe, it is. Listen, that picture, it wasn't a selfie, was it?"

"No, it can't be."

"So, who took it, then?"

"Hang on, let me dash back to my work room and check for you," said Parv, remaining exactly where she was. "I am checking registration serial numbers again for you now... No, that is definitely her phone. There are no other phones active on that VPN in the area right now," she lied. "It's unlikely she would have a passer-by take it. Someone who has seen her naked before, I guess. I'm trying to be subtle here, Brig," said Parv, when the opposite was true in reality.

"Don't worry, Grant's name is at the forefront of my head, too. He has clearly dumped me for her and gone away with her. It all makes sense now. Grant's awkward explanation that work had called him away was obviously a lie. Listen, I've caught them out before and now I can catch them again. Oh my God, Parv, this is gold dust. Two for the price of one. Come to mama!"

Brig's vindictive nature was rearing its ugly head again.

"Calm down, Brig, don't jump to conclusions," Parv pleaded. "Let's try to sort it out when I get down there in the morning, so don't do anything hasty, OK?"

Brig didn't respond. Parv decided to continue with her probing, worried now. Silence with Brig was always a dangerous sign.

"So, what are your plans tonight?" she delicately enquired.

"I don't have any," was Brig's stroppy reply. "What do you suggest, seeing as you've been here before?"

"West Bay is a few miles away. It's easy to find. You could watch the surfers there, that's your type of vibe, isn't it? There's more happening on a summer's evening for you there and more places to eat than in Skerrid Mawr, I would suggest. Try the big café that overlooks the sands there."

"Great, thanks. Will I pass by Norman Weaver's house if go that way?"

"Yes, it's just off the West Bay Road. Chances are the Union Jack will be flying outside."

"How typically boring."

"So, that's a done deal, then, Brig?" asked Parv hopefully.

"Yes, I'll have a look around this West Bay place. Is there any more news from that tart Tam?"

Parv felt relieved. Brig was going along with her suggestion.

"No, sorry, she has gone quiet right now. Her phone seems to be off. Be careful, Brig, and please don't draw attention to yourself. They aren't fools, you know," Parv requested, whilst fist-pumping to herself in the bedroom mirror.

"You know me, as if I would draw attention to myself," came her arrogant reply.

"Chances are I'll be with you around ten tomorrow morning... Sorry, Brig, I have another call coming in, so will say goodnight now, OK? Enjoy yourself, bye, bye."

The phone call was over.

Parv whooped loudly and picked up her VPN phone, relaying her news to the group.

Brig is agitated. She thinks that Grant took the picture.
I have told her to go to the West Bay Café tonight.
She knows where you live, Norm. Please be on your guard.
It's over to Liz and Rich for now. See you in the morning.
XXX

CHAPTER TWENTY-FOUR — PLANS

Without warning, Hertz lifted his bulky frame off his makeshift dog bed and headed straight for the caravan door. Tam knew from the wagging of his tail that it could only be due to Norm's impending arrival; anything else would have been met with three quick barks.

Norm appeared outside like a pack mule, his hands gripping several large shopping bags. Amey unlocked the door, allowing him to edge his way in sideways.

"Someone is looking after the house for me for now," he announced gruffly, dumping the bags down at the first point of space.

"Morgan?" asked Amey.

"No, it's Grant," said Norm, causing Tam to rock back in her seat.

Tam hadn't spoken to Grant since that fateful night. The thought of seeing him, especially now that Kee had arrived on the scene, would, at best, be awkward.

"Sorry it has taken so long to get over here. Things to do, of course... given yet another change in circumstances." Norm directed his gaze at Tam, obviously annoyed. "Anyway, Tam, what the hell were you thinking?"

"You gave me that phone. I used it," she defiantly replied. "I knew it would shake things up. Why?"

"Well, I can tell you why. The ripple effect has been huge. All our plans have gone out the window due to this vigilante action of yours. I have spent half the afternoon grovelling to everyone on both sides of the pond, with no explanation, thanks to your dalliance."

"Perhaps diplomacy isn't the answer to a bitch fight," came Tam's wine-fuelled response. "If only Daddy could hear me now, eh? He would probably have me court-martialled, before sending me to my room."

"Have you been drinking, Tam?"

"No, just too much sun."

"Well, I clearly saw that. Too much freedom lately for you it seems..."

"Norm, Norm, Norm," interjected Amey. "Remember that black and white photo in the kitchen? Me, naked on my horse? Just because you can't see what it means doesn't mean others can't."

"Well, I don't like that picture on the wall, if you must know."

"You can't see anything, just my back, so why would it embarrass you? You damned Westerners have no idea of how free we could be in the East. Trips to Rostock, in my day, were wonderful. No one even 'batted an eyelid', as you would say. Too much suppression by you British. Good for you, Tam," Amey added.

Tam could see that Amey was diverting Norm away from pursuing any possible reference to the Grant affair, which, she felt, he may have been about to add to the long list of reasons he was displeased with her.

There was an awkward silence before Norm picked up the thread once more. "Anyway, all that nonsense aside, I can tell you, Tam, that Brig has arrived in the village."

"Christ, she didn't waste much time!" exclaimed Tam.

"Well, what do you expect, sending out pictures like that?"

Tam noticed he didn't reveal how Brig had seen the picture. Surely, her idea of a mole within the group must now be a valid one.

"As a result of her being here, it goes without saying that none of us are safe, hence why you two are in this caravan. At least you heeded my warning."

Tam had to concede Norm's point. The game had definitely changed. She had brought this situation upon herself and, by Brig arriving, them as well. Tam felt she ought to offer an apology at some stage—perhaps not right now, though, as Norm obviously had more to say.

"From now on you are both confined to barracks, as it were. On a positive note, however, we have been able to utilise some means of controlling her, for now anyway," Norm informed them in his customary style.

"How?" asked Tam.

"I would rather not say until I know for sure."

Tam let out a loud huff of disapproval, placing her hands out toward Amey in a frustrated manner. "See what I mean? And what are 'our plans', then, Norm? You still haven't said anything to me about our plans. You're concealing things from me, things I ought to know."

Norm continued unabated. "All in good time, Tam. First things first. I understand you met someone today?"

"Yes, I did. Not going to play the big brother role on me now, are you?"

"No, it's your life."

"Oh, thanks for allowing me that. I suppose 'your people' have vetted him thoroughly, have they?"

"In fact, they have, yes. Amey gave me the registration from his van. We needed to know if he had any connections with Brig. The good news is that he's clean, no links to Brig as far as we can determine."

"Tell me more, then," Tam enthusiastically enquired.

"He's still here. His van is in the car park, I saw it just now," Norm informed her, slipping on his reading glasses to convey the findings from his phone. "He is Nat Keelor, hence the nickname Kee, I assume. Originally of south-east London, now living in Wales. Divorced, three kids, clean record, no political bias. Self-made businessman, still has active interests according to HMRC."

Tam smiled. It all made sense and fitted with what Kee had told her.

"Happy now, Tam?" asked Norm.

"Very," she replied, wondering when she would get to see him again.

Amey intervened. "Norm, why wasn't all this Brig business sorted out in London?"

"That was my original plan. We had worked hard with the parties concerned to convene next week, before these complications upset the applecart. Brig's blackmailing of Felton had to be stopped. The Home Secretary moved Felton away into 'gardening leave', which is why she probably turned her attentions to you, Tam, when he was no longer responding to her financial demands. The Americans were aware of it. Incredibly, they still said it was insufficient evidence for them to remove her. It was a ridiculous line to take, absolute rubbish, probably being fed to them by Washington. They were saying it was our problem, not theirs, hence the impasse. Only when I involved the Home Secretary did they agree to meet with us at all, to decide the best way forward."

"So, what effect did yesterday bring to the table, then?" Tam asked. "You never said."

Norm stood up and moved across to the window that looked out over the lake. He seemed choked by emotion as he answered her question.

"There are greater priorities than diplomacy, sis."

Tam felt touched. She realised that Norm had potentially sacrificed any political hold he might have had on the Brig situation to save her from immediate harm.

"I am so sorry, Norm. Like I said to Amey earlier, I never intended to cause you problems in your new life here in Skerrid Mawr. You always sort out other people's problems ahead of your own, and I do appreciate it, I really do," said Tam, standing up to give her brother a hug.

"It is good to see you two like this, and not arguing," said Amey, getting emotional herself.

"You're going to start me off in a minute," said Norm, likewise trying to compose himself.

"There is more to this, though, isn't there?" Tam asked him. "It involves Frankfurt, doesn't it?"

Norm sat back down and took a deep breath.

"Yes, it does. I wanted to keep this from you and Amey. It was upsetting for us all, and we will never forget that awful day. I knew there was only one person who could potentially stop Brig before it was too late—her own mother, Renate Brenzlig. Luckily, after all these years, she's seen sense."

Tam looked at Amey, who was clearly surprised at hearing Renate's name in the present context.

"Only thirty years late, Norm. Thirty years!" Amey vented.

Norm raised his palms knowingly. "There was a draft plan in place, before the latest attack on you last night, Tam. After I had you collected by Morgan, I brought forward arrangements for Renate to be moved to Britain, as next week's scheduled meeting was now untenable in the circumstances. Anyway, how did you know about the link to Frankfurt?"

Tam decided she needed to be economical with the truth, as he had been.

"Because I overheard your call this morning when I left the bathroom. When I came downstairs, I gave you the chance to say something, but you didn't. I knew then that you must have been working on something, other than my immediate problem. Your body language gave it away, I know you too well. I must confess, Norm, it greatly bothered me that you of all people weren't being totally open and honest with me. It had crossed my mind that Amey might know. However, she dispelled that theory when she found me at the beach."

"What did you say?" Norm asked Amey.

"Nothing, I didn't know anything, but you mentioned the anniversary of Frankfurt, and I saw some of the messages on your screens. Like Tam just said, you had to have something brewing. I knew you were angry—that is all I said to you, wasn't it, Tam?"

"Yes, Norm, that is all she said. You know the trauma of that day still affects me," said Tam, indignantly.

"As it does with us all," Amey agreed.

"None of us will ever forget it, or Renate Brenzlig's abominable act," Norm said.

Tam and Amey sat quietly, expecting Norm to elaborate on his statement. He initially seemed reticent to do so, before finally letting out a big sigh of concession.

"Yes, my plan was connected with that event, too. I can't deny it. Two birds with one stone, perhaps you could say. Without certainties, which I still don't have yet, I couldn't say anything to you, could I?"

Tam turned to Amey again, who was looking concerned.

"It's alright, Amey, it took me a little while to guess the likely family connection," she said. "It was only when she started messing around with Felton, I suppose. Strangely, Felton had told me she was causing Norm problems. Perhaps he was smoke-screening his affair with her by volunteering that, I don't know. Anyway, I have ways of finding out information, too, you know. I have a brain. Why else would she start things with Felton? He may have been good-looking once, but not now. It was just a way to get at us, probably driven to it by her mother's lies, no doubt."

Tam now looked at Norm, who was nodding along with her statement.

"Well, sis, the Americans reluctantly conceded the truth of her family background. It was only then that I knew I had to do something dynamic, yet as quietly as possible to protect you both, and the children, of course. My original aim was to work with the Americans to minimise any adverse publicity. However, they reneged on me, as someone across the pond started to pull some strings—I'm not exactly sure who, at this stage."

"Thank you for trying your best, Norm," said Amey. "We are grateful, aren't we, Tam?"

Tam nodded in agreement as Norm revealed the latest update.

"Your actions today, Tam, forced me to change the plans yet again. Thankfully, Parv was brilliant. She made a decision to rattle Brig's cage and, luckily for you, it worked. The flag was deployed to make you both come here, as we discussed. I couldn't risk Brig coming to the house and finding you, let alone me and Amey, too."

"So where exactly is Brig now?" Tam enquired.

"At Liz and Rich's place, Sandpiper, over in Mawdsridge. They are watching her as we speak. Parv has told her to go to the café at West Bay, and Rich will follow her this evening and keep tabs on her. Liz put a tracking device on her bike, so it shouldn't be too difficult to find her."

"Is Parv coming down?" asked Tam, not divulging her suspicion that Parv was in cahoots with Brig. It now seemed to serve no meaningful purpose.

"Yes, tomorrow morning. I need her to keep an eye on things for me, while I'm here."

"I think it would be a good idea for us to talk with Liz and Parv," Tam suggested. "Is that possible?"

"Why?"

"Because, Norm, I have more information. Information that you all need to know."

Before anyone could respond, Norm's phone rang.

He answered. "Hi, Liz. Nice to hear from you. Are you both OK?... We are all fine thanks, yes. Now, is Part One in place?... Good, good. Is she there now?... Just leaving—wow, that was lucky, had it been earlier, then we could have crossed paths. Imagine that, me and Brig face to face! Rich is on her scent, though, isn't he...? On her way to West Bay, OK, and hopefully not causing trouble... Not yet you say... give her time." He laughed. "Listen, I'm here with Tam and Amey. Tam has just told me she has information that you and Parv need to hear. It will be dicey to leave here, but I think it might be easier if we come over to you, whilst she is out of the way. It would be good for Tam and Amey to get out of this cramped caravan for a while, so shall we say in the next twenty minutes?... Great. No, none of us have eaten so that sounds ideal. Thank you, bye."

Without hesitation, Tam picked up her bag and made her way into her small twin bedroom to change. She felt more assured about the direction of the plans surrounding Brig and Renate, without knowing exactly how Norm planned to bring this to a conclusion.

The wine had made her hungry, and she hadn't consumed her sandwich earlier, so the thought of some hot food at Liz's now appealed to her growing appetite for satisfaction.

CHAPTER TWENTY-FIVE — SUGAR AND SPICE

Kee looked across at the All Angels' Church clock tower.

As much as he'd enjoyed visiting The Meadow Pipit, he knew he ought to pop his head into The Dragon's Tail at some point, still with the hope of seeing Tam there. Irrespective of whether she was there, he figured that Omni would have seen his van sat in the nature reserve car park on her way back to her pub from The Shack, so it might be prudent to call in. Failure to do so could mean her making his life trickier the next time he saw her.

Omni could even have information for him, particularly about Tam's whereabouts. She always had an ear to the ground, so it was worth a try, even if she mightn't be offering her full blessing to his liaison with Tam. Of course, he now had information on where Norm lived, so all was not lost, either way.

His revised plan to drive to the beautiful Afan Valley forest in the morning was now in doubt, given that he fully intended to knock at Norman Weaver's door at some point. The real question was whether to go there tonight or leave it until the morning, out of courtesy to Tam. She had been insistent about not following her or getting involved in her feud with this Brig girl. He'd mull over it on his walk back to The Dragon's Tail.

Kee pushed his plate away and got up from the bench seat, collecting his phone as he did so. Turning back toward the entrance, he waved to the helpful girl who had served him earlier.

She waved back and shouted, "Thank you! Hope you find Norman Weaver."

So did he.

The sun, the food and the cold beer had quickly impacted him, and he ventured somewhat uneasily to cross the Mawdsridge Lane. He was only halfway across when a motorbike appeared at speed from his left. It showed no signs of stopping, leaving him stranded in the middle of the road. The rider glared at him, and he glared back.

Her again. What was her problem?

Kee didn't appreciate her rude hand gesture, a single middle finger raised in defiance, as she sped away in the direction of West Bay.

"Are you OK?" came a shout from behind.

It was the pretty young girl once more, who had run across to check on his welfare.

"Yes, thank you, no harm done," replied Kee, a little shaken up but otherwise fine.

"OK, only if you're quite sure?"

"Yes, I'm good, thanks," he reiterated with an appreciative tap on her shoulder to acknowledge her caring attitude.

"Thank you for the drink and the tip, you are too kind. Please enjoy the rest of your evening, and take care," she said and turned to walk back to the pub.

"Wait. I should have asked your name. Mine's Kee."

"Seren," she replied.

"Listen, Seren, I'm often looking for staff to help with my mobile food and drink business, which I operate up and down the country. The way you looked after me tonight told me you're the sort of person I could really do with," he told her.

"Maybe. Depends, I suppose," Seren replied, naturally guarded.

"It would be cash in hand, and if you have any friends who you would want to include then that would be possible, too. It's all legitimate. I'm not asking for a commitment right now. However, I have some events this summer and may be short-staffed on one or two of them."

Seren took out her phone from her back pocket and asked for his contact details, which Kee was happy to provide.

"Thank you, Kee," she said with a winning smile. "I may be in touch. I had best get back now."

There, in this lovely young lady, was proof that politeness and manners did still exist and cost nothing, in stark contrast to the hateful woman on the motorbike.

As he ambled his way along the narrow pavement toward The Dragon's Tail, the incident with the motorbike played back in his mind once more. It seemed symptomatic of his recent experiences in life. Being taunted, challenged and disrespected for no good reason. It was why he felt happier alone at times. Kee even wondered if he had become a sad old man, something he'd thought he could never be.

The number plate on the bike was lodged in his brain. 26 DX 754.

Kee had a strange propensity for remembering unusual things like that. It had some meaning or significance. He knew it wasn't a personalised plate, nor a foreign one and neither was it an old-style British plate arrangement, the type before registrations took their current form in the UK. Something about it rang a bell, though. He stopped and searched the internet on his phone, only to find that his hunch was entirely correct.

Could this be the Brig Huddlestone character Tam had told him about? It seemed plausible, yet he had no way of verifying it. Nevertheless, he would mention it to Norm, or to Tam herself, if and when he saw one or other of them. It seemed significant.

Within a few minutes, he had found his way into The Dragon's Tail. The old building gave evidence that, in previous times, it had been a focal point of the village, even being the town hall at one stage, according to a parchment-style document hanging next to the bar. Its thick walls, small mullion-style windows, plus the tales of witchcraft and hauntings dotted around its interior, coloured one's imagination to that effect.

Kee approached the busy bar, purveying the choices that the pumps displayed. As he did so, a young woman turned towards him from the till. She was a complete contrast to the girl from The Meadow Pipit. In his younger days he may have got short shrift for staring at a buxom cleavage, but today he was staring more in disbelief than wonderment, and not at her bosom, but a reflective set of veneered teeth unable to be totally covered by her lips, bloated by too much filler.

Kee had been completely distracted by her oral enhancements, but his gaze now shifted to the poorly painted black lines that used to be the site of her natural eyebrows, and a pair of elongated false eyelashes.

Her natural beauty had been erased to look more akin to that of a drag queen than a beautiful young woman. How on earth was that construed to be attractive, he wondered?

"Yes?" she expelled somewhat impatiently, bringing Kee back into the moment.

"Oh... eh... Guinness, please."

"Thought so," came the indignant reply.

He just hoped that he didn't find powdery flakes of orange make-up on his froth, as she scratched her face with her dayglo nails.

As he sat on a barstool, he became transfixed by how the heavy make-up abruptly stopped at her neck, only relenting when, in his peripheral vision, he noticed a muscle-bound lad sitting at the end of the bar. Kee pretended he hadn't noticed him as his order was finally delivered, complete with a shamrock etching in the white froth. As he reached to collect it, he felt the slap of a hand on his shoulder.

"Put your card away, this one's on me," came the raucous tones of Omni.

"It's a wonder you make any money, giving old-aged pensioners like him free beer all the time," the barmaid commented curtly.

"Mind your own business, Shannel, alright? My pub, my rules. Go and collect some glasses or something will you, and take your boyfriend with you, if you want."

Omni waited for her to move away and out of earshot before she told Kee, "Pop upstairs if you fancy a shower. Daresay you are a bit smelly after all that activity today. Here's my key, off you go."

"Thanks, but no thanks. I've had a wash and sprayed deodorant in all the important places, so I will decline your kind offer," Kee responded, with a defensive hand, knowing her true intent.

"Pity, I needed a shower as well. We could have gone green and saved water, showering together."

"You're incorrigible, Omni."

"I know," she replied.

CHAPTER TWENTY-SIX — EVENING OUT

Tam sprayed herself with a few jets of her favourite perfume and pulled up her jeans. She couldn't see the need to don a bra, instead choosing to wear a baggy, white cotton tee-shirt, taking care to tuck her locket under the neckline. A quick freshen-up in the bathroom and she would be ready to head over to Sandpiper.

She could hear the muffled chatter of Amey and Norm in the back bedroom as she stepped across the lino and into the toilet closet. Leaving the door ajar, Tam stood at the sink, splashing her face with the cold water, concentrating it mainly on her tired eyes. As she dried off with the blue hand towel, she gazed into the mirror. The thought of applying make-up briefly crossed her mind, only briefly, before she opted to tie back her messy hair with a bobble and rejuvenate her dry lips with the lip salve from her bag.

"That'll do," she said to her reflection, before easing her way out and taking herself back to the window overlooking the lake, now with the excited Hertz at her feet.

Stroking his head gently, Tam wondered where Kee might be now. According to Norm, he was still here, so she just hoped he wasn't enjoying the pleasure of Omni's attentions. With a little luck, she might just catch a glimpse of him shortly. Tam smiled to herself as she tried to picture his reaction to finding her sketch. She dearly hoped he had found it and, better still, liked it. If he did, then she might suggest doing another one someday soon, this time on a full-length canvas.

Amey appeared.

"Sorry, Hertz, we cannot take you," she said. "Perhaps I will take you for walkies later."

The dog's ears shot up to the magical word, "walkies".

Norm was close behind.

"Let's go, come on," he said, flinging the caravan door open. It crashed against the buffering pad.

As Tam stepped out into the warm evening air, she was met with the smell of freshly cut grass, reminding her of the contretemps with the degenerate mower man earlier. Luckily, as she got into the back of Norm's car, he was nowhere to be seen. Sadly, however, as their short journey progressed, neither was Kee. Tam craned her neck out the window, trying to pick out Kee from the busy throng as they drove past The Dragon's Tail, only succeeding in seeing Omni setting down a tray of drinks for a large group of men, none of whom were Kee.

Maybe tomorrow, she thought, as they rounded the corner, turned down by the church and into Mawdsridge, arriving at Sandpiper moments later. As they alighted from the car, Liz was there to greet them, complete with her dyed red bob and matching glasses, a very different look from the one Tam remembered ten months previously. It suited her.

"It's so nice to see you again, Tam. It's been too long," said Liz, opening her arms with her walking stick in her hand.

"And you, too, Liz," said Tam, embracing her. "Look at your hair! Gosh, what a transformation. Plus, you were in your wheelchair the last time I saw you. You're doing really well, aren't you?"

"Getting there slowly and all that stuff," Liz responded coyly.

Tam stood aside to allow Liz to similarly greet Norm and Amey. Tam had thoroughly enjoyed Liz's company on her brief visit to Skerrid Mawr the previous August. A bright, vivacious girl defying the odds to recover from her injuries and remain so positive about the life ahead of her. She was a lesson to many more fortunate.

The warm smell of food wafted down the hallway as they followed Liz to her large kitchen, where the table had already been laid.

"Nothing exotic, I'm sorry, just some frozen pizzas," Liz explained. "Probably going to be another ten minutes, so just help yourself to the nibbles and please don't stand on ceremony. Amey knows where everything is, don't you?"

"Indeed, I do. In fact, why don't you give Tam a tour and I will finish things off for you?"

It was as if Amey was her mother figure. Perhaps she was.

"Good idea—Tam?" asked Liz.

"Yes, that would be good. I remember you telling me about the developments you and Rich had been planning; it would be great to see how things have turned out in practice," said Tam.

She followed Liz into a new extension. Liz opened the uPVC door, and there, in front of them, was a reasonably sized swimming pool. Instantly, Tam could feel the humidity in the large conservatory-type construction. Apart from the regular steps, Tam noticed that the pool also featured a hoist to accommodate those who were unable to walk in, and jet systems to provide both hydrotherapy and high-powered resistance for swimmers. She'd been to a similar pool recently herself.

"This is absolutely amazing, Liz. It was under construction the last time we met. You must be pleased with it," said Tam, impressed by all its modern facilities.

"If it wasn't for Norm then this would never have happened. I've spent so many hours in physiotherapy and hydrotherapy over the last few years; I know the benefits and how it helped me. When my parents were killed by that drunk driver, our world almost came to an end. As you may remember me telling you at Norm's housewarming, I almost died, too, and had to be given CPR. Rich would have been left alone."

"It doesn't bear thinking about," said Tam.

"Norm has been like a father to us since it happened, and all because he knew my father, Bryn, so well from their days together in the army."

"Of course, I remember Bryn, too, Liz. The fantastic way he helped Norm hone his skills to become a world champion and how he was always there to help others, like Michelle and myself, too. He was way ahead of his time in coaching skills, but remained a lovely, kind man throughout."

"Thank you for saying that, Tam. It means everything to me and Rich you know. Your brother supported us and helped my wider family to deal with everything, including our parents' will, as he was an appointed executor. I was stuck in hospital, and Rich had to live away from our family home with my Aunt Menna until it was feasible to return here. It sounds dreadful to say, but Norm dealt with more than he had to, including the insurance payouts and so forth. Money was the last thing on our minds. However, he made sure we were secure first and foremost, and then, when I became more able, he suggested that we had sufficient funds left to build a pool here to aid my own recovery and get back to the one sport I excel at—swimming. Coincidentally, I knew that the local health authority was struggling for pool time and that resources to provide further hydrotherapy services were scarce, so Norm made a deal and landed a business contract with them. Now, they can use the pool, and it gives me and Rich a steady income!"

Tam was awestruck. Norm had never told her the full details of this selfless act.

"In fact, I am taking a hydrotherapy qualification course right now, so I can supplement my swimming knowledge with new skills. Not only that, but we now host some of the baby swimming franchises here, too, so we have additional income that helps pay for all the overheads."

Tam was so impressed with Liz and her fighting spirit.

"So how did you and Rich get involved with my present situation, then?" she asked. "If you don't mind me asking?"

"Well, Rich was looking to join the local police force; Norm made it happen. He also offered him undercover supplementary work from time to time, too. He knows Rich is on the spectrum, yet he got him in and he has proved himself beyond everyone's dreams. Whilst emotionally he isn't the best, technically he's brilliant."

Liz's love of her not-so-little brother's achievements at such a trying time in his life was clear.

"And yourself, Liz—there's more to you than you're letting on, isn't there?"

Liz laughed. "Ok, Tam, you've sussed me. Dad taught me about ballistics; it fascinated me. He took me and Rich to the rifle range when we were young, under special dispensation, and I loved it. Now I get to work in ballistics from time to time, usually with the police force in Wales, and have done so for Norm's department, too. You are very astute!"

Tam was full of admiration for this determined young lady. Liz must only be a few years older than Ant and

Elinor, yet had faced the type of adversity many would never experience in a whole lifetime.

Liz cleared her throat, as emotions began to rise. "You see," she said, her voice hoarse, "Norm gave us a purpose, a reason to live. We really are forever in his debt."

At that moment, her phone pinged.

"Excuse me," she said, resting her stick to one side so she could retrieve her phone from her trouser pocket. She read the message. "Rich says he has arrived at the café and has confirmed her bike is there. He will find her and keep her there for as long as he can. He'll let me know when she's likely to leave. This is great news. It gives us a little more time. Right... I have just forwarded that nugget of information to the group. Now, let me quickly show you the annexe before we eat," she said, stepping back toward the door.

"Norm told me that your father had converted the garage," said Tam.

"Yes, Mum wanted it made into a small holiday let. Something to keep her busy in her retirement," Liz said as they exited the pool area and out the side door. They looped around the front of the house, across the wide, paved drive and into the annexe itself.

Tam knew that Liz's parents never got to fully realise that particular dream. So sad and so unjust.

The annexe itself was immaculate. Tam noticed the spacing within, the wide doors and the smooth flooring used throughout. It was clearly built with wheelchair access in mind, even before the accident temporarily confined Liz to one herself. Bryn must have been very forward-thinking to have accommodated such needs in the way that he had. The room was light, helped by three skylights and the neutral colour scheme used throughout. It smelt and looked clean. The only downside was its current inhabitant.

Liz called Tam forward and into the large double bedroom at the end of the building. Brig's bags lay strewn across the duvet.

"God, this is so strange," said Tam. "I only ever saw her once, at one of the American Embassy's so-called 'Welcome Evenings'. She wasn't very welcoming to me, though, only Felton. I wonder why."

"Look at this," said Liz, unfurling a small towel from within one of the pannier bags.

Inside was a small handgun.

"Oh, my goodness, she does mean business, doesn't she?" gasped Tam, who had never seen a real gun in her life, other than the low-calibre ones she had used in pentathlons.

"Without a doubt, Tam, without a doubt. The good news is it is no longer a live gun."

Tam looked bemused.

"Well, I took the liberty of popping in after she left, with my magical ballistics toolkit. Rich kept an eye out for me as I made it safe. She won't know, until she tries to fire it, that nothing will happen, so we can all relax a little bit easier. I can't find anything else in her things so, hopefully, that's it. She won't suspect a crocked young girl with a walking stick, will she?"

"Liz, superlatives fail me, you are a bloody genius."

CHAPTER TWENTY-SEVEN — THE POWER OF TRUTH

Returning to the comfortable lounge with Liz, Tam looked up to see the beautiful face of Parv on the large television screen that was mounted halfway up the wall. It was the first time Tam had seen Parv without her hijab. There she was, resplendent, with her slick black hair and a huge pair of brown eyes.

"We can eat and chat, we don't have a surfeit of time," said Liz, heading for the table. "Take a seat there so Parv can see you on the camera." She indicated where Tam should sit herself for the impromptu meeting.

"Hello, Parv," said Tam. "This is Tam speaking. How are you?"

"*Asra bekheir*. Good evening to you, Tam," replied Parv in her dusky accent. "I am good, how are you?"

"A little embarrassed, if truth be told. I feel the need to apologise to you for what happened today. I know that you have been brought in on my personal spat with Brig, and I fully appreciate your invaluable help."

"What is there to apologise for?" asked Parv.

"Because, initially, I suspected that someone may have been feeding Brig information."

"Felton!" shouted Norm, from the other end of the table.

"Norman, be quiet," said Amey. "Let Tam speak."

Tam looked at Norm, who held his hands up in apology, as she continued her explanation. "Felton is always feeding people information, but it's usually smarmy bullshit. However, in this case, I wrongly suspected someone in Norm's vigilante team—that person being you, Parv. I now know that is totally wrong and I wish to apologise for that."

"That's OK, Tam, quite understandable given my relationship with her, which was fairly common knowledge anyway," came Parv's slow, calm response.

"Thank you for being so understanding. It was actually Grant who told me about you and her being close. Given my bad track record in that regard with Grant, who was I to be on the moral high ground, eh? Nevertheless, I had to find out for sure. I knew if I used this precious VPN phone then something would probably stir. When I saw the flag at half-mast, I still believed it to be your doing."

Parv smiled at Tam's reasoning. "Well, it was my doing, but as an ally, not a double-crosser. Knowing what I do about all of this business, when I saw your photo, I decided to make a decision without first consulting Norm. It was risky and I knew that if it failed then my time in this country would probably be over, but it was an opportunity and a risk I was prepared to take. The good news was that Brig instantly bought it, without question."

Tam felt relieved that Parv accepted her explanation so warmly.

"You see, Brig has hoodwinked me too many times, and I prayed for an opportunity to do her down if one came along, and it did, today, thanks to you."

At that point, Amey interjected. "What exactly has Brig said to you, then, if you don't mind me asking?"

"Well, she had convinced herself that I had stayed at the annexe with Grant for your housewarming party. You see, it's OK for her to do what she wants with whomever she chooses, but not me. Anyway, knowing it wasn't true, it wasn't an issue for me. The good news, however, is that she's transferred her jealousy onto Grant."

"Why?" asked Tam.

"Because she knew your beach photo wasn't a selfie so wrongly assumed that Grant must be the photographer, especially after he cancelled their weekend away together. It was all so neat."

Liz cut in. "Hi, Parv, it's Liz here. Are you still tracking her phone?"

"Hi, Liz. Yes, I am. I have several tabs on her right now, including her phone, which pins her in West Bay with Rich. Incidentally, she is aware of where Norm's house is, and the tell-tale flagpole. If she tries to pop in there on her way back, she might get a shock to find Grant there!"

As they all politely laughed, Tam hoped that Grant's presence in the village wouldn't cause any problems, especially if he ever met Kee.

Parv spoke once more. "By the way, Tam, it was me, and me alone, who was monitoring the group VPN phones, at Norm's behest. If anyone has foreshortened the process it was me, not Norm. When I saw your picture appear, I made the decision to share it there and then, I hope you understand why now."

Tam now fully understood her rationale, as Liz picked up on Parv's thread.

"Subsequently, in your absence, Tam, we jointly discussed the best way to deal with Brig as quickly and as humanely possible. Our intention right now is to continue to steer her into our arms, without her knowledge. Seeing as she has a fascination with you, we will use that to our advantage—if you're agreeable to that, of course?"

Tam knew where this was inevitably heading. "How then, Liz?" she asked. "Are you saying that I am to be used as the bait in the trap?"

Tam noticed the split-second delay as Liz looked at Norm for some type of authorisation to proceed. Norm said nothing, preferring to help himself to more crisps from the table.

Liz looked back at her. "Rich will 'accidently on purpose' make reference to the fact he is meeting you tomorrow morning at The Steps."

"On what pretext would she possibly swallow that?"

"That you are his godmother and you are using the visit to meet up with him and head to Skerrid Beach for the afternoon. After all, Brig knows you were on the beach today, so it makes logical sense to go there again."

Tam felt the need to respond, but Liz sought to conclude her explanation of their latest plan.

"Now, despite what I said earlier about Rich, let me assure you he can play dumb extremely well, so why would Brig have cause to doubt him?"

Liz made the point well and it was hard to argue, given that she could offer nothing better.

All eyes were now on Tam. In light of this new revelation, she felt the time was right to announce some of the findings that she had been keeping to herself—and the unwitting Mr Argent, of course.

After taking a moment to compose herself, she began.

"I want to go face to face with Brig, not just be used as bait."

Tam could feel the ripple of silence go through the room.

"After you hear some of what I have to say, you will understand why. Now, I daresay you can fill me in on the specific details of your current plan, Liz, but it may have to be changed to accommodate my needs."

Liz looked across to Norm, who leaned back on his chair. "Go on, sis, say what you want to say," he said, a little condescendingly.

"The evidence I have gained will stop her in her tracks. It's just a pity that her mother can't be present to hear it."

Norm almost choked on his drink as she spoke. Amey thumped his back, perhaps thinking that he had a peanut lodged in his throat or suchlike.

Parv intervened. "Sorry to interrupt you, Tam, but—and I am sure that Norm will have no objections against me telling you—we are currently obtaining Renate Huddlestone's transfer from Salzburg, Austria as we speak. As Norm may or may not have told you, Brig's mother was due to be in London next week anyway, in a bid to talk some sense into Brig over the blackmail element. This was before we had to upscale and intervene last night. It is what we, or more particularly I, have been specifically working on."

Tam was trying to digest the information she was being furnished with and work out how she could best act upon it herself.

Parv had even more for her. "Yesterday, when we told the Americans about the attack on your house, we indicated that Renate was needed in the country, immediately if possible. Blackmail was one thing, but physical harm is another. They instantly agreed. Yes, Renate Huddlestone, nee Brenzlig, will be here, hopefully for eleven a.m. tomorrow morning. It is why I'm making the journey down early in the morning, to be on hand. However, I have much more to do here, in respect of the logistical arrangements, so I think I had best leave the call now."

Tam looked around the room. Everyone seemed to know that Renate was Brig's mother, yet no one had ever bothered to tell her. She felt extremely irritated by this admission. Even without the attacks, Tam felt that she, of all people, should have been informed of their undercover actions, given her ordeal with Renate in Frankfurt, and not kept in the dark.

Norm, having recovered from his choking episode, thanked Parv for her contribution as she signed off with her usual grace.

"Thank you, Tam, thank you all. Please take care. I am sending you my breath and my love." She kissed the palm of her hand and proffered it to the screen momentarily, before she left the call.

Using the hiatus, Tam turned to Norm to make her demands once more. "It seems only fair that I get to see Brig face to face, and Renate, if it's feasible. Please do not leave me out of things anymore."

"Is that it, Tam?" asked Norm dismissively. "You primarily want to see Brig face to face?"

"No, Norm, it isn't. Far from it, in fact. I knew that Renate was likely to be Brig's mother around six months after her arrival in London, when Felton kept mentioning Brig in the evenings. Then, inadvertently, the silly idiot started dropping hints about her background. It was at that point that I seriously started to consider the possibility of a connection. Believe it or not, I was more concerned about Renate resurfacing than Brig's affair with Felton! What I really want, I suppose, is explanations and apologies. Not just to my face, but a joint confession to the whole world."

"OK... well, I did ask I suppose. Not sure if the latter will happen, though."

"Well, it bloody well should. It means more to me to get the truth of Frankfurt out in the open than anything else, to release the metaphorical thirty-year noose from around my neck."

Amey spoke. "This is all so sad, yet inevitable. I feel responsible in some way, Tam, I always have."

"Oh, Amey, don't ever think that," said Tam, taking her hand. "You know I always wanted the best for you, Norm, and my own kids, of course, which is why I am saying what has been on my mind for such a long time. The truth hurts and there is more I need to say, and do, to get us to where we *all* need to be."

"So, what are your plans, then?" asked Norm. "How will this all work?"

Tam let out a sigh of relief. Finally, he was listening, taking her needs seriously at last. She stated her position, now armed with facts that Norm was unaware of. Facts that would openly show her determination to not let sleeping dogs lie.

"Well, during these awful months of dealing with Felton's philandering and my suspicions involving Renate being Brig's mother, I decided to take up an offer we received thirty years ago."

Amey touched Norm's arm. "What does she mean, Norm?" she whispered.

Norm shook his head. "I don't know."

Tam's smile broadened. "Oh, I think you do, Norm. Don't cover things up anymore. Amey has the right to know that you have been treading the same path as I have been. However, I think that me and my helper are probably one to two weeks ahead of you—on a par with the Americans, I would say."

Liz raised her hand, like a child in a classroom. "Can I ask you if this is to do with the Freedom of Information Act in Germany?"

"Yes, it is. The thirty-year period expired recently, as Norm would have found out. You have just confirmed it.

The difference is that I have been in contact with a certain Anton Himmelmann, whose own private application for information regarding the Frankfurt affair was fast-tracked, ahead of anyone else's, including the Americans'... and yours."

It was Norm's turn to be taken aback.

"Sorry, who is Anton Himmelmann?" asked Liz.

Norm interjected. "He was the police official in Frankfurt back in 1992. The one who, initially, accused Tam of creating the commotion that robbed Amey of her gold medal."

"Correct, Norm, he was," said Tam. "But he conclusively proved otherwise, didn't he?"

Norm nodded in agreement.

"Then, of course, the massive cover-up then took place, orchestrated over his head by his peers. Basically, Renate Brenzlig, as she was then, escaped justice via the diplomatic power of a certain Jeph Huddlestone. He got her to America scot-free, if you will."

"It's amazing how much power some people can wield, isn't it?" said Liz, very calmly.

"Indeed, it is, Liz, indeed it is," said Tam. "Now, if you recall, Norm, he always said to keep in touch, and I did— on and off over the years, hoping that his influence could provide some answers for me, you and Amey about the cover-up. Sadly, nothing was forthcoming—until recently, that is. Apparently, the incident in 1992 saw him promoted to another department, just to gag him and to stifle any further interest he might have in the case."

"I never knew that, sis," said Norm, clearly not surprised at the strings that can get pulled from behind the scenes.

"When Himmelmann and I first spoke about the matter, he told me that he was never satisfied with the outcome and would register his interest under the FOI act, in advance, for the official German government papers on the matter. He promised to let me know if and when that submission ever became successful. Well, that time finally arrived. Having retired from the German police force, he was no longer under any pressure from higher-ups, so was free to challenge the system."

"My Christ, Tam, you have been busy. Didn't you think to tell me?" vented Norm, a little aggrieved.

"Of course I was going to tell you, once I had printed out copies of the findings and given them to Argent first. When the manure and lilies arrived on my doorstep, I knew that I had to see him on the pretext of the divorce case and then pass him Himmelmann's findings in a sealed envelope, along with strict instructions only to open them should anything happen to me. If anything had actually happened to me, then at least Ant and El would have known the truth, as would you and Amey."

"Tam, this is all so fantastic, so clever of you," said Amey.

"I needed contingency and some way to the truth, at least. When that brick went through my window last night, I was truly terrified. It was obvious that I had to get away from there as quickly as possible. That was my first concern—hence calling you, Norm. There was no way at that moment that I could calmly discuss Himmelmann's findings with you over the phone, was there?" Tam stated in all earnestness.

"Yes, yes, I understand that, but we talked this morning, didn't we? You could have said something then, surely?" said Norm, standing from his seat to pace around the room.

"Yes, I could have, but I overheard a telephone call you were having with someone this very morning, probably Liz or Parv, I now assume. You distinctly mentioned Frankfurt, yet you failed to mention it to me. I gave you every chance to, and you didn't take it. Like I said to you, in good faith, I needed time alone, to think."

"Well, it was an unusual way of thinking, in my book."

"Perhaps to you, it was, yet not to me. I still felt, as I said to Parv just now, that there might be a spy in the camp, so decided to keep my thoughts with me till dinner tonight. My intention was always to discuss it with you, at your house later. It was during my journey to the beach, where I encountered the wondrous 'Our Lady of the Dunes' carving and then met the beautiful and inspirational Kee, that I felt empowered to do something, something that would provoke a reaction."

"You certainly did that, Tam!" said Norm, turning his back and making his way across to the window, clearly in a huff.

"Obviously, this isn't exactly the situation I had in mind when I did it, but thanks to your marvellous team, you have it under control, as you always do, Norm," said Tam, trying to praise, not patronise.

Norm sat himself down next to her on the end of the settee.

"Alright, Tam, I get it, I get it now. Perhaps I should have been a little more upfront with what was going on and kept you in the loop. You were traumatised in Frankfurt, we all know that, and I fully understand you being in contact with Himmelmann and why. It was selfless, I get it now."

It wasn't very often that her brother conceded the point to anything he wasn't in control of, least of all to his 'little sis'.

"Thank you, Norm. I never wanted to hurt you, or anyone. It was my chance for me to step out of your shadow and do something for us Weavers for once. I have been dormant too long. At least you have Renate on tap, as it were, something I never bargained on."

Norm's demeanour changed for the better. He stood back up and paced around the table, his enthusiasm now obvious as he spoke.

"Yes, we can really see this home now. If Rich can get her where we want her and Parv can weave her magic with the logistics, then we can get it all tied up neatly. However, I sense you know more than the fact that Renate is Brig's mother, Tam, so what did you discover? What is it that we don't know yet?"

Tam stood up and moved across to sit next to Amey at the dinner table.

"Are you sure you are ready for this, Amey?" asked Tam, gently rubbing her arm.

"It has killed me for too long. We all need to know the truth."

Reaching back across the table, Tam took a long drink from her glass.

"The crux of the matter is that Renate's actions were based on false information. She believed that you had taken her place in the German team. An 'Ossi' replacing a 'Wessi', as you might say. It was this that drove her fury, according to transcripts from her police interrogation. However, she was tragically wrong. Renate's place in the team was taken by another Wessi, Ziggy Stauber, not you."

Amey sat staring across the room, in some sort of daze.

"Are you sure of this, Tam?" she uttered, as she turned to look Tam in the eye.

"I am afraid so. It is absolutely true, sadly."

Amey dropped her gaze down to the table, pushing around a salt cellar that lay there.

"Can I ask a question, please?" asked Liz.

"Of course, yes," replied Tam.

"Why didn't Renate ride in the team? She must have originally been selected, to be subsequently made so angry by her exclusion."

"Yes, it is a question that I have certainly asked myself, and so have Norm and Amey over the years, no doubt. The simple irony is that the American officials put in an initial objection to Amey competing. It was based on the premise that any sporting success from the old East Germany must involve steroid abuse, something that was often levelled at all Iron Curtain countries. The German authorities vigorously protested this, causing the whole event to be put into doubt in the days leading up to it. However, after some heated debate amongst the organisers and the participating countries, it was agreed that blood tests would take place, on the basis that every competitor was tested, not just Amey Vogler," said Tam, rubbing Amey's shoulder.

"*Ja*, that is correct. I didn't know that it was because of me, though." Amey shrugged.

"Well, when the results were collated, it was found that not only was Amey clear, but Renate Brenzlig was pregnant!"

Amey interjected then. "No one could compete if they were pregnant, it was part of the rules. Such things were, ordinarily, down to honesty back then, not a blood test!"

"Renate was not allowed to compete, and a replacement, in Ziggy, was found and utilised," Tam explained, drawing on the reports Himmelmann had sent her. "The teams weren't confirmed until two days before the event, so Renate's name did not appear on the German team sheet, while Amey's did. Clearly, Renate didn't want to see Amey stealing her glory and decided to sabotage the competition. She didn't bargain on me seeing her do it, though."

"Wow, that explains so much," said Norm. "So why couldn't the authorities have been open from the outset about this?"

"It looks like pride, honour and reputations had much to do with it. You of all people know how it works behind the scenes."

Norm conceded her point with a wry grin.

"It was only after the event that Jeph Huddlestone, the top American diplomat with whom she had been fraternising, got involved and took her to America with him. As Himmelmann said to me, reputation was everything, so it was easier to officially say that no culprit was found, just to keep honour intact on both sides of the Atlantic."

"So, why did Brig resurrect this vendetta against the Weavers?" asked Liz.

"Because Renate hasn't been honest with her, has she? Brig must have been brainwashed from a young age to have become the vengeful monster that she now is. She needs to be stopped from causing any further problems, for her own sake, if not ours. She needs to know this undeniable truth, and I need to be the one to tell her!"

CHAPTER TWENTY-EIGHT — SO GULLIBLE

Rich arrived at West Bay on his e-bike and headed for the café with his long-lensed Canon camera across his back. Scanning the car park, he spotted the distinctive blue paintwork of Brig's motorbike close to the café building. He dismounted and proceeded to connect the safety lock for his bike to a post as near to hers as possible.

He poked his head into the café, hoping Brig would be sitting down quietly so he could approach her and pretend that their meeting was purely coincidental. Unfortunately, she was not sitting down quietly; instead, she was standing up, loudly remonstrating the girl at the till.

"What do you mean you don't take this type of card? What kind of frickin' third-world country is this?"

"We don't take this card. Look at the notice," said the young girl, pointing above her head to the sign showing the accepted means of payment. "Cash is fine, obviously," she croaked, now sensing this would escalate further.

A hush had descended within the venue.

Brig was having none of it. Seemingly oblivious to the queue now building up behind her, she stood her ground.

"Listen here, missy. I have offered you payment and you have refused—"

"Do you mind if I serve the next customer, please?" the till girl bluntly interrupted, gesturing to the next customer to step forward and blatantly avoiding Brig's protestations in the process.

"Yes, I do." Brig pushed her way back in front of the till, before she was interrupted again, this time by a man standing two behind her in the queue.

"Oy, love, if I wanted cold food, I would have bought a bloody sandwich," he said in a strong local accent.

A murmur of appreciation could clearly be heard, and two people clapped to elevate Brig's embarrassment and anger even further.

Rich had no choice now other than to dash to the till and solve the problem by tendering his own bank card. The last thing he needed was for the police to be notified; it would blow his cover if his work colleagues appeared.

The sarcastic voice in the queue piped up, once more. "Hooray, well done, mate, now take your bunny boiler girlfriend out before I throw her out."

"But she's not my girlfriend... "

"Thank you, my sweet, all done," the cashier quickly confirmed, passing his card back as Brig lifted her tray away from the madding crowd and sought refuge outside, mouthing an expletive directly at the heckler as she did so.

"Sorry, sorry, she isn't my girlfriend, really," Rich pleaded to the man, praying he wouldn't now be a target for this hefty guy.

He followed on as quickly as he could, trying to catch up with the indignant Brig, who was strutting to an outdoor table.

"You give in too easily," she informed him, whilst placing her card into the outside pocket of her leather jacket, a pocket that clearly contained at least two other payment cards. "Two more minutes and they would have given it to me for nothing, like they do in London."

"You're lucky they didn't call the police," Rich told her.

"The police? They wouldn't do anything cos they couldn't do anything. Don't worry, kid, it's too complicated for the likes of you," she delivered harshly.

Yet, Rich did know. He knew all he needed to about her.

Brig put her tray down before completely unzipping her leather jacket, removing it and laying it down neatly upon the tabletop. Her tight white vest seemed two sizes too small, according to Rich's eyes and those of other interested men, leaving little to the imagination.

Having not appreciated her callous put-down, Rich sat down with his back to her, facing the beach instead. He swivelled the camera strap around his chest, removed the cap from the camera lens and switched it on.

"Anyway, Rich, what are you doing here?" asked Brig, interrupting his flow.

Rich looked back over his shoulder and raised his camera, as if to say "stupid". Brig was looking down and didn't see.

"Well, I love taking pictures, especially here," he said. "The views across the channel to Somerset, the surfers riding the waves, the coloured sails of the kiteboarders, especially in this type of evening light can be outstanding. Why, what are you doing here, Brig?"

"Oh, you know, taking in the sights, if you can call them that, and trying to get some decent food. 'Trying' being the operative word," she replied, deriding the food before her.

"You're Parv's friend, Liz tells me?"

"Yes, I am Parv's friend. Anything else Liz tell you?" came her curt response.

"No, just making friendly conversation. Parv is a very pretty lady, isn't she?"

At least this caused Brig to raise her eyebrows. Parv was pretty, *her* pretty.

"Can I level with you, Rich?" she said, shovelling another forkful of salad into her mouth.

Rich declined to answer in case she bestowed another insult or derogatory comment his way.

"I am seeking some old acquaintances, all of whom are dying to see me."

"So, you will be surprising them, will you?" asked Rich, whilst clicking away on his camera.

"You could say that, Rich, yes."

Rich heard her but didn't respond, he just continued clicking away, much to the consternation of Brig who wasn't used to people ignoring her. She demanded attention.

"Why don't you take some pictures of me? You must agree I am full of action—look."

Rich looked round to find her pouting her lips and pushing her arms together making her breasts burst forward in a highly provocative fashion.

"Sorry, I don't do that sort of photography."

"That's a crying shame, Rich, cos I do. Say, you really are a shy one, aren't you? Women like me scare you, don't they?"

Once more, Rich declined to be drawn into her taunts. She was right, they did scare him.

Unabated, Brig continued to tease him. "You're a big, fit guy, well able to deal with the likes of me. I'm sure the girls clamour for you," she said. "Perhaps you haven't met the right girl who can educate you. Girls aren't shrinking violets anymore, you know, we get what we want. Girl power. I think you need some personal training, with me. What if I were to ask you to come running with me in the morning?"

"Is that another suggestive comment?" he replied.

"Aw, you are so sweet, Rich. No, genuinely, I think you would benefit from my company. Well, we're almost living together in the same house now. You could always 'knock me up' in the morning, if you like."

Rich turned his back on her once more, disgusted with her gutter talk. He understood alright, even if he didn't outwardly show it.

"Sorry, Rich, I think I said that all wrong. Please, I really am going to get up and go running. Why don't you join me? You look fit—perhaps you could put me through my paces, eh?"

Rich was becoming increasingly annoyed by her implications. However, he knew she would be no match for his own fast running pace and, with that in mind, he could confidently parry her less-than-subtle approach.

"No, I can't make it, sorry. I have to meet my godmother at eleven o'clock. I haven't seen her for a while, so it wouldn't leave me enough time to do both."

"Who is your godmother? Would I know her at all?" she asked, clearly fishing for information.

"Oh, you wouldn't know Tam. How could you?" he said, deliberately dropping the name.

"Yes, it was a silly question, really. Shame, I expect she is a lovely person. Are you both going somewhere nice, or is it a family occasion?"

"It's probably only the two of us. She loves swimming and windsurfing and so do I."

"Are you returning here to West Bay?" Brig enquired.

"No, it's too busy with tourists, as you can see. We're staying local, back at Skerrid Beach. We'll meet up at The Steps around eleven and then go to Omni's Shack to rent some boards."

"'The Steps', what does that mean?"

"Everyone knows them around here. The Steps is where you get a great view of the beach and the sea. Later, on the way back, I suggest you take a good look to your left as you pass the golf course—you can't miss them on top of the dunes."

"OK, thanks. Yes, I will look out for them. Maybe I will finish my run and meet you there. I'm sure I could teach you a thing or two, if your godmother doesn't mind, that is?"

"I am sure Tam would love to meet you. Tam likes everyone," he fed her, now enjoying his role.

Knowing Brig had taken it all in, he turned his gaze back to the sea and broke out a smug smile.

"I never asked you what you do for a living," said Brig. "You and your sister live in a very big house for two so young. It must have cost a lot of money. I can't imagine that the BnB pays you a fortune, especially in the winter."

Rich knew she had deliberately changed the subject to avert suspicion.

"Liz works from home as a physiotherapist for the local health board. You know from her pronounced limp that she is still injured from a car accident, so they come to her for treatment, and I am a freelance photographer."

"It still doesn't add up, unless you earn a fortune with that camera, that is," Brig commented.

"The house was paid for by the insurance companies, if you must know, when my parents were killed in the same car crash. I was the lucky one who escaped. We get by."

For once, Brig was speechless.

Rich turned away from her, continuing to take photographs of the brightly coloured sails being used by the kite surfers along the beach below, leaving Brig to consume her remaining food.

The silence was short-lived.

"I guess taking photos can be interesting. What stuff do you do?" Brig asked.

"Weddings, sporting events like football, rugby, underwater pictures of swimmers, plus kite sailors, like you can see here. You just need the right equipment." It was a comment he immediately regretted making, giving Brig cause to restart her smutty talk.

"I bet you have all the right equipment, Rich, and it must put you heavily in demand. Let me know if you ever fancy a trip to London—and bring your camera, won't you? Plenty of sights I could show you."

Rich let out a sigh. Would this tortuous evening never end?

"Hey, you still haven't taken a picture of me yet, Mr 'Professional Photographer'. C'mon, you can email it to me. Say, you know what? I could even put it on my personal website. My subscribers would love it. It might lead to more work for you, so I'm doing you a favour here—I am very popular. Good money for us both, and certain 'fringe benefits', shall we say?"

Brig stood up and walked around the bench to stand between Rich and the sea. "Tell you what, Richy boy, I will sit on my bike, and you take some photos of me with the sea in the background. As you say, there's great light to use. How about that?"

Brig made her way to her motorbike and suggestively mounted the wide saddle.

"I can always slip my vest off, you know."

Rich refused to respond.

"No? OK, well, if you don't take my photo right now, I'll take it off anyway."

"Please, don't do that, people know me, it is embarrassing," he said, getting his camera ready as he caved to her demands.

"Good boy. Right, are you ready?"

Begrudgingly, Rich took the photos she demanded, if only to assuage her threat of being semi-naked.

"When I get back, I'll give Liz my email address and a link to my website," said Brig. "You can have seven days free, when I get the photos, of course. I think that's fair. Now, get up and pass me my jacket and helmet—if it's not too hard, that is," she added salaciously.

Anything to get rid of her, he thought, as she slipped on her leather jacket and drew the zip up to just below her neck.

"If I don't see you before, have a lovely time with your godmother. I am sure it will be memorable," she added, placing her helmet on and clipping the safety strap together.

Rich stood and watched as the throaty motorbike disappeared from sight.

Placing himself back down onto the bench, he pulled his phone out from his back pocket and wrote a text to the group.

Game on everyone. Heading home. Godmother is GO!

CHAPTER TWENTY-NINE – STRONGER TOGETHER

Tam was buzzing as she made her way into her bedroom.

Not only was she going to take the battle to Brig, but, on the short drive back, she had caught a brief glimpse of Kee in his bright orange shirt, standing imperiously in The Dragon's Tail's car park. How she would have loved to have stopped and joined him. Maybe tomorrow or, better still, tonight! Sitting on the narrow single bed, she tried thinking of ways to slip out of the caravan, just to tell him she was OK and about the developments in the ongoing Brig situation.

Lying to Norm was no longer an option, yet, by the same token, Tam was sure if she were to be honest and raise the subject now, he would block her suggestion anyway. He would say something along the lines of "Don't spoil things now at this late stage" or "That Brig is a madwoman and she might see you." Frustratingly, he would be right. It was a reckless thought.

"Tam, Tam! We are ready to play Skat now!" called Amey from the living area.

Tam returned to the lounge to find Norm and Amey sitting at the small dining table, with the easy sounds of classical music sedating the mood.

Skat was a card game with German origins that Amey had introduced to them many years ago. Despite not having played it recently, Tam had never forgotten the rules or the suits, which differed from a standard pack of cards, namely acorns, hearts, leaves and bells. The game used a small, thirty-two-card deck, where seven was the lowest denomination, and was very similar in strategy to Bridge with bidding, but more akin to Trumps in actual play.

Amey had always been passionate about the game and played it to a very high standard.

"Norm, I know I should have asked at Liz's, but what is happening exactly tomorrow and who is doing what?" asked Tam as she took her place at the game.

"Well, all being well, Grant and Morgan will be up and about early. Initially, they will be working with the local constabulary to set up roadblocks at either end of the West Bay Road. They will return to the house and then, in Grant's case, head over to The Steps, pending our arrival for eleven a.m. Morgan will place himself on the golf course, which will also be closed, and await the arrival of Renate in a helicopter. Both will be hidden away from Brig's view."

"Will Grant and Morgan be armed?" asked Amey as she dealt the first hand.

"Of course. Whilst we know Brig's gun has been neutralised, we cannot assume that she might not have some other weapon about her person, even if it is just a kitchen knife."

"So, in a worst-case scenario, would Grant shoot to kill or injure?" Tam asked casually, sorting her hand.

"Injure, preferably. She's no use to us dead, to be honest, and it wouldn't go down well if we did take her out completely. Grant will make his own assessment—after all, that's what his training was for. Furthermore, he will be able to hear our conversation as I'll be wired up. Liz will be monitoring us, too."

They each made their bids, which Amey noted down before laying down her first card, the Queen of Hearts. Norm followed with an eight whilst Tam took the spoils, delivering a King.

"You said that Parv will be here by ten in the morning, so what will her final role be in all of this?" Tam asked of Norm.

"Good question, sis. As it stands, we want her to go with Brig to The Steps. Now, given Brig's intent, she may not let it happen. If that occurs, Parv will then alert Liz, either by the VPN phone or a knock on her door, whichever is best at the time."

"You've been very thorough as usual, Norm," said Tam, placing her next card on the table.

"I have told Amey to remain here, and originally, you were to stay here also. It goes against my principles, but you clearly have more to say on this whole subject, so best I hear it whilst you are in front of Brig, I suppose."

Tam gave a little punch in the air. Such minor victories over her dear brother were few and far between.

"It would be better if I were to hear it now, just so I am prepared," intimated Norm.

"I am sorry, Norm, but no. This is my chance to floor the infallible Brig. Now, assuming Rich does get her to agree to meet us at The Steps then everyone will find out at the same time. By the way, don't bother trying to contact Argent—he doesn't know what I have to say, as it isn't all in the documents he has in safekeeping."

"It certainly looks like you're holding all the Aces this time," said Norm, seemingly conceding defeat on the subject.

For the umpteenth time, he picked up his VPN phone, desperate to hear from Rich. On this occasion he was rewarded.

"He's done it. Here's his text." He showed it to Tam and then to Amey. "What an amazing lad. Right, I must get back to the house. We have to tie up some loose ends now that element has been sorted."

"How do you know that Renate and Brig haven't been speaking by phone?" Tam volleyed at him. "Surely, they must be in regular contact with each other? If so, we could be running into a trap, set by her not us—and where is Jeph Huddlestone in all of this?"

"Good, relevant points, Tam. We dealt with these aspects weeks ago. Jeph is unable to travel due to poor health. Secondly, the Americans agreed to monitor any contact between them, hoping Brig might reveal her shenanigans to her mother or father through a phone call or text. Had she done so then they would have stepped in sooner. Surprisingly, she hasn't called them at all. Additionally, we agreed with Renate and the Americans that Renate would be fitted with a tag and would only be able to visit Austria, so she could see some of her relatives again. Had she strayed over the border into Germany then she would have been picked up immediately. It seems that, for once, she wants this chapter of all our lives to end and, potentially, apologise for her wrongdoing."

"Hallelujah," said Amey, waving her hands in the air.

"Tam, I want you to wait here until Rich collects you in the morning," said Norm. "It's what we agreed in Operation Godmother, so Brig won't think anything of you being with him—it's what she's now expecting to see."

Tam noticed Amey struggling to get out of her chair and reached across to help her to her feet.

"Ouch! I was going to take Hertz out for his last walk but I don't think it will be possible. My hip feels a little too sore after my walk this morning."

"I can do it, just around the campsite, if that's OK, Norm?" offered Tam, with an ulterior motive in mind.

"OK, keep to the campsite then—no further, you hear?" said Norm in his stern, brotherly voice, the one he'd often used toward her when they were children. "Apparently, Brig's on her way back from West Bay as we speak. Leave it a while, perhaps when it gets darker."

As Amey and Norm hugged each other, Tam stifled her inner excitement. The thought of seeing Kee again tonight would complete her day... as long as he was in his van, of course, and not with Omni.

CHAPTER THIRTY — SKIRTING WITH TROUBLE

In the busy Dragon's Tail, Kee found himself watching the first half of an international football game on the oversized television that was mounted high on the wall of the old pub. Many faces he recognised were in for the match, standing two deep at the bar and filling every available seat, too. They were, unknowingly, providing him with a buffer from Omni's attentions as she pulled pints at the bar, chatting with local punters and visitors alike. Nevertheless, she kept her beady eye on him, or so it felt.

As the halftime whistle blew, many of the guys made for the toilet, leaving Kee there like a sitting duck. Within moments, Omni had made her way from behind the bar and stood squarely in front of him.

"I would bloody hate football, were it not good for business," she said, picking up some of the empty glasses from his table.

"It isn't that great, to be honest. I think I'll be off once I've finished this one," he said, lifting his half-full glass.

"You can't, you flipping lightweight. It's Quiz Night— look, it says so on the board, see?"

Kee groaned. He shouldn't have tried to assuage Omni by his mere attendance; there would always be more she would foist upon him, and not usually a quiz either.

"You can be in my team, 'The G-Spotters', if you like. All the answers are to do with the letter 'G'."

"The letter 'G'? Ooh, that sounds exciting," mocked Kee.

Without batting an eyelid Omni, continued her recruitment drive. "Well, I had a tip from Selwyn Roberts, tonight's quizmaster, that it could involve Germany, you know. I did ask Amey, our local resident from 'the Bundesland' last week, but she wasn't up for it. Shame that, really—we could have won quite easily with her in the team, and you knowing her sister-in-law now, of course," she pointedly added.

Kee had known it would only be a matter of time before Omni brought up the subject of Tam. If only Amey had said yes and brought Tam along, too, it would have been more than bearable to stay. Sadly not.

"Kee, are you still with us, love? Oh, hang on a minute, you've gone all gooey thinking about Tam, haven't you?" Omni taunted.

"Ok, Omni, you win, I'll stay," said Kee, caving in to her pressure.

"Righto, then," said Omni, walking away smugly, having got her way.

Kee took the opportunity to get some respite from Omni, taking his drink outside into the perfect evening conditions to be found in the small beer garden, which sat on top of a low wall just above the West Bay Road. Placing his drink on the edge of the weather-beaten wooden table, he looked across to the vast dunes to his left. He marvelled at the lengthening shadows that lay upon their wide undulations as the lowering sun created a crimson hue in the sky. In the distance were golfers, trying to squeeze out every drop of daylight no doubt, to complete their round on the links. Above, the distant drone of a light aircraft somewhere high in the sky.

It was serene. It would have been the perfect evening to spend with Tam. He checked his phone to see if he had any further messages from his kids, a change of heart perhaps, but no.

Looking up, he noticed an impressive silver horse lorry approaching from West Bay. It had been a day of horses, including when the magnificently talented Tam had saved the day for someone else's child.

Suddenly, without warning, the dazzle of a single headlamp appeared alongside the lorry, attempting an ill-judged overtaking manoeuvre at considerable speed. Kee looked to his right, only to see two cyclists, riding side by side, heading straight into its path.

Surely not—the same damned blue motorbike he had clashed with earlier was edging its way past the lorry, now blatantly on the wrong side of the road. It seemed, to his eyes at least, that a collision was almost inevitable.

There was nothing he could do other than watch in horror as they converged, neither aware of the other. Somehow, at the last possible moment, the motorbike managed to swerve across the front of the lorry, in an attempt to avoid a head-on collision. The shock of its appearance forced the cyclists to swerve left, missing the motorbike by inches, sending them careering into the low wall alongside the pub, upon which Kee was perched.

Somehow, the lorry managed to avoid them by effecting an emergency stop attempt, which sent it across the grassy verge opposite. The sickening thud of horses hitting the side walls within could be heard. It all seemed to happen in a split second and all came to a shuddering standstill just as quickly.

Kee jumped down from the wall to stop any further traffic before attending to one of the cyclists lying prostrate on the tarmac. As he did so, the other cyclist got himself up from the floor, his knees and elbows badly grazed and bleeding.

"I'm OK, I think," said the first rider, resting face-up as Kee approached him.

Kee slowly extricated the bike away from his legs to allow him to get up. His injuries seemed similarly superficial, like the other cyclist's, as Kee slowly hauled him up onto his feet.

On the edge of the road, he could see that horse lorry driver was out, opening the side door to check on the horses. Kee hoped the silence was good news, with no serious injuries within.

Omni briefly appeared by his shoulder and, upon viewing the carnage, instantly returned inside for water and some clean bar towels. Kee, along with others now present, ushered the cyclists to the side of the wall and sat them down to check them over once more as Omni reappeared.

"Will you call the police, please?" asked the second rider.

"Call them if you like," interrupted Omni. "They won't do anything, unless anyone got the registration number or can identify the driver, that is. He's probably long gone by now. If he had any decency he would have stopped. Shall I get you an ambulance, though?" She dabbed at his grazed elbow with a damp towel, causing him to flinch.

"No, I think I am OK, thanks, just a few cuts. I'm angry more than anything. I've only had this bike a couple of weeks," he stated, as Omni now dabbed at his knee, in an attempt to wash any grit from his wound.

Kee spoke. "It wasn't a car that overtook, it was a motorbike. I saw her overtaking the lorry, right by here." He gestured toward an adjacent farm gate.

"Her?" asked Omni

"Yes, 'her'. I saw her earlier. Same colour bike and the same noisy exhaust pipe."

"So, where did you see her, then?"

"Er... around the corner, shall we say?" Kee coyly replied, realising his Freudian slip had immediately placed him in deep trouble with Omni.

"Hang on a bloody minute. You were in The Meadow Pipit, weren't you?"

"No, outside The Meadow Pipit, if you must know, but that isn't important right now for God's sake, Omni. Let's get these lads sorted out, they must be in shock."

"Aye, you're right in this case, *mun*, but you're not off the hook, matey, not by a long chalk."

Kee raised his eyes to the heavens, wishing he had kept his mouth firmly shut.

The horse lorry's engine started up, leaving Kee to assume all was well as it eased its way off the grass verge and away from the scene.

The second cyclist was now being attended to by two of the regulars and patched up with plasters from a first aid kit. Like his friend, he was more concerned with the state of his bike than his own condition.

Kee took hold of the man's badly scratched bike and grasped its front wheel between his knees, twisting the handlebars back into their rightful position. Other than the scuffs, in his qualified opinion, it seemed to still be in good working order as he span the wheels and moved the gears forward and back to check for any adverse effects that the crash may have imparted. He repeated his checks with the second bike, which also appeared to still be fit for purpose.

"I can drive you home if you like, lads," offered the driver of a transit van, patiently waiting for the scene to clear.

His offer was declined with thanks, as the cyclists jointly decided to complete their relatively short ride home, standing up and clipping their special shoes back into their respective pedals.

"Guys, if you want to call in tomorrow, there's a pint on the house," Omni called, as they set off rather gingerly. "We can pass over any photos we have taken, if you need them for an insurance claim or a police crime number, OK?"

A raised arm signified acknowledgement of her kind offer as they headed away, West Bay bound. Despite everything else he might think of her, Kee knew, deep down, that Omni was a truly kind woman, just not the woman for him.

With the incident cleared, he sensed it would have been an opportune time to slip away himself, were Omni not standing watching him yet again. He was stuck.

He reluctantly wandered back into the pub and returned to his seat to watch the conclusion of the game. A fresh pint of beer and a bowl of curry quickly appeared before him. He was being killed, not by her kindness, but by the inevitable indigestion from eating two meals in such a short space of time!

With the game nearing its conclusion, Kee heard that the quiz had been cancelled, so he plotted his escape once more as the pub slowly emptied of customers. Omni, however, had different ideas, depositing herself in a vacant chair opposite him.

"Would you like to stay in my empty caravan?" she offered, dangling a different set of keys before him. "Or there is still that spare bed upstairs, of course."

The inebriated guy next to him overheard. "How do you get all the special offers, then, mate?" he asked, causing raucous laughter around the table.

With all eyes on him, Kee refused to answer either Omni's invitation or the impertinent question, finishing his drink as if to signify his exit.

"The lady really has left her mark on you, hasn't she?" said Omni, conceding defeat.

"More than you will ever know," declared Kee, getting to his feet and placing his empty glass on the bar. "Goodnight, Omni." Kee blew her a kiss as he made for the door.

Stepping out into the warm night air, he looked across to the ambient light on Sker Lake, totally unaware that Tam was just two minutes away, in that very direction.

It had been a long day for all the right reasons, and not the day of solace he was expecting to find.

He figured it was now too late to knock on Norm's door, to warn him of Brig's potential presence in the village, so he would have to go in the morning. Hopefully, the beautiful Tam would be there, too.

CHAPTER THIRTY-ONE — NEED YOU

Tam had decided to follow Norm's advice and only take Hertz out for his final walk of the day under the cover of summer darkness. However, she fully intended to stray beyond the boundaries agreed with her brother—getting a message to Kee was now her immediate priority.

Judging by the position of the sinking sun, her soiree could still be a good thirty minutes away. It was frustrating; she wanted to go now, whilst he might still be awake.

Luckily, Amey broached the subject of Kee and the day as a whole, something she was more than happy to discuss.

"When do you think you will see Kee again, Tam?" she asked, opening a window to remove the pressure of the warm air trapped in the caravan.

"Who knows?" Tam replied, pouring out the remnants of the red wine. "Perhaps tomorrow, you never know."

"He seems like a very nice man. He has a kind face—well informed, too. He impressed me with his knowledge of East Germany and sport in general, it was very refreshing. Far be it from me to say, but he seems to be your type of man."

"Aww, thank you, Amey. He was so lovely to me today," said Tam. "He gave me space. Not once did he pester me or give me the type of corny chat most men deliver. To him I was just another person, one he just happened to offer to chaperone, yet he left me to my new experience without staring or passing comment about my less-than-perfect figure."

"You still have a wonderful figure, Tam. Why are you so hard on yourself? Look at me, old and lined, yet I don't care who sees me naked, as long as it doesn't offend anyone."

"Nice of you to say, if not completely true," said Tam, patting her stomach.

"So, what inspired you to go au naturel, then? Why today, in the face of all your troubles?"

"It has always been on my mind I suppose, because of you."

Amey looked pleasantly surprised with her response.

"That picture of you in the kitchen is so evocative. I'd never have thought I could possibly emulate you, yet the circumstances conspired for it to happen today. Of course, the weather was perfect, plus both you and Norm were busy, so the opportunity presented itself.

"In all truth, I needed to escape from my world and my overthinking mind, for a while. This was radical, something out of the ordinary, something that would distract me, however irresponsible and dangerous it might have first seemed," she fervently explained to an entranced Amey.

"You mentioned Hannah and the statue of 'Our Lady' at the nature reserve earlier, how did that influence you?" asked Amey.

"That wooden carving really caught my eye. Its strength said so much to me in that very instant, I was literally in awe of its magnitude. Then Hannah appeared. She was lovely, not the sort of person I expected to be running a nature reserve. She exuded confidence. Given she must be around my age, she looked stunning for a lady of her build, not dowdy or drab. Her platinum blonde pixie hairstyle showed me that she was being who she wanted to be, something which, to date, I have failed to be in my own life. That had to change. It spurred me on. Look, I even did a sketch of the carving... Here," said Tam, rummaging in her bag and offering the sketch across to Amey.

"You haven't lost your artistic skills, Tam," said Amey, impressed.

"It's yours, Amey, I would like you to keep it."

"*Danke*, I will keep it here in the caravan."

Amey took a drawing pin from a drawer and, affixed the sketch to a small corkboard that was propped up against the tiles in the kitchen area.

"It will always make me think of you now, when I am here on my own," she said, standing back to allow Tam to see it residing alongside an aged photograph of Norm with his gold medal around his neck.

It made Tam feel ten feet tall.

As the sun finally started to drop down below the horizon, Amey collected her wine glass and sat alongside Tam, who had moved across to the slim, albeit faded, cushioned bench.

"Tell me more about Kee. I am fascinated by the impact he has had on you today."

"Quite simply, he didn't try to be anything other than himself," said Tam. "Initially, he was the guarded one, being evasive about his background. It was only later I found out exactly why."

"Evasive, but not like Felton's evasive, obviously!" said Amey.

"No, not like Felton at all, quite the opposite. On our way back from the beach he actually broke down, revealing his own sadness. It touched me deeply. It explained why he had been so empathetic on the beach when I had told him of my own trials and tribulations over the last year or so."

"He must trust you, to tell you something so deep. That bodes well, Tam. Dare I say it, even Ant and El would love him by the sound of it, wouldn't they?"

"They would. You know what, I can honestly say that I lived more in one short day with Kee, a relative stranger, than I have with Felton in twenty-five long years."

"Good for you, Tam. You deserve it." Amey clinked her wine glass against Tam's.

Tam felt the pangs of hurt lifting from her soul as she confided more in Amey. "You know full well that Felton and I stopped loving each other years ago. Our relationship was only ever a physical one until Ant and Elinor were born. The loss of my figure and the allure of younger, prettier women turned his head away from me after that point. Somehow, I deluded myself that the definition of love was a handsome man in a well-paid job, living in a nice area of London. In fact, they weren't even my aspirations at all, they were my father's wishes for me. Every day thereafter became another day of mundane existence. Only the children and taking on a part-time, albeit boring, civil service job, gave me any respect for myself. Now I can see how much time I have truly wasted over the last few years and how I could quite happily make a new, fulfilling life here in Skerrid Mawr. Look at you, Amey, blessed with the forests of Thuringia, the countryside of Sussex and now the beauty of a Welsh coastline. What a great life you have had."

"And Kee, where would he fit into all of this?"

"He, like you, has shown me what life could be," said Tam, finishing her wine.

"How so?"

"To be free and happy with someone who is your friend and equal. Not only have I seen that in your relationship with Norm, but also in your friends on the beach today.

If ever I saw a definition of love, it was them. They were beautiful in every way. Their age and body size didn't matter to them anymore, as long as they had each other."

"Indeed. As we used to say back home, 'you are never too old to love, once you find it for yourself.'"

"What an amazing expression. My goal wasn't to find love, you know, but I can't deny it may have found me today. Am I being reckless and stupid?"

"A little, perhaps," Amey replied with a grin, surreptitiously handing her Hertz's lead.

Tam felt a tingle of excitement run through her body, triggered by Amey's perceptive inference. Looking out across the lake, she could see that only the last vestiges of sun were apparent in the amber sky.

"We know Brig is back at Liz's, so go now, under the cover of the incoming darkness, to Kee. You know where he is to be found," instructed Amey.

"Oh, Amey, thank you," Tam said, reaching out for her navy hoody. "I don't want him to leave here without him knowing that I care and would like to see him again. For all I know, he's not interested, so I would like to find out, either way."

"Norm will go mad if he finds out, so don't let me down. Remember, Kee may be out or asleep even, so why don't you write him a note, just in case?"

"Good idea." Tam took her notepad from her bag once more. "Are you sure you won't come with me?"

"I am quite sure. You need to do this yourself. However, can I suggest that you take the longer route, behind the caravan and up to the main road that way?"

"Why?" asked Tam, mildly concerned.

"Because it will avoid the main entrance, just in case that Gary guy is hanging around. He lives above the shop, so best beware, *ja*?"

"Yes, I certainly don't want his attentions again."

"Good. Listen, just as the road arcs back towards Linda's shop you will see a path that branches off to the left. If you take that route, it will bring you out by The Dragon's Tail," Amey explained, as Tam quickly scribbled her note to Kee. She was tempted to leave her telephone number, however, with her phone still off, that would not achieve much for now.

"Here, put it in this plastic food bag, it will keep it dry from any dew," said Amey, waving said item at Tam.

Tam carefully placed the note inside the bag, now keener than ever to get out of the door.

"If Norm should phone me, then I will say you are asleep. I will wait up until you return. You have fifteen minutes or until I finish my second cup of tea, whichever is sooner."

Dear Amey. How sweet and selfless she was to be aiding and abetting Tam in this way.

Tam took the lead and clipped it to Hertz's collar.

"I promise that I will be as quick as I can," she said to Amey before stepping out into the humid air with Hertz.

Amey securely closed the door behind them, and they headed down toward the edge of the site, looking back briefly to see Amey waving from the brightly lit window. Tam was so blessed to have her as her sister-in-law.

Taking the advised clockwise route, they reached the very edge of the site, within a stone's throw of the lake. Tam could hear the water lapping lightly against the bank, her senses otherwise overwhelmed by the strong, distinctive odour of the bracken, which ensconced the outer perimeter of the park.

Low-level lighting posts then helped to illuminate their way up to the spur path, the one that Amey had mentioned. Stepping onto the shale surface, Tam was able to orient herself by the upstairs lights of The Dragon's Tail.

Upon reaching the West Bay Road, she stopped and looked across to the large ground-floor window of the pub. Levering herself onto tiptoes, Tam strained her neck to the left and to the right, to see if anyone was left inside. She truly hoped and prayed that Kee wasn't still there.

Suddenly, she caught sight of a lady who had come close to the window, seemingly cleaning down tables. Tam's heart jumped as the woman momentarily stopped. She seemed to be peering out, toward her and the dog. Tam quickly realised it must be Omni, so turned her face away, lifting her hood up over her head to mask her face. As much as she liked Omni, she didn't want to risk being seen by her right now. Coaxing Hertz away, she paced along the uneven pavement toward the nature reserve car park as rapidly as she could.

As Tam steered Hertz past the front of the building, she could make out the shadowed form of the carving. Even silhouetted, its influence was strong enough to send a tingle up her spine. She wanted to stop and look longer but there in the distance sat a silver VW campervan with a mountain bike affixed to the rear door, kept company only by the illumination of a dull orange streetlamp. This had to be Kee's van.

The crunch of her footsteps on the loose gravel seemed sure to give her away. Reaching into her pocket, she took out the carrier bag containing the note, deftly lifted the wiper blade and placed it beneath. Once more, her heartbeat pummelled away in her tight chest. What if she accidentally set off an alarm or Hertz were to bark? She would surely be discovered. In reality, she wasn't totally averse to that outcome, if it meant she could talk to him again. She was close, so, so close to him once more.

Then, before she had the chance to even contemplate her next action, a raucous snore was heard from deep within the van. She had to stifle her cry of delight, afraid she might wake him. Thankfully, he was here and not anywhere else.

"Sleep well, you gorgeous man," she whispered, her fingers lightly touching the van, mimicking the way his fingers had left their mark on both her skin and her soul some hours before.

"Hertz, it's time to get back," she whispered to her obedient companion. His tail wagged vigorously in agreement, bumping against the front tyre of the van.

As they gingerly edged away from Kee's van, Tam's attention inevitably turned across the now deserted West Bay Road, toward Norm's house, the safehouse where she had slept the night before, such a tantalisingly short distance away. Now, of course, it was potentially an 'unsafe house'. Tam feared for her brave, ever-reliable brother, even if Grant was there to keep him company. How she wished they could all have been there again tonight, without this awful spectre hanging over them all.

Having now called Brig's bluff, Tam knew full well there was no going back.

CHAPTER THIRTY-TWO — REALITY STRIKES

Sleep had proved elusive for Tam in recent months.

Despite warm thoughts of Kee, her slumber was dominated by inauspicious thoughts of the morning ahead, causing yet another restless night. It certainly wasn't the ideal preparation for a confrontation that could define her life from hereon.

She had toyed with various scenarios, none of which ended in an outcome that she would truly consider a triumph. Violence was something Tam abhorred, yet it seemed inevitable.

Norm would certainly be armed, as would Grant. If Brig were to draw her gun, albeit knowingly neutralised by Liz, would they shoot? No one, not even Brig, deserved such an awful outcome.

Tam knew she would find it hard to engage in any form of physical fight with Brig, too. Not because she couldn't, but rather because the thought of accidentally causing serious harm to another human being went way beyond her beliefs as a pacifist.

She recalled an incident that had cemented her beliefs, something that had happened to her when she was fourteen with Tasha Withers, the schoolyard bully. Tasha had been giving most girls in her class a tough time through her attempts to extort lunch money, with threats of impending harm otherwise. It drew uncanny parallels with Brig Huddlestone.

One cold February morning, Tam found herself being targeted by this girl. Not one of her classmates came to her aid; they just stood and watched, obviously glad it wasn't them this time. As she refused to concede to the demands, Tasha attempted to land a punch and Tam ducked. Tasha stumbled forward and turned for a second attempt. Without a second thought, Tam landed her own blow squarely onto Tasha's chin, causing the girl to fall and hit her head on the hard playground floor. Tam stood there stunned as the teachers arrived and tended to an unconscious Tasha, blaming Tam as the perpetrator! None of it was what she wanted to happen; it was forced upon her and she lost, being instantly suspended before a swift expulsion. It was all so unfair, castigated for one fluke punch. What if that was to recur later today and she unwittingly inflicted a similar fate on Brig? Where could that put her—in prison?

Yes, Tasha Withers had recovered, but the fear of inflicting harm, even in self-defence, remained in Tam's thoughts. Now it only served to fuel her nervousness, the stomach gripes worsening as she pulled the thin duvet up to her chin once more for comfort.

There was a gentle tapping at her door.

"You know, it is time you got up now, Tam," said Amey. "You need to be ready for when Rich arrives."

Yes, she knew. In reality, she just didn't want the day to begin at all.

"OK, Amey, I will get up," Tam feebly replied, not really meaning it.

"You know where I will be," Amey called, as if it were any other day.

That perky demeanour reminded Tam of her own mother's inappropriately cheery morning calls when she was a youngster, usually when she had an important exam or an injection at the doctor's surgery. Perhaps Amey had forgotten what an important day it was going to be, for goodness' sake. This awful mess directly affected her, too, even though she would not be present at The Steps; how could she be so matter-of-fact about it?

Tam's mind drifted back to Norm, at the house. No doubt he would be putting his final battle plans together, distributing orders to his "foot soldiers", Grant and Morgan, and liaising with all the parties involved as only he could.

Yet the onus firmly remained on her shoulders now; it was her that Brig was primarily coming to see. Delaying her rising would not make the problem go away; it had to be faced, and eleven o'clock wasn't too far away.

"If you don't hurry up, your tea and this Ruhrei will be cold," came a plaintive cry.

As she sat up, the smell of Amey's scrambled eggs drifted into the bedroom, hastening the need to head for the toilet. She didn't want to be sick, but the very thought of eating right now made her border on retching.

Sitting on the toilet, with the door still wide open, she ran the tap and doused her face in an attempt to cool herself down, taking care to breathe through her mouth to avoid the smell.

"Are you OK, Tam?" said Amey, appearing at the doorway.

"No, not right now. Give me a minute."

Amey receded away, leaving Tam to slowly recover.

"Don't worry, I have given the eggs to Hertz now," Amey informed her. "We will need to take him out for a quick walk; it's his routine, of course. Shall I take him and leave you here alone for ten minutes?"

"No, please wait," Tam responded, now confident that the worst had passed. "I think the air will do me good. It's just nerves."

Tam stepped across the narrow hallway and back into the bedroom, quickly changing into the previous evening's clothes, wanting to get outside as soon as she possibly could. Ignoring Amey, she made straight for the caravan door and the fresh air of the morning, almost gasping as she did so. Leaning on the plastic balustrade of the caravan balcony, she prayed that she didn't encounter Gary the mower man again. Not him, not today. She really wasn't in the mood.

As she waited for Amey and Hertz to appear, her thoughts flitted to Kee and she wondered if he had seen her note. She prayed it hadn't fallen off the windscreen. If it had, he wouldn't appear at The Steps, due to ignorance, not choice. Then again, perhaps he had seen it and chosen to scrunch it up, throw it away and leave anyway? The least she should have done was put a telephone number on it. What an idiot she'd been not to. Then, at the very least, she could have lived in hope that he might call or leave a message sometime in the near future. Idiot.

Amey finally appeared with Hertz pulling hard on his lead.

"Let's just head along the lakeside, maybe it will calm you down?" she suggested, locking the door.

As they walked down to the lake, Tam tried to dispel her negative thoughts, hoping that she would be wrong on all counts, namely, that she could successfully deal with Brig and, furthermore, that Kee had got her message.

Amey had her own thoughts about the morning ahead; it wasn't what Tam expected to hear.

"You know, Tam, all this has been a long time coming. I might seem calm to you, but inside, not so. Remember it was me that spent several painful weeks in Frankfurt University Hospital. As a result, I have endured many years learning to cope with that day, trying to rebuild my shattered dreams. Thankfully, you and your lovely brother have been instrumental in my recovery every day since."

Tam knew that Amey had struggled for many years on a combination of medications, all a consequence of Renate's malicious action that fateful day.

"Naturally, I worry that you, Anthony, Elinor, Norm or even me, could get hurt today by Renate's maniacal daughter. Who knows what she is truly capable of?"

"Who knows indeed?" said Tam rhetorically.

"Don't you think it bizarre that, soon, the instigator of this whole saga, my equestrian adversary, Renate Brenzlig, will be right here, in Skerrid Mawr, both of us within touching distance of each other, after all these years?"

Tam agreed. It certainly wasn't anything that any of them could have feasibly considered before.

"Whatever happens, I would love the chance to see her and ask why... why she did what she did to me back then, and how she created such a monster in Brig."

It was deep-rooted emotion. Tam chose not to interrupt her flow.

"If we could ever put our differences to one side, then I am sure it would help a hardened Ossi, like me, to forgive. Germany needs to know the truth about what happened, and I feel it should be me and Renate, together, who tell this to our homeland to complete our reunification, be that today or someday soon."

Tam had never seen, or heard, such an outpouring from her sister-in-law which included forgiveness and reconciliation. Amey, of course, was right—she did deserve the opportunity to find a resolution to this feud, for everyone's sake.

CHAPTER THIRTY-THREE — GONE

Liz appeared in the front room as Rich, somewhat awkwardly, was leaning out of the front window. His unflattering choice of bedwear, namely oversized blue chequered boxer shorts, was not offering his best side by anyone's stretch of the imagination.

Wearing her usual towelling robe, her hair still wet from her shower, Liz asked him, curtly, what he was doing.

"Looks like we've taken our eye off the ball for two minutes," he reported. "She's slipped the net."

"Oh no, please no. What makes you think that?"

"I thought I heard something like a door closing, and I got up and came straight down here to look. I didn't want to rush outside dressed like this, which is why I am trying to be inconspicuous."

"Is her motorbike still there?" asked Liz, pushing him to one side to look for herself.

"Yes, it is. The chances are she has gone out on foot. Sorry, Liz, it was my fault. I didn't think she would get up this early, given Parv will be arriving in a short while. In hindsight, I should have set my alarm and been watching, especially as she said she might be going for a run. I honestly thought she was bluffing."

"OK. We need to think quickly. Let's knock on her door to check first," Liz said. "We have no time to waste—we've put everyone at risk with our stupidity."

"We should have put cameras in there, like I told you," Rich called out as he made his way to the desk in the corridor to collect the spare key.

"Well, we didn't have time to do it, did we? No use crying over that now. You had best check her phone for movement, too," said Liz, following him out into the shaded, north-facing side of the property.

Before they could knock on the annexe door, they were distracted by a shout from across the road.

"Problem, guys?"

It was Tony, one of the neighbours, putting out the dustbins as his wife, Bev, watered the small front garden with an elongated hose, complete with adjustable spray head.

"We weren't sure if we heard our visitor going out. We're just checking in case she has," Liz explained.

"Well, you were right the first time, Liz—we saw her going out about fifteen minutes ago, didn't we, love?"

"Aye, we did. Kitted out she was, in painted-on spandex. Left nothing to the imagination, shall we say?" confirmed Bev, with an accusing look at Tony.

"Not my fault, love, is it? I didn't ask her to wear that outfit," Tony replied defensively.

"Well, you certainly feasted your eyes on her long enough, didn't you? I saw you. Anyway, Liz, she jogged up toward the All Angels' Church. I said hello but she totally ignored me. Probably those ear things they wear. If she were my daughter, she certainly wouldn't be wearing that outfit, let me tell you, right now!"

"Alright, Bev, that's enough," interjected Tony. "They want to get on, see." He pointed over to Rich, who had moved away to try the annexe door with the spare key.

"Any classes today, Liz?" added Tony, following Liz across to the annexe.

"No," replied Liz, now frustrated at his insistence to continue the discussion. "The maintenance people were due, but they cancelled at the last minute," she lied as Rich stood aside, allowing her to lead the way—with Tony still in close attendance.

"Hey, Rich, I wouldn't mind a go on that bike, though," Tony kept on. "Smart one that is. I had one similar to that, years ago it was, before me and Bev met—a Triumph it was, possibly a Tiger Cub, can't remember exactly. Anyway—"

"Sorry, Tony, we've got to find her, it's really important. See you later, thanks, bye," replied Rich, firmly closing the annexe door on him.

Lying on the bed was Brig's phone. Liz could see it had been switched off. Now, with both the motorbike and phone still here, they had no way of tracking her movements. This was definitely an emergency. Liz knew she had to get a message out, but who knew exactly where Brig would be heading?

"Don't worry, I've sent a brief message out to the group," said Rich. "Can't see her doing much at this time of day, especially dressed in running gear. It's the eleven o'clock meeting that will matter."

"If you say so," said Liz, "but her unpredictability scares me."

Soon, Rich had news.

"Parv has responded already. She has crossed the Severn Bridge and is around forty-five minutes away. Parv says that Brig does jog quite a lot, so hopes that is all it is."

"Good, we need Parv here for Brig's return. I need to check for that gun again," said Liz.

She slipped her hand into Brig's case and carefully extracted the towel she knew it was wrapped in.

Liz's face fell as she unfurled the towel. The gun was gone. Even though she had neutralised it, this made Brig's intent to harm clear.

"Rich, put another alert out now. It has to be Norm's house she is heading to. She doesn't know about the caravan."

"Will do. It would have been easy for her to have located Norm's house last night, with that damned flagpole," he said, keying in the message into the group chat.

Liz went into the kitchen area, checking in case any of the knives had gone, too. Luckily, they were all present.

Rich read out his post:

Norm, we believe she is heading to your house.
Her gun is gone, we assume with her.
Whilst it won't work, it shows her intent.
Morgan and Grant, you must intercept her.
Tam and Amey, please be on your guard.

Moments later, he conveyed the two immediate responses received to Liz:

Grant: *On our way back now.*
Norm: *I will be ready for her, don't worry.*

"What has Amey said?" asked Liz.

"Nothing, which is extremely worrying. My phone says the message has been delivered to Amey's phone. However, I can see that she hasn't read any of the messages yet. It means her phone is probably off. For all we know, Liz, they could be in the caravan like sitting ducks."

CHAPTER THIRTY-FOUR — ISOLATED

"Bloody fool!" shouted Norm, berating himself.

He had just received Liz's message.

"Why didn't I make contingencies for this? I mean, I covered all bases but not my own. How many years have I been doing this for others, yet I go and mess it up for myself?" His mithering continued, causing the cat to depart his chair and slope away to the kitchen.

Norm strode purposefully to the cupboard in the hallway, unbuttoning his shirt as he did so. "Right then, Weaver, get yourself ready, she could turn up here at any time," he muttered, laying his shirt to one side before taking out a hefty bulletproof Kevlar vest, one that had been intended for use at The Steps later.

Placing it upon his bare chest, he attempted to fasten it but only succeeded in trapping his copious hair in the Velcro straps. It made him wince, and he had to stop, unfasten, correct and re-fasten it, adding fuel to his frustration.

If Brig did arrive, then his strategy would have to be to play for time. Whilst this wasn't in the original script, his hope was that Grant and Morgan would get back to the house sooner rather than later. He'd seen that they had both read the message. At least the golf club wasn't that far away, only a few minutes in fact. If there were to be a fracas with

Brig, he would prefer that they were here to intercept her, rather than him facing her alone.

Struggling back into his baggy lumberjack-style shirt, he flipped the catch on the side door, allowing it to swing gently open. If Brig got there first, then this 'open door' policy could serve to lull her to a position where he could control the play. His express aim would be to get inside her head in an attempt to pacify any aggressive intent she might have. Conversely, should the two lads arrive back first, then they would have time to determine her whereabouts within the village and to plot an appropriate course of action.

He had this under control, as long as it wasn't the caravan she was heading for.

Injuring or even killing Brig, was, of course, an option to him. However, he knew that this would cause untold problems, both diplomatically and nationally. He wanted to reduce his problems at this time of life, not increase them. No, he decided, he'd exercise restraint; after all, he had worked hard to establish a basis for trust with both the Americans and Renate in the hope of bringing Brig's misdemeanours to an end at the agreed time and place, that being eleven o'clock at The Steps, not here and now.

His head was swirling, his mouth dry as the adrenalin kicked in. A toe-to-toe contest was something he hadn't taken on for many years, let alone against a young, female maniac, over thirty years his junior. He knew from Grant that she worked-out and would be well-trained in self-defence or, in this case, offence.

Could he even bring himself to hit a woman? It wasn't something he had ever contemplated before.

He peered at the barrel of his old gun, which lay beneath a mess of papers on the table in the middle of the room. It only had blanks in it; best leave it that way. The temptation might prove too great, otherwise, if he were to make the rounds live. At least he knew Brig's gun had been nullified, should she come wielding it in his direction.

Perhaps, if she was heading here, Brig might be thinking that she will find Tam and Amey present—logically, this seemed the most likely option. It was what he had originally feared might happen, especially when the photo had been deliberately brought to her attention via Parv. If Brig had done her homework, then tracing his home address wouldn't be difficult. He took some crumb of comfort in the fact that his half-mast flag tactic had worked and that Tam and Amey were safe at the caravan. Well, hopefully so.

Taking a swig of his lukewarm coffee, Norm sat down and switched off two of his three monitors so he could concentrate on watching the four CCTV cameras that shared the remaining screen.

Within a minute of monitoring, the hairs on the back of his neck rose as someone appeared.

No one else was expected, not even Susie the post lady. It must be Brig.

He observed her tentative movements as she crept along the path to the side door. She stopped and looked up. She must have seen the camera that angled down from above, because she stepped forward and out of its view. Switching from digital visual to human audible, Norm listened intently for any clue to her exact position. The lightest of squeaks told him that the soles of her shoes were now upon the tiles of the hallway. Two more squeaks followed before a pause. Then two more.

She must be just behind the other side of the door, a door that was ajar. Three slim fingers appeared, clutching onto the door's edge, before they quickly retracted. Staying silent was Norm's way of unsettling her. The door swayed ever so lightly. Was she now too afraid to come in? The tension was palpable.

"There's no need to be coy, Brigette, I know you are there," Norm said, projecting his voice loudly while keeping his gaze steadfast on the door.

The door opened, and there stood Brig Huddlestone, in his house, with her pistol aimed in his direction.

"I thought this was too easy. I mean, you're not known for being lackadaisical, Weaver," she croaked, seemingly shocked that she was still under his power, despite her being the one holding the gun.

"Shall I turn away so you can shoot me in the back, bit like your mother would have done to me, given the chance, eh?" Norm asked, testing her mettle.

"I *will* shoot you if you keep mentioning my mother like that, old loser."

"OK. That was a little remiss of me, I agree," said Norm calmly. "Now, I suppose we had best observe protocol, don't you agree, Brig?"

"Only you and your ilk care for inane protocol these days, we don't care," she replied indignantly.

"We? And who is we? I think you will find your statement to be untrue, Brig. Your counterparts are very amenable to protocol, as you will soon find out, no doubt."

"Just cut the crap and get up, slowly and with your hands up... This is a hold-up scenario, of course," Brig countered, using his own style against him.

As requested, Norm raised his right and then his left arm, as slowly as he possibly could, before rising to his feet.

"You know, Brigette, I give people chances in this world, including the likes of Grant... and Parv, of course," he said with a mocking smile.

Brig sneered at his jibe.

"In all honesty, I didn't know anything about you when you first got appointed, only what others told me. Most disappointing, really. Usually, I get informed, even by the

Americans, when someone like you is likely to cross my path. However, it now seems that someone in Cheltenham or Whitehall slipped up. Slipped up badly."

"Where is all this trash going?" said Brig, impatient.

"I will get to that, just wait." He held his palm toward her. "Whether your appointment in London was deliberate or inadvertent, I have yet to find out. The chances are it had something to do with an inept civil servant, called Felton, with a liking for young, attractive women, like you," he said, trying to imply that she was just one of many Felton had appointed, mainly for his own personal pleasure.

Brig seemed to know what he was saying was true, based on her silence.

"Thereafter, as you probably know, the ranks were closed on me. I had no further say in the matter. So now there's a new 'middle-aged wave' of 'head treaders' up in London, controlling the show. Unfortunately, for me anyway, it was headed up by my awful brother-in-law, Felton, in my absence. Both he and his band of fools think they are very clever. They are not. They're all imbeciles, in fact."

"At last, something we can finally agree on," Brig responded with contempt.

"Even if I had been invited into their crass little circle, it isn't one that I would have wished to be part of, which is why I was most annoyed to be put out to pasture. Home Secretaries can do that to people like me in Britain, you know?"

"I wouldn't know, would I?"

Norm was praying that Morgan and Grant would appear through the door at any given moment. Their absence meant that he had to continue to buy time. He could sense Brig would soon twig his ploy, and he didn't want it to end badly, especially not in his own house and not before Renate was given the chance to talk sense to her, which was still his ultimate intention.

"As a consequence, I subsequently relocated down here. Funny that, there's a similarity to your dear mother there—relocating. However, in her case, she fled to a totally different country to avoid prosecution for her callous act. I would call that 'defecting', wouldn't you?"

He hoped that, by taunting her, she would start talking and, in so doing, protract her stay long enough to be captured by Grant or Morgan.

"I wouldn't say that if I were you, Norm. Don't compare yourself to my mother, not now, not ever."

Norm sat back down, allowing her the high ground, sensing that she might revel in her hold over him, and more importantly, talk. Where the hell were they?

"You're a bright girl, Brigette; I cannot deny that. Don't you realise all this nonsense is spoiling things for everyone, including your parents and, moreover, yourself? You coming here today will only go against you, which is a shame. Listen, all these misunderstandings will get sorted through the proper channels, given time." Norm put it to her like a barrister pleading his case.

"Don't think so, Norm. You know what, I thought Felton was clever initially, and difficult to break, but his brains, like so many men's, are so easy to pick. 'Sleep your way to the top' is what I say. Imagine my surprise when I found out the full extent of his connections. It was like a dream come true—the Weavers are mine for the taking," she vented, relishing her opportunity to show her hatred toward his family.

"What, you mean a dream for you, or a dream for your destructive mother?"

"Aww, poor little Amey didn't get a medal at all, did she? Just a comfy bed in a Frankfurt hospital."

Norm flinched in anger; he found the topic deeply emotional. That terrible day in Frankfurt that both he and

Tam had borne witness to was never far from his mind. His tactics to pacify Brig were now giving way to outright temper.

"That gun in your hand is a bit small for a starting pistol, isn't it?" he jibed. "Like the one she fired at Amey that day, in a fit of jealousy and rage."

Brig's face went red as he continued his tirade.

"The West Germans were made to look stupid in front of the whole world that day thanks to Renate's actions, no one else's. Not exactly what she intended, though, was it?"

"No, it wasn't!" Brig screamed at him, rising to his bait.

He was getting under her skin.

"Understandably, she was a proud horsewoman and so loyal to the West, yet so jealous of an East German who had all the credentials to give a reunited country the kudos it sought. You don't know the irony of all this, do you, Brig? No... because she never told you the truth, did she?"

"What truth?"

"Your mother was unable to compete at Frankfurt under WPO rules because she was found to be pregnant... with you!"

"No, no... she couldn't have been. The dates would be wrong. You are the liar. Your family are the ones who caused all these problems. Little wonder she did what she did. Oh Lord, the glory of taking you all out." She smirked.

Norm shook his head and then caught her gaze shift to the messy table as she switched her gun to her other hand. As he attempted to stand, she reached over and pulled his own gun from under the paper and fired two quick shots into his chest at close range, sending him reeling into the corner of the room.

"And with your own gun, too," she said with disdain before throwing it under the table and quickly making her exit.

CHAPTER THIRTY-FIVE – THE FIRST RESPONDER

Stretching out from his sleeping bag, Kee pulled back the flimsy curtain to see the sun radiantly poised in the sky to the east. There, just above the hedge line, a house stood at the end of the common, the one he now believed must belong to Norman Weaver. The white flagpole that the girl from The Meadow Pipit had told him about stood boldly before it, bedecked with a large multi-coloured flag sitting limply at half-mast.

Whilst he couldn't identify the flag, he suddenly wondered if that was what Tam had seen the afternoon before. If it was, then things were starting to make more sense.

Kee knew he had to get up and knock at the door, first to establish if it was Norm's house; secondly, to see if Tam was actually there. Lastly, if his suspicions were true about the motorcyclist, to warn whoever was present that a person he believed to be Brig Huddlestone was in the village.

Unzipping the sleeping bag, he swivelled his legs away from his makeshift bed and onto the cool floor. Reaching across, he flicked the switch of the small travel kettle and watched the resultant orange glow impatiently as it boiled.

He badly needed tea. The after-effects of Omni's garlic-filled curry and several pints of beer had left his mouth feeling like a camel's armpit, as his old dad used to say.

As the noise from the kettle gently rose, he gazed back through the window, catching something in his peripheral vision. On second glance, he could see it was a woman, exiting a side gateway from the very house he believed must belong to the Weavers.

She seemed to be in a hurry as she broke into a jog and disappeared into a side lane. Now he was worried, seriously worried. Even at a couple of hundred metres, that figure hadn't looked like Tam, or Amey for that matter. She was younger and her hair was fair for a start. If it was Brig, then what would she be doing there—other than no good?

His concerns were enough to prompt him into a more immediate plan of action. He had to get dressed and get up there as soon as he could. Nothing could stop him now, or so he thought.

As he dragged his crumpled shorts from the previous day over his bare backside, the unmistakable rattle of an approaching quad bike could be heard.

"Not Omni, not now, please," he plaintively cried out loud.

Sure enough, it was Omni.

As he buttoned up his equally crumpled shirt, the bike skidded to a halt by his van. Reluctantly he drew the sliding door aside, her ruddy face appearing in front of him, even before the door was fully retracted.

"Just seen PC Bob Evans at a police roadblock down by the golf club. There's something funny going on, let me tell you. Now, he doesn't know what it's about, they won't tell him, but they have had to seal off the area. Apparently, there's another one stopping vehicles on the other side of Mawdsridge, too," she volleyed out, hardly stopping for breath. "See, I was just nipping down into West Bay, but they said if I goes out, I can't get back in. If you notice, there aren't any golfers out this morning. Look, *mun*, come out here, look for yourself," she said, grabbing hold of Kee's arm and leading him onto the stony ground.

"OK, OK, it could be anything," said Kee, not willing to divulge to Omni any details relating to what he had just seen. The thought of involving her was too much to contemplate right now. All he really wanted to do was get rid of her as quickly as possible and get to Norman Weaver's house.

Omni's information validated his suspicions. Tam had warned him that trouble lay ahead, and this was clearly why.

"You know what this means, don't you?" asked Omni.

"No, tell me," came Kee's frustrated reply.

"It means Sammy won't be at The Shack if she can't get through, so you will have to help me. I can't do it all on my own."

Kee was dumbfounded. This was the last thing he needed right now. His temper started to rise as she unwittingly wasted his time, time he knew he didn't have. However, his patience was about to be tested even further as he noticed Omni craning her neck toward the front of his van.

"Got a ticket for overparking have you?" she remarked.

"Eh?"

"Look, on your windscreen, *mun*. Ooh, sixty-pound fine unless you pay it early, love," continued Omni as Kee swiftly moved, albeit barefoot, to extract the docket from under his wiper before she could get hold of it.

It read:

Don't ask how I found you
I need you more than you know

Meet me at The Steps at 11 a.m.
(and don't talk to any strange women)
Tam X

Kee stifled his joy as best he could.

"Well... who's it from, then? Not the council or the police, is it? What does it say, then?" came the relentless barrage from the nosey Omni.

Kee held his hand up to halt her onslaught and slowly read the note back to himself once more to be sure it was genuinely from Tam.

"Nothing that concerns you, Omni, OK?"

"It's that Tam girl again, isn't it?"

"Maybe... and I can't help you at The Shack, sorry."

"Why, got a better offer, then, have you?"

"No, in fact I was planning on heading up to the Afan Valley, if you must know. According to you, I can get out of the roadblock, so it isn't a problem for me, is it?" he smugly lied, adding, "Anyway, what's the point of opening The Shack if no one can get through?"

She thought for a moment.

"You got a point, I suppose, but then again, coastal path customers can still get around."

Before Kee could respond, a sleek, black car whistled past them at very high speed.

"Jesus, he's bloody shifting," remarked Omni. "There is definitely something funny going on, never seen it like this, *mun.*"

"Hadn't you best get off, then? You'll have customers waiting," he said bluntly.

Omni muttered something rude under her breath and gave him the evil eye as she stroppily walked back to her quad bike. Kee waited for her to enter the dunes before grabbing his footwear and his phone. At least now he would be out of sight from her.

Quickly locking the van, he squeezed through a gap in the hedge and crossed the relatively short distance to the Weaver house.

Omni was right, it was quiet. Nobody on the golf course, none of the usual traffic on the West Bay Road and very little activity from the houses leading up to Norm's. He almost felt conspicuous under the warm sun, his trepidation growing.

Recalling what he'd seen from the van, he opted to call in via the side entrance of the house, where he'd last seen the girl, rather than the front door. By now, he could clearly see along the lane that the unknown female must have turned down. Despite all his previous visits to Skerrid Mawr, he had never ventured down that particular lane nor did he know exactly where it led to, other than possibly toward the back of The Dragon's Tail.

When he reached the side of the house, he could plainly see that the door was half open. He knocked several times and awaited a response. Nothing was forthcoming.

He pushed the door with his right hand, and it obediently opened wider.

"Hello, hello... is anyone here?"

The silence was deafening.

"Hello? If this is Norman Weaver's house can someone let me know, please?" he called.

Still nothing.

What was he getting involved in? Tam's warnings were now at the forefront of his mind. This wasn't good. Nevertheless, he was here, he had to look inside to ease his curiosity, if nothing else.

Tiptoeing along the corridor, he peered into the kitchen.

"Hello, is anyone here?" Kee asked once more.

Ahead, a door lay wide open. Beyond it, a computer monitor seemed to be active, but there was an empty chair. It was far too late to walk away now.

"Hello, is anyone here? I'm here to help you," he called, not knowing what to expect.

As he remained still, he picked up the faintest of noises.

Not sure if it was a voice or his imagination, he stepped across the room's threshold, now able to see beyond the table in front of him. There, down in the corner of the room, the figure of a man lay slumped face downward.

The groaning was now more audible. His first thought, as he rushed to the man's side, was that he must have fallen due to a heart attack or stroke. He had only ever encountered a situation like this once before and, on that occasion, had the benefit of a defibrillator to revive the victim from probable death. This was different. Very, very different.

CHAPTER THIRTY-SIX – THE FOLD

Amey had barely put the key in the caravan door before the loud roar of a car could be heard. Instinctively, Tam looked up to see a black vehicle descending the hill at great speed, quickly screeching to a halt alongside them, causing Hertz to bark loudly.

The doors of the car flung open. Morgan and Grant quickly alighted, looking all set for some type of riotous clash in their padded regalia. Their heads turned left and right as they checked the immediate area around the caravan.

"Have you seen her...? Brig Huddlestone...?" Grant asked, almost panting as he did so. "She slipped out from Sandpiper, and we can't trace her."

"No, we haven't," replied Tam, instantly concerned.

"Liz alerted us to it about five minutes ago. We were at the golf club making final preparations for the eleven o'clock meet. Didn't you see the message?"

"No, I was told to keep mine off—by Norm himself—and Amey's phone is still inside the caravan, I think," explained Tam, and Amey agreed it was.

Grant and Morgan exchanged a look for a fraction too long. It was an ominous sign.

"Have you been back to my house?" Amey desperately enquired, slumping down onto a plastic chair, clearly fearing the worst.

"No, we came here first, on the premise that she is primarily targeting you, Tam, and, secondly, that you two would be all but defenceless to any attack. We know Norm should be able to look after himself."

In Tam's mind, "should" was a big word in this new context.

All three of them looked at Amey, who had gone pale.

"Amey, are you OK?" Tam asked.

"Not really, no. Get me home, please, now... Get me home," she said, standing up and handing her Hertz's leash.

Instantly, Amey became unsteady on her feet. Tam stepped in and clasped her hand to stop her falling.

"It will be alright, I'm sure Norm is fine," Tam tried to assure her, whilst, deep down, feeling the same.

"There's still no reply, Grant," Morgan informed him, waving his phone in the air.

"OK, everyone in the car, now," commanded Grant, his strong arm now taking Amey's weight off Tam.

Morgan dashed to open the two rear doors, and the tailgate of the large SUV to accommodate Hertz, who jumped in without hesitation.

Tam sat in the back, and Morgan closed her door, as he had done back in London two days ago, and placed himself behind the steering wheel, whilst Grant continued to help the unstable Amey into the more spacious front passenger seat.

The engine revved loudly as Grant joined Tam in the back, and his door had hardly shut before Morgan had swivelled the car through 180 degrees and up the tarmac slope.

"God, I feel sick," said Amey, lowering her window as they joined the West Bay Road before a quick left turn took them toward her home.

Tam looked at Grant, who was now anything but calm himself. She observed his gentle rocking motion, clearly keyed up for conflict, his hand checking and re-checking that his gun was at his fingertips.

"That girl is dead meat if I catch her..." he snarled.

"You two, stay here. It could get messy," shouted Morgan as the ninety-second journey came to an abrupt halt on the grass outside the house.

Morgan and Grant leapt out of the car, Morgan veering right toward the front window of Norm's office whilst Grant stayed left. If there was someone in there, moreover Brig, they now had her exits covered. But what of Norm?

Tam placed a hand on Amey's shoulder and felt Amey's hand settle upon hers. It felt cold.

"Don't wait for me, Tam, I will be alright. You need to go, I know you do, so go. Go for me."

With a squeeze of her hand, Tam pushed her door open and headed after Grant for safety, as quickly as her legs could muster.

Morgan's head lifted, like a cat who had spotted movement in tall grass. He stooped to avoid being seen and scurried across to them, as if under military fire.

In a loud whisper, he said, "Man down and person present. We need to get in, now."

"Tam, keep down and wait in the kitchen till we tell you otherwise. Got it?" came Grant's blunt instruction, to which she gave a thumbs up, without any intention of keeping to it.

With Grant leading, she skulked down behind them, watching as they both drew their firearms and edged their way over the threshold. Once in the smooth hallway, both men moved as deftly as they could in an attempt to avoid giving their presence away.

The door to Norm's office was wide open, but Tam's view was obscured by Morgan's tall frame.

Holding her breath as she followed after them, she watched as they lightly trod their way into the room. Then, a loud click was heard, prior to Grant suddenly bellowing out his orders.

"Get away, get away now! Face down! Don't look at me, face the floor, do it NOW!"

Straining to see, Tam couldn't work out who was on the other side of the table in the ensuing commotion—but it looked like a man that Grant was dragging to one side. Standing astride the intruder, Grant beckoned for Morgan to take over and effect the arrest, his firearm still aimed at the person's head.

There, in the corner, Tam could see the crumpled figure of her brother. She recognised the patterned shirt; it was one she had bought him for Christmas two years ago. Her heart went into her mouth. As Grant stepped into the available space behind Norm, she thought she caught a faint groaning noise.

"Is he alive, Grant?" she asked.

Grant got down to Norm's level to assess the situation. Another groan could be heard.

"Yes, he's alive. Boss, can you hear me? Boss?" he asked, preparing to turn Norm over.

Tam thought she heard the faintest "yes" in response to his question.

"I am going to move you. Do you understand?"

Norm's arm rose slightly, as if inviting Grant to continue.

"Do you have any pain in your neck or arms?"

"No, I'm OK, just get me up," Norm's croaky voice directed.

Tam felt a palpable sense of relief. By the looks of it, her brother had survived whatever attack had befallen him. Her attention turned to the likely attacker, the man Morgan had under his control.

"Morgan, can you move him away?" Grant said. "I need more space."

As Morgan grasped the man's collar, she could now see the back of his head.

It looked uncannily like that of Kee. Surely it couldn't be Kee, could it? What in God's name would he be doing here?

Grant was helping Norm up. Norm's face looked ashen, a symptom of shock, as he was manoeuvred into his favourite chair.

"I'm OK, I'm OK," he murmured groggily, still not fully taking in who was there, including Tam.

Grant pointed under the table. "Your old gun is under the table, boss. Did he use that to shoot you?"

"Yes and no," Norm replied, now realising Tam was in the room and acknowledging her with a weak smile.

Grant reached under the table and brought the gun into view, smelling its muzzle.

"Well, it's been fired, that's obvious."

"Yes, it was, but not by him. By her... Brig," Norm informed him softly.

All Tam could hear was the name Brig. She moved as far forward as space would allow, reaching out to touch Norm's fingers.

"Blanks, not live ammo," he added. "And had they been live then this vest would have saved me." His mouth was still dry, by the sound of it.

Tam picked up a half-empty bottle of water from the table, unscrewed the top and offered it to her courageous brother.

"So, who is he?" asked Morgan, pointing down at his compliant prisoner.

"Please, Morgan, let him up. He's a hero," Norm instructed.

Morgan relinquished his grip on the man and instead reached down to assist him.

As he rose, Norm spoke again. "This, as Tam knows full well, is Nat Keelor, or Kee as he is better known around Skerrid Mawr. He became famous yesterday for taking 'that' photo. He is a good man, prepared to risk his neck for me, in your absence. A rare breed. For that, I thank you with all my heart, Kee."

Tam welled up.

"Sorry, mate, just doing my job," Morgan said, brushing Kee down as best he could.

"Yeah, no hard feelings, OK," said Grant, reaching forward to shake Kee's hand.

The pride Tam felt was way beyond anything she had ever felt before. Norm was endorsing Kee, not just to her, but to his own men.

"What are you doing here, Kee?" she asked, rushing across to hug him. "I didn't even tell you where I was staying."

"You didn't need to tell me, Tam. After you left me yesterday, I found myself in a skirmish with a motorcyclist outside The Meadow Pipit, a female motorcyclist. The number plate was odd and I made some investigations. It made me curious. Later, as the sun was setting, I witnessed the same motorcyclist cause an accident outside The Dragon's Tail—"

"How did you know it was Brig Huddlestone, though?" asked Norm before he could finish his story.

"As I said, her motorbike. It was registered on an unusual plate, one that I found out only diplomats can use. Given what Tam had told me about her difficult situation with an aggressive, young, female American diplomat, I was able to put two and two together."

Tam was impressed by his intelligence, as was Norm, judging by the nodding of his head.

"My original intention was to call here last night, to warn you all that she was in the village. After too many drinks I realised I might make a fool of myself, so decided to leave it till this morning. I found out where you lived, Norm, from a lovely young lady at The Meadow Pipit. The flagpole confirmed it."

His last comment caused a light ripple of laughter.

"So, what prompted you to call here at the exact time that you did, then?" Grant asked.

"Out of my van window, I saw a young woman with fair hair leaving your house from that direction," he said, pointing to the side door. "With the greatest respect, Tam, I knew it wasn't you, so became concerned that she may be aggravating things, hence me calling in when I did. The doors were all open, it was like the *Marie Celeste*, totally abandoned. Halfway down the corridor, I could see that a monitor screen was on, therefore assumed someone must be in here. It was only then that I found you in the corner. That was when you guys arrived, of course."

"Very vigilant of you, Kee, for which we all sincerely convey our appreciation," said Norm.

"Here, here," said Grant. "Great job you did there. Selfless."

"You're welcome," Kee replied, with humility.

The impact of seeing Grant and Kee together in this room, let alone the former showering the latter with compliments, wasn't lost on Tam. However, now that all seemed well, she was burning to ask Kee a sensitive question.

"Did you get my note, Kee?" she enquired, blushing slightly.

"Yes, just before Omni almost got her hands on it. Imagine the consequences if she had!"

"It doesn't bear thinking about. She may have eaten you alive."

"True. I have to say, however, when these guys weighed in, I didn't think I was going to make it to The Steps by eleven, more like the local jail."

As Tam smiled, she noticed the other men exchanging glances.

Norm raised his hand. "Yes, now... umm, regarding The Steps at eleven a.m. You weren't to know this, Kee, but there are national security aspects to everything that we have been involved in, aspects that I cannot directly discuss with you. Now, by virtue of Brig's actions here today, our plans have changed. Therefore, resultantly, I will be standing back. You, Tam, are to take the leading role in the subjugating of Brig Huddlestone, along with these guys and a fine young lad called Rich."

Tam had never expected to be handed such a responsibility; she'd always assumed Norm would be leading from the front.

Norm continued to his brief, without even asking her if she accepted his challenge. "We have to assume that Brig is back at Sandpiper, over in Mawdsridge, by now. She must also be preparing for the eleven a.m. meet in her own narrow-minded way, believing she is infallible and that we are stupid," he said, slowly taking off his damaged lumberjack shirt. "Grant, I want you to take over the operational aspects and take Kee with you. He deserves to be there at the end; he is part of things now." He doled out his instructions as if nothing had happened to him.

Grant gave a quick salute, accepting his allotted task.

"Kee, I want you to listen to Grant and do whatever he tells you, when he tells you. My own contribution is to give you this Kevlar vest. I don't think you will need it, but it works." He grinned as he gingerly undid the Velcro and passed the vest to Kee via Grant. "Can you do that for me?"

"Yes, of course," said Kee. "It would be my pleasure."

Tam couldn't believe that Norm had accepted him into the fold so readily. The thought of having Kee present at The Steps lifted her once more, even if it were alongside Grant, of all people!

"Morgan, I want you to message the group right now and briefly explain what has taken place. We need Rich here as soon as possible to escort Tam to The Steps, exactly as Brig will be expecting. Make sure that either Liz or Rich puts her motorbike out of operation, too. How they do it is entirely up to them, as long as it doesn't arouse suspicion. We do not want her to be mobile now, just on foot."

Tam could see that Kee, like her, was impressed at how her brother's mind worked so quickly and so clearly, especially after what he had just been through.

"Oh, and I will redirect some police cover here and get one of the medical teams in, too, just to make sure she hasn't caused me any trauma," he concluded, pointing at his hairy chest and then his head.

As he spoke, the deep thrum of a helicopter could be heard in the distance.

"Haven't you forgotten something?" came a quivering voice from the doorway.

They all turned to face the tall figure of Amey.

"Me!"

CHAPTER THIRTY-SEVEN — SAY NOTHING, DO MUCH

At Sandpiper, Liz could hear Rich making derogatory comments to himself as he dashed back downstairs. She wished she had some positive updates on Brig's location for him. Sadly, she didn't.

No news was bad news for Rich, who continued to admonish himself, having let Brig out of his sights on the very morning that it really mattered. Liz knew he had gone to such lengths to set up Operation Godmother for Norm, and now it was cast in doubt, due to what he seemed to feel was his own stupidity. He wasn't solely at fault; Liz acknowledged that she had been lax, too.

"Rich, you have to calm down. She can't have gone far. If she had, then the boys at the roadblocks would have seen her, wouldn't they? They have her description and she's on foot, not even on her motorbike," reasoned Liz. "I am as much to blame as you. We have to be pragmatic about this. Surely, she isn't going to pass up the chance to meet up with Tam."

"It makes me look stupid to Norm and the entire group now, doesn't it?" Rich angrily responded.

"Norm knows she's a slippery cow, so try not to fret, you will only get yourself in a state, eh?" said Liz, holding the palms of her hands out in front of her in a pacifying manner, as their mother did when Rich lost his temper as a child.

As Liz checked her watch for the umpteenth time, her phone pinged.

It was a message from Morgan. It wasn't good news.

"Norm has been shot," she said, causing Rich to instantly revert into an episode of self-loathing once more, his fingers going through his hair as if he was going to rip it all out in temper.

"Wait, wait!" she bellowed. "He is OK, he was wearing a bulletproof vest but is obviously shocked. Christ knows how she managed it—her own gun doesn't work—but that's for another day, not now.

"On that basis," she continued, "Brig will likely be back here anytime, I'm guessing, and we must play it straight and pretend we don't know anything about anything or she will twig, you hear?"

"What about me going to the caravan to get Tam, is that still happening?"

"No. It says here that you'll need to go to Norm's to collect her."

"OK, but if I go out via the front entrance, Brig will see me, won't she?"

"Good point. Can you see if you can get the old back gate open so you can go across the paddocks? She won't be anywhere near that, I hope."

Rich nodded. "Shall I do it now?"

"No. Can you get out to her motorbike and render it useless first? They don't want her to be mobile; she needs to be on foot to give us the best chance of controlling her. Let down her tyre or something before she gets back. Do it first. Quickly, go on," she instructed, gesturing to the front of the house.

Without a moment's hesitation, Rich was gone, grabbing a pen as he ran through the living room to the front door. Liz followed on behind as quickly as she could, ready to warn him should Brig reappear.

She watched as he undid the dust cap of the front tyre and jammed the end of the pen into the valve, praying that nosy neighbours Tony and Bev weren't curtain twitching across the way.

Rich gave a nod to Liz that the job was done and scampered, with overly bent knees, back to the front door, slamming it firmly behind him.

"That was bloody close, she's back!" yelled Liz, sloping away from the window and out of sight. "Let's get back into the garden as if nothing has happened, remember? You go and try the gate first and I will keep watch."

She limped back into the sunshine, positioning herself next to the low-level, white-glossed picket fencing that divided the two patios while Rich ran across the grass and into the corner of the garden. She watched as he wrestled with a rusty top bolt, twisting it up and down numerous times in an attempt to free it from its housing. The seconds ticked by, until finally, it relented. Grasping the top of the old wooden gate, Rich pulled against the ivy that entwined it to the top of the fence. The ivy was thick from years of neglect, and he edged his fingers behind it to snap it away as best he could, working his way down the entire length of the rotten gate. The dust it gave off made him cough loudly as it started to give way to his efforts. His relentless pushing and pulling finally freed the gate, and it opened sufficiently for him to proclaim success.

"Leave it now, Rich, she's in her bedroom," said Liz. "It looks like she's heading out here. Quick, sit down and make out you're reading a magazine or something. I'll head in and report back to the group." She passed him a stack of magazines from inside the door, which he deposited onto the rattan table before him. Brushing himself down, Rich pulled up a chair and a sudoku book, opening it to a random page to cover the rush.

Moments later, Brig duly appeared, wrapped in a towel, her hair dripping wet, whistling some inane tune whilst looking very pleased with herself. Liz ducked back behind the long, lightweight drape to veil her presence. She needed to hear what Brig had to say for herself and observe her as covertly as possible. Edging the drape to one side, Liz could see over the head of the now-seated Rich, and directly at the root of all evil.

"Enjoy your run, did you?" asked Rich, somewhat politely.

"Do you know what, Rich, I did, very much so. It went way better than I expected. You missed it all."

"Good for you," he responded, not looking up from the sudoku book.

"It made me very hot, so much so I needed to take a cool shower to calm me down. Then again, judging by the size of my nipples you could probably have guessed. You are staring at my nipples, aren't you, Rich?"

Liz knew Rich was not equipped to deal with such teasing; being on the spectrum meant he struggled with anyone who encroached on his space at the best of times, let alone an overbearing powerhouse like Brig Huddlestone. She hoped he wouldn't respond inappropriately and say something that might blow their cover.

"Did you see a helicopter?" asked Rich.

Liz immediately wondered where the hell this was going.

"No, that's a bizarre question, why?" Brig responded.

Liz held her breath.

"My phone app is tracking an air ambulance. We often see them heading into West Bay when there has been an incident. There's one on its way, but the app can be a little slow to update, hence my question."

Liz smiled. Rich was teasing Brig without her knowledge, trying to provoke a response based on the fact that he knew that Norm had been shot, was OK and that a helicopter was due in the village with Brig's own mother on board. Either way, it seemed to strike a chord with Brig, who upped her jubilant mood.

"You are a very strange boy, aren't you? Not your best chat-up line, though, I would suggest. Either way, I just hope it doesn't prevent you from meeting your grandmother today," she responded with her usual guile.

"Godmother," he corrected her. "It's my godmother, like I told you last night."

Liz marvelled at his calmness.

"Oh yeah, last night. I look forward to seeing those pictures. Where is your camera now, Mr Freelancer, or are you keeping it for your trip to the beach with her?"

"No, it's in my room. Why?"

"Because I can add to those quite easily," Brig said, dismantling the knot that held the towel in place and allowing it to drop provocatively to the floor to reveal her lithe body. "By the way, a little birdy told me that your godmother likes to go au naturel, too, so just be careful or you might get out of your depth. Stick to younger, fitter models like me, you sexy hunk of a man."

Liz was incensed and could hold back no longer. Stepping out from her cover, she made her way to the edge of the fence, causing Brig to flinch in surprise.

"Looks like you've dropped something!" Liz bellowed, removing her glasses to give Brig the full force of her stare.

"My towel, you mean?" was her stark response.

"No, your dignity. If you weren't Parv's friend, I would pack your bags myself and then throw you out, right now!"

Brig looked at Rich, then back at Liz, before recoiling into her bedroom, firmly pulling the French doors behind her.

Liz turned to Rich.

"Well done, you were brilliant," she whispered out of Brig's earshot.

"And so were you, Liz. Wow."

"Right, there's no time to lose. Parv will be here soon, and they need you at Norm's, so go now. Whatever happens with that awful excuse for a woman, look after Tam and yourself, won't you? Make sure you both come home safe, please."

As Rich made for the corner of the fence, Liz called out, "Mum and Dad would be so proud of you, Rich," blowing a kiss in his direction.

Rich gave a thumbs up as he proceeded to squeeze himself through the small aperture he had created earlier, disappearing into the paddock beyond.

Liz took a deep breath, hoping that Rich would be successful in his part to rid the country of the blight called Brig Huddlestone.

A shrill noise rang out as she stood alone on the patio; it was the front doorbell. It must be Parv arriving at long last; Liz just hoped she could get to greet her before Brig appeared. More importantly, she needed to close and securely lock the rear doors to her own house first, as any incursion by Brig could be disastrous were she to see the computer screens detailing their plans. Liz swiftly locked the doors and shuffled as quickly as she could to the front door.

She opened the door, and there stood Parv, a woman of outstanding beauty and intelligence.

"Hello," they chorused.

As they hugged, Liz whispered to Parv that Rich had left and everything was back on track. Parv acknowledged this immediately and made a zipping motion across her lips as the annexe door opened. Brig appeared, glaring daggers at Liz.

"I think you'll find it's me she is here for, not you, loser landlady," she spat out.

Liz withdrew from Parv, who shot her a cheeky wink of understanding.

Maintaining her position, Liz stood at the doorway to watch, in an attempt to rile up Brig even more.

"Come here, darling. Lovely to see you, as always," Brig called to Parv, who then made her way across the drive to greet her. They kissed each other on either cheek, Brig directing her poisoned stare at Liz as she looked on.

"I thought you might have gotten here earlier," Brig stated, loud enough for Liz to hear, "cos I am running late, as it were."

"Well, I did the best I could. I did warn you that I wouldn't get here any sooner," said Parv, defending herself from Brig's less-than-welcoming statement.

"Why don't you go in, unpack and get a shower whilst I'm out?" said Brig.

"Where are you going, then, Brig?"

"I need to loosen out my muscles from my run, as I went much further than I thought."

Liz understood her cryptic comment; Brig was revelling in self-gratification.

"I'm going to walk up to that pub on the corner, grab a coffee to go and then head over to that lake across the main road. I should be less than an hour so can bring you something back, if you want," Brig offered.

Parv looked less than impressed. Liz knew that Parv also knew that Brig was blatantly lying.

"Oh, and there was me thinking that we could breakfast together," said Parv, feigning hurt.

"Tomorrow perhaps, not today." Brig stepped away from Parv, toward her motorbike.

Liz froze, praying that she wouldn't notice the flat tyre. To her relief, Parv noticed the deflation and immediately called Brig back.

"Give me a proper kiss, then, Brig, if it's not too much to ask for?" she said, in a pleading tone.

Luckily, Brig made her way back to Parv, grabbing her face and planting a kiss on her mouth.

"Changed your mind, then?" asked Parv.

"No, I haven't, and while we're about it, clean your teeth—your mouth stinks."

With that derisive comment, Brig went on her way, not even noticing the flat tyre.

Liz waited until she was out of sight and then ventured back to Parv. "With any luck, within the next hour, she will be on that helicopter and out of all our lives, forever."

CHAPTER THIRTY-EIGHT — TAKING THE MANTLE

It had been fifteen minutes since Kee and Grant had departed Norm's house. The sight of them leaving alongside one another was something Tam could never have comprehended, let alone in bulletproof vests. They seemed to be chatting away as if they were father and son heading off on a fishing trip or suchlike.

Whilst the last few days had been a whirlwind of emotions for Tam, she now knew it had effectively become the culmination of a thirty-year spat between two families— the Weavers and the Huddlestones—the conclusion of which was fast approaching in a small Welsh village called Skerrid Mawr.

With the invaluable support of Norm's elite group, Tam knew that she possessed a gilt-edged chance to bury the demons of Frankfurt and bring an end to family hostility, simply with the power of truth.

She peered out of the front window, observing a small influx of police personnel taking up their positions, a little too late in her view, but welcome nevertheless. Ultimately, they were there for her family, arranged by her courageous brother, who was now wired up to various devices that the medics had installed on his hairy chest and arms. Amey chatted with them, offering them tea and biscuits as only she could at a time like this.

Kind Amey. How so very much Tam wanted to stop her hurt and give her a gift that all their money couldn't buy: total freedom from hate.

The deep voice of Rich, her companion for the morning, could be heard over the hubbub, arriving at the side door, like so many had done over the last thirty-six hours or so. His tall frame appeared, with a mock salute to the ensemble packed into Norm's office.

"Rich, good man. You remember Tam from the housewarming, of course?" said Norm.

"Yes, I do. Sorry I missed you last night, Tam," he said with an apologetic nod in her direction.

"Good to see you again, Rich. I wish it were in better circumstances, but I want to convey my heartfelt thanks for going to so much trouble on our behalf," said Tam, approaching him for a hug.

"Oh, it's no trouble at all, happy to help. Your brother and Amey have been so kind to us since... well, you know," he said. Yes, she knew.

Such a handsome but shy boy, thought Tam as she hugged him, rubbing his back. She felt so sorry for his condition and the awful family tragedy that had befallen both him and Liz. It made her thankful that her own trauma was relatively limited in comparison to theirs. For this young man to have cared so relentlessly for his sister over the last two years, and then to have taken on a force majeure like Brig Huddlestone yesterday, left her full of admiration.

"Sorry to interrupt..." said Morgan, tapping on his watch. "We only have eleven minutes to get to The Steps, boss."

Norm spoke in his usual authoritative manner. "Listen, sis, the time is now here and you do need to get out into position, as Morgan says. Remember, in all likelihood, Brig will be ahead of you, so be prepared. Grant has confirmed that he and Kee have taken up their covert positions and, rest assured, they will have you covered when you get to The Steps."

Tam felt greatly lifted by the news.

"Morgan will be right behind you and Rich by your side at all times along the route."

Morgan lifted his slim rifle as confirmation. The sight of firearms had never sat well with Tam, but she appreciated that they were a necessary contingency measure today.

"Rich, I suggest that you cut straight across the common, veer to the left of the car park and straight onto the golf course fairway itself. This will lessen the chances of you accidentally bumping into Brig, based on our assumption that she is heading there from the nature reserve side of the dunes."

"Got it, Mr Weaver," Rich confirmed, like a timid schoolboy to his teacher.

"Just so you know, both Grant and Morgan have comms equipment on board and will be continuously relaying information back to Liz, me and the helicopter, too. The Americans will only make their presence felt when either Grant or Morgan decides. All being well, and avoiding any more incidents, they will hand her over to the Americans when the time is right."

Tam felt reassured by Norm's plan, marvelling at how he could think so clearly given all he had gone through in the last hour.

"And Renate, where will she be?" she asked.

"Renate will remain in the helicopter unless, in our opinion, she is needed to conclude proceedings with Brigette. All clear?"

Everyone nodded.

"On that basis, then, I will leave Brig to you now, Tam. I'm intrigued by this secret you have kept to yourself. I still can't imagine what it is," he added.

Tam refused to be drawn as she leant across to plant a kiss on her steadfast brother's cheek.

"Ready, Morgan?" Norm asked as she stepped back.

"Ready, boss," he replied, with a clenched fist.

An emotional Amey came forward with open arms. "Please take care, Tam. Don't let her get the better of you, or us, anymore," she pleaded, welling up with emotion.

"I will, Amey, I promise."

"Sorry, Tam, we must go," said Morgan, tapping his watch once more.

Tam released Amey, keeping her own emotions inside as best she could.

At this point, Morgan invited Rich to walk out with him, heading out through the front door. It allowed Tam to gather herself and follow on for, arguably, the most momentous event of her life.

Morgan and Rich lifted the blue and white cordon tape aloft as an invitation to Tam to walk onto the grass of the common. As they crossed the eerily quiet West Bay Road, Tam looked across at Kee's silver van. It stood solitarily in the car park, as it had done the previous night.

What a remarkable man Kee truly was, having acted in the way that he had, for her family's benefit. His selfless traits were now irrevocably tattooed upon her heart.

With Rich and Morgan continuously checking left and right for any threats, she let her mind wander into what type of conversation Grant and Kee might have been having as they walked this very pathway together some minutes before. All good, she hoped.

As she kept pace with Rich, the reality of the situation, with her at the epicentre of it, began to sink in. She knew she had to be strong and not buckle under Brig's inevitable taunts.

Above the scrub, the top of The Steps soon peeked into view. Tam was but moments away from a long overdue meeting with her nemesis, Brig Huddlestone.

"Hey!" came a sharp call from behind, causing Tam's heart rate to instantly increase, thinking it may be Brig ambushing them.

It was Morgan, who had drifted several yards behind them without her even noticing.

"*Pob lwc*, Tam... Do what you have to do. I will be watching at all times," he said, before quickly ducking out of sight.

"He said 'good luck' to you, in Welsh," Rich informed her, as she blew out a sigh of relief.

At least it was nothing more than that.

"Come on, Rich, let's get this done once and for all," said Tam, moving up to the highest point in the dunes thus far, the plateau that housed The Steps.

CHAPTER THIRTY-NINE — THE STEPS

Tam cast her gaze across the closely mown grass, peering past The Steps to see if anyone was present. Eerily, there was nothing.

Grant and Kee had hidden themselves away well. They certainly weren't providing a single clue as to their whereabouts. Perhaps that was their intention.

Looking inland, there were no vehicles zipping along the West Bay Road, or any smarmy golfers approaching the tee area upon which she now stood, nor any sign of the venomous Brig Huddlestone. It was just her, Rich and a slight breeze.

Standing on tiptoes, she could make out the upper floor of Norm's house and the sight of a freshly raised Union Jack, now residing at the top of the glossy white pole. Dear Norm, how she loved his little idiosyncrasies. It made her smile.

"Something funny, Tam?" came the unwelcome voice of Brig from behind them.

Tam felt the rush of adrenalin coursing into her veins as she turned to face Brig.

"I suggest you step away from your freaky little godson, if, indeed, that is who he is. Don't want any non-Weavers getting hurt now, do we?"

In a show of collective defiance, Tam took half a pace to her left, ignoring her request, to place herself alongside the towering Rich.

"Did you teleport yourself here, weird boy?" Brig asked. "I mean, you were ogling my naked body less than half an hour ago, weren't you? Did he tell you that, Tam, how he lusted for my body?"

Tam shook her head without answering.

"Not that such a thing would shock you, Mrs Goody-Two-Shoes, would it? At least you bothered to put clothes on today, you haggard old bitch."

Tam tilted her head in defiance of this verbal attack, goading her to continue.

"According to my people in Vauxhall, your smutty picture is trending all over Whitehall," Brig taunted. "I can see what Felton meant about your surplus cellulite. Disgusting. What were you thinking? Shouldn't someone of your age be taking up embroidery or something?"

Tam raised her hand and glided it over her head, in a deliberate attempt to further rile Brig, eyeballing her all the while.

"Guess what, Tam? Felton's career will be over once the media get hold of my story—and they will get hold of it, if I have anything to do with it. Apparently, they pay good money for dirt on such prominent fools."

"It's already over, so don't kid yourself, Brig," Tam vehemently responded. "Not that I care anymore. We don't need him, or his money."

"Well, Mrs Kendall, I think you need to clear your sullied conscience first, don't you?"

"Sullied conscience?"

"Yes, don't act all clean and virginal on me, you're as bad as he is. Tell me, how does it feel to be a blatant liar?

Someone who chose to ruin my mother's life by siding with the Ossis and then tried to take the only man I ever cared for," Brig delivered with her usual harshness. "You, like your brother, are vindictive and smug."

Tam refused to fold under her verbal attack, remaining outwardly calm, crossing her arms to feign boredom. Underneath, her heart was racing.

"How I enjoyed discovering your identity, gaining passage to England and then meeting up with the gullible Felton. He was so easy to control... if you know what I mean. Even the simple, young ones like your so-called godson are putty in my hands."

Tam noticed Rich clenching his fist. She laid her hand upon it. The last thing she wanted right now was Rich punching Brig full in the face, however much Brig might deserve it.

"Ignore her, Rich. Justice will be served, don't worry," Tam assured him.

Brig sniggered. "Yeah, right. Now, here's a final little tip for you, Tam... For future reference, when it comes to men, I find that if you dish out a couple of compliments and a little flattery, it serves to loosen their stupid male tongues. Before long, you'll have them singing like canaries. Now, here I am as proof, ready to take the spoils."

"All British men?" responded Tam indignantly.

"Granted, your late brother had some credibility, but even he and his sycophantic friends weren't sharp enough for me. Way too old and slow, that's why 'your people' dumped him out here. At college in the States, I did my research on you lot before plotting my onward path to London. Mother hated all three of you, and Daddy already had the fast-track connections to get me here. American intelligence, you could call it. Infiltration was a breeze," Brig stated, seemingly proud of her actions.

"So, you think Felton was exclusive to you alone, do you, Brig? You were only one of many notches on his bedpost. In fact, I hope you had regular tests at the clinic—God knows what diseases you were all passing around," rebuffed Tam. "For your information, he was no longer interested in me, and we had been in separate rooms for years."

"Not totally true, though, is it? That fateful night you overstepped the line with Grant, remember? Felton himself told me exactly what happened between you when we met up for lunch the very next day."

"What?" Tam gasped.

"Oh, yes, we met for a hastily arranged lunch to discuss 'business'. The price of my silence had just gone up. There was no way he could risk your indiscretion getting out into the corridors of power, as it would reflect poorly on him. Pure gold."

"How did you know about my meeting with Grant? There's no way Felton would have told you," said Tam, reeling like she was on the ropes of a boxing ring, desperate to fight back.

Brig took the chance to ram home her advantage, landing another blow. "The truth is, Tam, I followed your car that night. I knew Grant was working at your office and I didn't trust him. He had mentioned a girl who worked there—it wasn't you, it was someone much prettier. I didn't think he could stoop so low as to end up with you, of all people! You aren't even his type. You're plain, and you're way too old."

Tam held herself together as best she could whilst Brig continued to dig away at her.

"Funnily enough, you never even noticed me sitting near the bar, albeit with a bandana and glasses. You ordered your drinks, stood as close to me then as you are now."

Tam felt rocked by this revelation, one that was impossible to deny.

"A few sneaky phone snaps, taken as you ate your meal together, and a discreet enquiry as to which room you were in gave me everything I needed to contact Felton. Once you both disappeared upstairs, I left for home. I didn't need to go further—but obviously you did, you slut."

Tam raised her eyes to the heavens. Brig wasn't finished just yet.

"Perhaps, in hindsight, I should have sent my text to Felton immediately, but it gave me the night to think about how much this was all worth. Information is king, closely followed by cash, where I come from," Brig crowed, thoroughly enjoying the reveal.

Tam looked down at Rich, who had now sat himself down, cross-legged on the sand, looking away, pretending not to hear any of it. She was feeling cornered.

Brig's tirade wasn't over.

"The other problem you created for yourself was that Grant was exclusively mine. You tried to take him away from me. It's unforgiveable, Tam, and a very big mistake."

Sensing weakness in Brig's position, Tam retaliated immediately. "So, is Parv also 'exclusively' yours, too?"

There was silence. Tam had definitely delivered a side blow.

"Parv is a plaything, and also good for information," Brig stuttered. "Women like Parv can be as gullible as men. Anyhow, no one knows about Parv and me. How do you know? Oh... don't tell me... she worked for the late Norm, too?"

Tam smiled smugly. "Yes, how else did you get to see my photo, eh? How else did you get to know where I was—and why are you staying at Sandpiper of all places? Need I go on?" Tam jabbed away, now feeling she had comprehensively turned the tables on her adversary, as Brig failed to respond.

Tam took the golden opportunity to slam home her attack. "Parv is a gorgeous, savvy girl and very loyal, but not to you anymore."

It was now patently obvious that Brig's temper was starting to boil as she started to kick at the edge of the sandy path like a child having a tantrum. Tam decided to ride this wave of momentum for all that it was worth.

"You know what, Brig? You look a bit like your mother when she got rattled. Yet you look nothing like your father, hasn't that ever crossed your mind?"

"What did you say?"

"I said you look nothing like your supposed father, Jeph Huddlestone. Sure, you have some of your mother's features, but not her chin, for example. Wonder where that came from. It certainly isn't Jeph, is it?" Tam taunted.

Brig stared at Tam, seemingly unable to speak.

"Tobias Pfelzen, have you ever heard of him?" Tam asked coolly, knowing she had Brig on the back foot.

"Tobias who?"

"Pfelzen, Tobias Pfelzen. Your real father. Surely, your mother told you about him... if she ever told you the truth, that is?" Tam jibed.

"No, Jeph is my real father. What is this nonsense?"

"He might have acted like a father, perhaps, yet it is Tobias who is your true, biological father."

"Yeah? And how would you of all damned people know?"

"Your chin has a distinctive small cleft in it. Neither Renate nor Jeph has that feature, but Tobias does."

"That proves nothing, and where is this all bullshit leading?"

Tam knew she had the upper hand—she'd triggered Brig's curiosity.

"There are pictures I can show you that I have recently received from a former police chief in Frankfurt called

Anton Himmelmann. The likeness is uncanny, including your hair. Now, I daresay there used to be a picture of him in this locket."

Tam drew upon the silver chain around her neck, until the heart-shaped locket appeared, glinting in the sunlight.

"It must have fallen out when your mother snagged it on the scaffolding poles that fateful day."

"What fateful day? What the hell are you talking about?"

"When she shot a starting pistol at the World Pentathlon Championships in Frankfurt in 1992, causing Amey Vogler to fall from her horse and, in so doing, ruining Amey's chances of winning a gold medal, both for herself and Germany."

"Nonsense. Mother told me about Frankfurt and the ignominy of being replaced by an East German in the team, just to appease the Ossi part of the country, at her expense, nothing more."

"I am afraid your mother has lied to you on several counts. I was there. I was the only one who clearly saw your mother, from underneath a temporary grandstand, shoot that pistol. Then, in her attempt to escape from me, a witness to her deed, she caught her neck on the poles, leaving this chain on the floor. As I chased after her, I was intercepted and, with the starting pistol in my possession, the Frankfurt Police tried to make me culpable for the incident. They put me through hell. The trauma has never left me and neither did the chain."

"This is ridiculous, all lies made up by you!" shouted Brig, marching right up into Tam's face.

Rich stood up, ready to intervene. Tam raised the palm of her hand toward him and held her ground.

"The whole reason she got away with it was because there was a top-level cover-up. Jeph Huddlestone used his diplomatic sway to take Renate out of the country just a few days later, to avoid prosecution. Has anyone ever been found guilty of the shooting in the last thirty years? The answer is no, in case you were wondering."

Tam was on a roll, not allowing Brig to respond until she had fully driven her point home.

"Papers that I have seen confirm that your mother could never have ridden in the competition anyway—she was pregnant, with you."

"Your stupid brother told me this earlier, what of it?"

"Well, I bet he never told you that her replacement in the team was actually a West German, Ziggy Stauber, not Amey Vogler, did he?"

"Woah, hang on now, no damn way on this planet is that so. They wouldn't have done it, I'm telling you."

"It's true, Brig, it's all true. Even Norm doesn't know the full facts yet, only Himmelmann and I do. What is now beyond doubt is that Amey Vogler was always going to be in the team; your mother got it badly wrong."

"This is getting too ridiculous to believe. How dare you continue to call my mother a liar, and that Jeph is not my real father!"

"So why have you held a vendetta against us, then?" said Tam. "After all, it's no accident you are in the UK, coercing my husband and connecting with Norm the way you did. Like you said yourself, you knew damn well who we were. Your mother sent you over here to finish her dirty work."

Brig pulled out her pistol, causing Tam to stop her accusations.

"Well, we are one Weaver down, and soon it will be two," Brig said, clearly believing she had regained her power once more, by virtue of the gun.

"I don't think so," said Rich casually.

"Shall I shoot you first, then, freaky boy?"

"Well, you can try, but my sister disarmed it last night when you were in West Bay with me. Also, for your information, you shot Norm with blanks, and he was wearing a bulletproof vest, too. He tricked you. Norman Weaver is alive and recovering from shock, nothing more."

Tam marvelled at Rich's level-headed response in the face of adversity.

"What about that air ambulance earlier? That must have been for him, surely?"

"No, it wasn't an air ambulance at all—we just told you that, you sucker. It was a British helicopter containing American officials, and your mother, of course," Rich informed her with delight in his voice.

For the first time, Brig looked visibly shocked.

"My mother... How?"

In a calm voice, Tam said, "Your mother, and Jeph for that matter, knew things had gone too far with your blackmail against Felton and me, let alone everything else. According to Norm, Renate was due to be brought to London from Austria next week for a secret meeting—a meeting you would have been made to attend under American law. However, when you damaged my house, it left Norm no other choice but to make arrangements to bring her to the UK sooner, and to Skerrid Mawr today to coincide with our meeting here, right now. The truth had to be told before someone, yourself included, got seriously injured. Sadly, it didn't prevent you from shooting Norm. Luckily for you, he is, like Rich said, recovering well."

Brig refused to accept Tam's explanation.

"Mother would have told me about this, she wouldn't hide it from me. We recently spoke on the phone, for Christ's sake."

"Well, obviously she didn't," replied Tam, maintaining her passive tone, like a mother to a daughter. "She, like Jeph, was bound to secrecy. Ironically, it was to protect you from yourself. Had she told you, then it would have jeopardised the fragile relations that exist between London and Washington right now and, in the process, made things worse for you."

"So, is this Tobias man here, too?" she asked.

Tam sensed the lowering of her guard. The barrage of facts had hit home.

"No, Tobias doesn't know about any of this yet, let alone about you. No doubt, he will be told once you and your mother are under American control. There is a possibility he will be invited to undergo DNA tests to satisfy these claims. If it proves positive, it may actually allow you and your mother the unlikely possibility of being allowed back into Germany," said Tam in an attempt to pacify her further.

The thoughts that she had planted were now clearly starting to resonate with Brig as she stood there, unresponsive.

"He has children of his own, so technically you have half-brothers and a sister," Tam added. "He currently resides in Walchsee, Austria. Your mother must know he is your true father, but she has hoodwinked both you and Jeph into believing otherwise. I'm so sorry to be the one to tell you."

The silence was deafening.

Brig stood back and looked at the gun.

Tam prayed that Grant or Morgan would not intervene. Injuring Brig, or worse, killing her, would not serve any meaningful purpose to anyone. They had to wait.

Thankfully, in a gesture of surrender, Brig threw the gun to one side and ran her fingers through her hair. Tam's gaze remained fixed on her as she raised her head up once more.

"So why did Grant take that picture of you, on the beach?" she asked, looking defeated, almost hurt.

Before she could answer, Grant stood up from behind the bank of the tee block, his rifle over his shoulder. Brig jumped in surprise.

"I didn't," he said. "He did." Grant beckoned to someone to stand up and make their presence known.

The slim figure of Kee then appeared by his side.

"Oh no, not you, the frickin' idiot that ran out in front of me yesterday evening," Brig directed at him.

"No, get it right—you almost ran me over, remember?" replied Kee, as if ready to start a fight of his own with her. "Then, later on, I saw you recklessly overtake that horse lorry, causing two cyclists to swerve and crash."

Tam was glad to see he would take no nonsense.

"Ought to add that to all her charges," said Grant with disdain, as he approached Brig with a set of handcuffs ready.

Brig spat at him, scoring a direct hit on his black bulletproof vest.

"Naughty, naughty," he responded, clipping one cuff to her arm and pressing his nose up against hers. "Listen up: I never, ever cared for you, Brig. It was no coincidence we lived in the same tenement block; the boss put me there, rent-free, to keep an eye on you. Just as well he did, eh?" he said as he pulled his face away from hers.

"I thought you loved me, Grant, really loved me."

"There's only one person who loves you, Brig... yourself. By the way, Parv doesn't care much for you either. Had it not been for her, then you might have succeeded in your quest against the Weavers. You want to learn to give love back in the right way and then someone might, perhaps, actually love you."

Brig muttered an expletive as Morgan entered the fray, his rifle on his back.

"They're waiting for you, Brig," he announced, giving the nod to Grant to complete her removal.

"Wait," said Tam.

Everyone looked at her. Swivelling the locket into position, she inserted a fingernail into the clasp and released it from around her neck.

"I want you to have this, Brig, to show to your mother, who, if she has any compassion, must have mourned its loss this last thirty years. I kept it in case I needed to prove my innocence back then, telling no one, including Himmelmann and Norm. My hope was that, one day, I might be able to return it to her and we'd let bygones be bygones. That day is now."

Tam held her open hand forward.

"Can I wear it?" asked Brig quietly.

"Of course you can, yes," said Tam, gently moving behind Brig.

As Brig held her chin up, Tam placed the silver chain around her neck and fastened it, tapping at the locket to make it slide around to the front. She watched as Brig gently rubbed her fingers over the engraved 'T'.

Tam knew her work was done.

"*Pob lwc*," she said as Grant led Brig away, with Morgan in close attendance.

In the middle of the fairway stood two American military policemen, obediently waiting for her arrival. The faint noise of whirring blades could be heard in the distance, a signal that her reunion with Renate was now imminent.

"You were very generous to her, Tam," said Kee, taking her hand. "She doesn't deserve such humility, from you or your family. It speaks volumes to me of your integrity."

His welcome touch and kind words reassured her that her handling of Brig had been just and true.

"Deep down, she wasn't to blame—her misguided parents were," Tam replied, in all honesty. "Perhaps they will all learn by this."

"It's safe to turn your own phone on now," interjected Rich, picking up the gun that still lay on the grass. "I will see you back at Norm's shortly, no doubt."

With that, he started walking away, seemingly allowing her time with Kee at the very place it had all started for them, just one day before.

"Perhaps you ought to check your phone, like the lad said," Kee prompted.

Tam wasted no time in switching her phone back on; she was desperate for news from the children. Her phone pinged almost immediately.

Auntie Amey said you were staying with her for a few days.
Hope you are having a wonderful time.
Can't get hold of Dad as usual, but who cares?
El
XX

Closely followed by another...

Auntie has sorted out a few more days for us with her family in Thuringia, if we want it.
They are lovely people, so will get a flight back on Monday or Tuesday. Enjoy your weekend.
Ant x

"Good news?" Kee enquired, probably having read the smile on her face.

"Yes, the best possible news. My kids are safe, thank God, and blissfully unaware of the full extent of what has happened over the last couple of weeks. I'll tell them more when they get back home—with the exception of some details, of course!"

"What do you mean? About Grant, or me, or both?" Kee asked lightly.

"Not about Grant, no, most certainly not!" said Tam, giving him a playful slap. "You, yes. I would love to tell them about you, if that's OK?"

"You know it is. So... when are you planning on returning home, then?" asked Kee in his usual warm tone.

"I'll probably stay here for the weekend, at least. There will be much to sort out, as you might expect, on so many levels."

"Yes, you will need to be here for Amey and Norm, of course, I understand that. There are things I should be attending to, I suppose," said Kee, somewhat glibly.

"That tells me you are leaving, Kee," said Tam, reading between the lines.

Kee gave a wavering hand gesture. "Sure, I have things to do—if I want to do them, that is," he said, inviting a response from Tam.

Without thinking, she took hold of his hands.

"Please stay, for a day or two at least. Amey thought you were adorable, and I am sure Norm would like to meet you properly and thank you for helping him, and all of us. After all, you were instrumental in bringing this family conflict to a conclusion. There's plenty of room, honestly—you won't have to sleep in your van."

"Well, I'm sure Norm would love to thank me for disrupting his plans by taking a naked photo of his sister which ultimately led him to being shot by a madwoman! Nah, I don't think so, do you?"

"Listen, Kee, the likes of Brig and Felton were the only things stopping him from retiring. Essentially, after this weekend, they are gone, out of all our lives forever. They are someone else's problem from now on. So my brother's commitment to this country is now complete. Amey will be ecstatic. The Weavers are all free to enjoy themselves now, so please stay, for me, at least... Yes?" she implored him.

She hooked onto his gaze, unwilling to take no for an answer.

"OK, tell you what, I'll cut you a deal. If I stay over this weekend, it will be on the basis that I will cook you all a meal, to pay for my keep, if you will. That invitation extends to Rich, Liz, Grant, Omni, whoever you like, with some provisos, namely: you help me buy the ingredients for the meal of your choice and assist me in buying some new clothes in West Bay as soon as we can, because these ones stink."

"Agreed," Tam instantly replied.

"Secondly, me and you spend some quality time on the beach together tomorrow... alone."

"Absolutely agreed."

"Finally, you, and your kids if they want, can help me cook for tens of thousands of people next weekend."

"Where on earth?" asked Tam, a little bemused.

"How does Glastonbury sound?"

AUTHOR PROFILE

Born in South East London in 1962, author Nick Davieson moved to South Wales as a youngster when his father accepted a job back in his own homeland. Along with his two older brothers and sister, he regularly returned to Lewisham to spend school holidays with his grandparents, so has always thought of himself as British.

Nick was educated in the traditional comprehensive school system and achieved successful grades in all his chosen subjects. Sport was always at the top of his agenda and, apart from football, he achieved success in the lesser-known sport of cycle speedway, becoming a national junior champion at seventeen years old.

It was always his ambition to run his own business and, alongside his wife, Karen, did so successfully in the document archiving industry for over twenty-seven years before acquisition. His version of success was always to find time for sport and to support his own children growing up, never missing a nativity or sports day and spending many hours at Pony Club events with Karen and their three children.

His accountants coined it "The Lifestyle Business" way before the flexibility of the modern working environment evolved. Nick is a keen runner and triathlete to this day.

WHAT DID YOU THINK OF *SKERRID MAWR?*

A big thank you for purchasing this book. It means a lot that you chose this book specifically from such a wide range on offer. I do hope you enjoyed it.

Book reviews are incredibly important for an author. All feedback helps them improve their writing for future projects and for developing this edition. If you are able to spare a few minutes to post a review on Amazon, that would be much appreciated.

Publisher Information

Rowanvale Books provides publishing services to independent authors, writers and poets all over the globe. We deliver a personal, honest and efficient service that allows authors to see their work published, while remaining in control of the process and retaining their creativity. By making publishing services available to authors in a cost-effective and ethical way, we at Rowanvale Books hope to ensure that the local, national and international community benefits from a steady stream of good quality literature.

For more information about us, our authors or our publications, please get in touch.

www.rowanvalebooks.com
info@rowanvalebooks.com

Printed in Great Britain
by Amazon

4af0372a-1333-48c0-9884-f4e761a700c2R01